ALL

THINGS

UNFORGIVEN

ALL

THINGS

UNFORGIVEN

A Novel

Raj Karamchedu

SAARANGA BOOKS

For

Mary

Contents

Part One

Part Two

Part Three

"TRUE! – nervous – very, very dreadfully nervous I had been and am; but why will you say that I am mad? The disease had sharpened my senses – not destroyed – not dulled them. Above all was the sense of hearing acute. I heard all things in the heaven and in the earth. I heard many things in hell. How, then, am I mad? Hearken! and observe how healthily – how calmly I can tell you the whole story."
– Edgar Allan Poe, *The Tell-Tale Heart* –

Part One

1

"Kill me, Kill Every- one!"

It happened in the summer of 1996, on the fourth day after Arya returned home, having finished five years of study and work in America.

Sometime in the early evening hours there was a scuffle of some sort in the inner room of the house, an ordinary apartment in the city of Hyderabad, where this incident took place.

Loud shricks were heard from inside, and within moments Arya was seen in a most extraordinary condition. With his hair disheveled, and with a look of a madman on his pale, distraught face, he was seen running from one room to the other, with a knife in his hand.

Those who claimed that they saw what exactly happened described it this way. There he was, they said, with the knife in his hand, his broken eyeglasses slipping on his nose, kneeling before a motionless figure of a heavyset woman, who appeared as though she was staring at him intensely, fixing her gaze on him without blinking an eye.

Even those who were watching the incident from outside the apartment, through an open window, said there was indeed a knife in his hand, and that the heavyset woman was none other than Anasuya, the young man's mother.

Such was the sight that as soon as they saw it everyone dispersed, and there was an eerie silence in the hallway and on the stairs.

The truth is, even as Anasuya saw the knife in Arya's hand she was unable to realize why he was holding it. After a second or two she became conscious that she herself had fallen down on the floor, but she thought someone else had fallen, not she, and someone else's body, not hers, was being pummelled by his feet. From somewhere inside the house she heard a pleading voice that kept saying, *"Kill me, kill everyone...!"* - almost moaning at some point. She saw that Arya's mouth was moving in a strange way, and realized that it was Arya himself who was saying these words. She saw his face, the very same diamond-or-a-pearl face of her child who used to cling to her legs after being severely chided by her. In that moment she saw a mark of crime, dancing all by itself over his head, laughing at her, as though it was a mark of her own sin, flying out of her and landing on him, her unfortunate son.

She closed her eyes, and felt something blunt crack her temple and strike the back of her head. A moment elapsed. Anasuya was afraid. She experienced a strange feeling and opened her eyes.

Seeing Arya's feet now striking her stomach, she at once, as though in a pleasant condition, made a movement to rise on her knees. What she really wanted to do was to clutch his arms, not letting them go, and to press her trembling head to his feet, soaking them with her tears of guilt, seeking his forgiveness.

But at that moment there was a struggle somewhere in the room, and she fell back, thinking to herself, *"Me?* All this happening to me? Me, who wished to study and improve myself?"

"Poor boy...!" Anasuya said, talking to herself later.

2

The Matchmaking

THE FACT IS, THAT WISH to study and improve herself, the same that still dug in and worked its way in the pit of her heart even as Anasuya fell under the pummelling feet, was always there in her; and, having taken hold of her from the very beginning of her school days, it agitated her young desires, translating in her imagination everything that she was into everything that she wanted to be.

From her very early childhood days Anasuya – who, in her later years, turned into a pretty young woman with black gleaming eyes, with which she teased her children on occasion – possessed a peculiar mix of boldness, combined with a sudden shyness.

When she was still a teenage girl in school, a certain tendency, one that often can be seen in young girls at a tender age, to see the world around them in all its poignant beauty, descended all by itself into Anasuya. And this quality, by which girls in that state appear all at once irresistible, was causing Anasuya to get all tangled up with everything in her sight.

In their neighborhood there was one schoolboy, under the sway of a similar transformation in his own youthful bloom. The boy, distressed at seeing his advances on Anasuya coming to a cold end, and evidently having made up his mind to die in her hands, wrote her a note and slipped it into her schoolbag.

When Anasuya opened it, it went like this, "...so you must go to a shop, buy a sharp knife, put it in your bag and come to school – and then saying sweetly 'Oh, I want to sit next to you and put my arms around you,' you come near me and put the knife in my heart, and then twist it, and then keep it that way," to which Anasuya replied, on the same page, "I won't do that, I will just give the knife to you and ask you to do it yourself."

Somehow the boy's friends came to know of it and they cracked up laughing, but they were also surprised at Anasuya's boldness in even writing back.

Once when Anasuya was twelve she was in a rickshaw with Vasundhara, her sister-in-law, when her attention was diverted to an elderly woman on the far left of the busy street. At first, seeing the city clothes on the elderly woman, Anasuya was about to look away, but then observing the woman's limp all her hesitation disappeared. She stuck her head out of the rickshaw and opened her mouth to say, "Wherever are you going, Amma?" But in that same instant she was embarrassed for some reason and did not speak these words. By then the elderly woman had already walked to a distance, and before Anasuya said what she wanted to say their rickshaw drove past her.

When they returned home, Anasuya became unusually

quiet at first, but became angry when one of her brothers said, "Who knows who it was, but why concern yourself with such trifle matters...?"

That's how it was with Anasuya. Something about some stranger impulsively attracted her attention, making her restless.

IT WAS ONE SUCH RESTLESS, youthful day in Hyderabad, sometime during the middle of 1962; and as the sixteen year-old Anasuya listened to all the talk in the front room, her big black eyes anxiously widened, she didn't know what irritated her more, whether the words of Sarangapani, the visitor, or her own mother's willingness to be impressed by them.

Earlier that morning, just as Anasuya was preparing to go to school, this Sarangapani, the elder son of a Srivaishnava Brahmana family from Pillanagrovi village, opened the green gate of their house, and saying, "What do you say, Seshamma, it appears that he insists you buy him a bicycle," he stepped into the house, and went on and on, "Whatever else I may think of my brother, on this matter I see that he is perched high up on the tree. Only a new bicycle will bring him down!"

Anasuya knew that even before the guest came inside two or three beaming faces from the kitchen had at once peered into the front room, and that their condition had suddenly brightened at the sound of Sarangapani's voice.

"What of a bicycle? As long as the boy is as bright and red-cheeked as you say, then what of a bicycle, we may give him a scooter itself!" said Seshamma, her mother, who then stopped whatever she was doing and went out to receive the guest.

And then not even a moment passed when Pandurangam, her forty-year-old elder brother, the very same whom Anasuya feared greatly and did not enter the drawing room in the mornings while he was still at home, even when she needed the ink pot for her pen, he too was seen going into the front room, with his golden-silk shawl shining brightly on him.

"Look here, Pandurangava, the matter has come down to the bicycle," said Seshamma, addressing her favorite son – the matter being the proposal for her daughter Anasuya.

Pandurangam stared at Sarangapani, the man who brought the question of bicycle into their midst, for a second, before emanating a soft smile.

"If the boy studied properly, has no habits of smoking and drinking, then a bicycle is a small thing," Pandurangam said in a silky thin voice. He then directly addressed Sarangapani, "Have you come alone?" but without waiting for a reply, he turned to no one in particular and issued orders to, "bring some coffee and tiffin," for the guest, and concluded with a renewed smile, "A job will be assured. Our sister will somehow manage."

Pandurangam always believed that his position, as the Chief Accounts officer in the city, amplified the meekness others experienced in his presence. Hence he always spoke with the calm reassurance of one who was forced to descend from a great height, but having reluctantly done so, conceded to display his benevolence as long as he was here.

At these words, a faint, almost imperceptible, frown briefly came over Sarangapani's face, and he smiled softly. But a moment later, thinking, "What does it matter that I have to sit here and listen to his condescending talk? Is it not true that he is indeed at such a high position, so much higher than I can ever be?" he dismissed his indignation.

Vasundhara – the wife of Pandurangam – a good-looking woman of thirty five, with a sharp chin and bright eyes, dressed in orange saree with golden-yellow patterns on it, came in with the plate of puffed rice.

Seshamma then resumed, "Did these men get to such a status all by themselves?" referring to her other sons and sons-in-law. "It was Pandurangam himself who begged Lord knows how many government officers on their behalf! You can see for yourself what sacrifices he makes!"

Vasundhara stood back near the door. On her face was an expression of ambivalence, common in daughters-in-law.

"When it is in our Pandurangam's hands then is there any doubt?" Seshamma continued. "Let the boy pass the degree examination today, and then see if he will not get him a job tomorrow!"

"Whatever did you imagine, Seshamma?" Sarangapani exclaimed, as though injured by the very question, raising his aggressively proud finger. "Just last week itself he passed the engineering degree, in no less than first class!"

Then, carried away by the same emotion, Sarangapani cried, "State, state-wide, he ranked first!" hardly able to contain his excitement. "No one in our whole district came even close to my brother's marks!"

At once his expression softened. He got up from his chair, stood in front of Seshamma and bent forward, a grim intentional look now occupying his face. With a firm pressure he placed both his palms on Seshamma's chair, and said, "A boy like that, such a bright and young boy, I am placing in your hands, Seshamma, and thereafter it is all up to you!"

Having said these words, Sarangapani leaned back and abruptly relaxed, beaming at everyone in the room, just as someone who placed on the table every precious possession he had, and was himself impressed by it.

"Let it be that way then! As you wish then!" replied Seshamma, visibly pleased, her enthusiasm elevated by the force of Sarangapani's words.

She then leaned forward, and with the vigor of someone who had just taken over the ownership of that very precious possession, said, "Look here, Ranga!" staring brightly into Sarangapani's eyes. "Now listen to me. I say to you today, now, on this auspicious day, on this blessed morning hour, that from now on your brother is like my own son. We are not giving away our daughter, but we are gaining a son!"

With these words she embraced Sarangapani. Sarangapani wiped his eyes with his shawl.

A few moments of silence elapsed. Vasundhara came forward, took the plate complaining he hadn't even touched it and offered more coffee. Sarangapani submissively took the new coffee glass, and enquired if children had already departed for school.

HAVING SERVED THE GUEST, VASUNDHARA left the front room, and without knowing why, entered the large study room, where Anasuya was sitting at the desk, already in the long dress she usually wore on the school day.

At the sound of the footsteps Anasuya closed the book, and with that familiar derisive twist of her mouth, she looked coldly at her sister-in-law, and abruptly left the room.

Later that afternoon, when the house was quiet, Vasundhara came into her bedroom and stood in front of the enormous almirah, sighing heavily. She was moved by a recollection in her own heavy heart. She recalled the despair that had overwhelmed her, when, as a new bride nearly ten years ago, she had entered this house as though entering a dark tunnel. As with many daughters-in-law who enter new families, Vasundhara had also experienced the dread that from this enormous dark tunnel there was no way out.

Now, imagining that such a dark tunnel also awaited Anasuya somewhere else, Vasundhara felt a slight lessening of her own agitation. But the next moment this feeling of kinship in dread for Anasuya gave in to the pity that rose in her heart.

At Pillanagrovi, at the same hour that Sarangapani had hurried to the bus stop, Rushi was lying on his back, on the stone-slab bed in the front yard, already awake and remembering his achievement in the engineering degree examination. "You have to have self-reliability first," he said to himself, experiencing a feeling of one who was elevated to a great height from which everyone appeared benign, harmless and even distant.

Then hearing the voice of Janakamma, the wife of Sarangapani, and seeing the thick smoke that began to come out of the kitchen, Rushi remembered the special mood of everyone in the house these days, and remembered the purpose of his brother's early morning rush. "Now *this,* Lord, what an ordeal!" Rushi thought. Recalling the people of that other house, he tried to summon Seshamma's face in his imagination, "Daughters are usually prettier than mothers..."

Inside the kitchen Janakamma broke a few more dry sticks, and a moment later the yellow fire from the woodstove cleared up the smoke.

Abruptly displeased by his thoughts, Rushi rose.

Rushi was a young man who displayed a special brightness and a tendency to excel in his studies, but this excellence was sporadic. While it was customary for the male members of the family to memorize the scriptures and develop the mastery to recite them, Rushi showed no such interest. From his earliest childhood he possessed a striking talent for artistic painting and sketching, though no one saw him practice, and his father did not teach him either. At school he did not show any particular adoration towards the teachers, but he was well-liked.

There was only one primary school in Pillanagrovi village. Mud walls separated one class from the other and children sat on the floor. When Rushi completed fifth grade his father insisted that he be sent to higher secondary school, even though it was ten miles away.

So they bought the young boy a bicycle, and every morning his mother Kanakamma wrapped his tin box of lunch in a soft cloth, watched him ride his bicycle to school, and sighed with heaviness in her heart.

In the late afternoon, on his way back, Rushi would not go straight home, but would ride for a while, stop near the fields, and rest his bicycle against a tree by the dirt road. He would then sit in the shade, open the school library book and read until the evening cacophony of birds disturbed his concentration. Then he would get on the bicycle and ride brightly, replaying dreamily in his head what he had just read, smiling at the empty tin box swaying on the handle bar.

While the villagers revered the father, and were even enchanted by his gentle manner with which he dismissed their petty lapses, drawing their attention instead to the tales that caught his fancy, it was Rushi they were fond of the most.

"Just the same as his father," they said, referring to a quality of tenderness he possessed, which he retained even at his present age of twenty.

By mid morning, having bathed and soaked his healthy body, pouring buckets of cold water over his large shoulders while one of the children teased him by hiding the soap, Rushi entered the kitchen with his bare feet. He uttered a few quick words of prayer under his breath, and unable to reach the cadence that he usually heard in the recitation of Sarangapani, he sat on the floor and playfully began calling his young toddler nephew Kittu, who had just discovered running.

"Wasn't it only yesterday that you finished the college? So where are you off to now this early?" asked Janakamma. "Well, go if you want to, but what's the use of wasting your time with the little one if you are in a rush?" she said, filling his steel glass with water.

"Let him go where he wants to," came a voice from the adjoining room, of his mother Kanakamma. "How many more days he will go fancy-free anyway, even as we speak isn't our Ranga talking to the girl's people in the city?"

Pretending to ignore these words, evidently aimed at pinpricking him, but experiencing an elevated mood nevertheless, Rushi took a long time eating his meal, playing with Kittu.

Kittu climbed up on him, sat on his strong forearms, and began to laugh as Rushi kept opening his palm and, just as the little boy was about to catch the blue marble in it, closing his unyielding fingers.

"See that face, how red it turned at the mention of marriage!" said Kanakamma. "I don't know how the girl turns out to be, but all the world's shyness is in this boy's cheeks."

Then complaining at Kanakamma and Janakamma that a man alone can hardly survive such an onslaught that came from all sides, Rushi took his bicycle and came out.

Throughout that day Rushi experienced a heightened awareness of his present condition. During the phase of his university days Rushi believed in the theory of the nobility of loving all humanity, but when he applied himself to it he experienced nothing but the coldness of the other, which disappointed him. But now, just a few days after his graduation, he did not remember that antipathy; instead, a joyful enthusiasm now infected his views of the world and for the people around him; and his current reminiscing was filled with moments when he ran with other caste boys, sat with them on the cane fence, smoked cigarettes and walked with them while talking voraciously and dreamily about some new thing he had just observed.

That was how it was with Rushi.

3

The Marriage

EIGHT DAYS AFTER THE VISIT by Sarangapani agitated her, Anasuya completed her tenth-grade final examinations, and unable to resist her desire to see the new movie, she closed the novel she was reading, got up from the sofa, and hearing people talking outside, stepped out of her room.

It was before noon and the female members of the family had just gathered in the vast bedroom. Children went from one room to another with a slight after-meal slumber and sat wherever they wished: a bed, an arm-chair or on the floor, lazily playing with toys and picture books. The house servants were speaking freely to each other, exchanging personal matters in playful tones, with which they sometimes speak when the mistress of the house has no more orders to give. Pandurangam had not yet come home for the afternoon meal.

Voices were heard from one of the inner rooms.

"...then the boy can stay with us, what is in it?" Seshamma was talking with animation as usual.

Though Anasuya was aware that since Sarangapani's visit the family behaved as though something special was about to occur, their conversations frequently mentioning "Sarangapani," and occasionally another name "Rushi," she decided that this matter was not any of her concern. But somewhere within her a feeling of annoyance began to rise.

She approached the small side bedroom, and softly opened the door to see if Vasundhara was there.

"Have you finished reading your book already? Come in, come in, it's just me here alone," spoke Vasundhara's voice, seeing her.

Anasuya stepped in and saw that Vasundhara had just finished cleaning her veena, and was setting it quietly by the side of the bed.

Anasuya whispered brightly, "Ey, Vasu...?" but even before she finished speaking, it was plain that even Vasundhara was thinking the same thing – the new movie.

"But Amma is sure to say no if we ask her now," Vasundhara said gravely, remembering Seshamma's mood. "Besides, tomorrow they will visit us. And they are bringing him and everybody!"

"Who are coming?" Anasuya frowned. "Who are they?"

Seeing that her sister-in-law was about to turn cold in anger, Vasundhara took her hand, pulled her toward the bed, and with a rising whispering voice, said, "If you already start behaving like this then how will it be when they see you tomorrow!"

"Who is asking them to come? No one tells me anything!" Anasuya said, pulling her hand away, and sitting on the bed. "Did anyone ask me? Even so, why should I marry now anyway? I am still in school. I want to study!"

"How are studies and marriage tied in this case? Won't they allow you to study after the marriage? Why should they not?"

Saying these words Vasundhara looked at her sister-in-law with an expression of a womanly delight that filled her ever since Sarangapani's visit. Seeing that Vasundhara did not comprehend the turmoil in her, Anasuya became even more irritated.

"But what of all that now!" Anasuya said, suddenly raising herself from the bed. "Are you coming with me to the cinema or not?" her pale, defiant face staring directly into Vasundhara.

An hour after this exchange, by which time the two girls have reconciled, they obtained Seshamma's permission. Seshamma ordered Gopalam, Anasuya's brother, to accompany them and insisted that they go to the matinee show so the girls return home by evening.

THE AFTERNOON WAS ALREADY HOT, so they went in rickshaw while Gopalam followed them on his bicycle.

Though Vasundhara tried all she could to elevate Anasuya's mood and distract her from thinking about the next day, the two girls ended up talking about the very same topic in the rickshaw.

While Vasundhara was speaking reassuringly that Anasuya could still study even after the marriage, Anasuya drifted into an involuntary recollection. Years ago, when Vasundhara herself was still new in the house, she was often seen in the mornings with her eyes swollen red from crying and lack of sleep. Now such memories added to Anasuya's despair, and gave rise to even more apprehension about her own present condition. At once she experienced an overflowing pity and kinship for Vasundhara.

By the time the rickshaw reached the cinema theater, the crowd was already inside the gates, with bicycles and rickshaws going in, and men and children jumping off them and rushing to the ticket lines.

Guarding her shining black-and-green dress while climbing upstairs to the second class door, aware that several pairs of eyes were looking at her, Anasuya went inside the hall following Gopalam's lead, tightening Vasundhara's hand in her grip at the sudden darkness which engulfed them as they entered.

When she sat down on the seat and settled, Anasuya once again remembered the circumstances in which she found herself at home.

Then a young boy, of no more than thirteen or fourteen years of age, appeared in a soldier's uniform on the screen. At once emerging from a despairing crowd of men and women of the village, who gathered at the center of the scene, he jumped on the black horse. Holding its reins, he swerved the agitated animal towards the audience and swore to fly at once to the king's court and punish the queen's cousins who trampled on the old man causing his death. Despite his high sounding words, and the youthful energy with which he kicked his horse and sent it flying forward, it was evident that he was just a boy who wished to appear as a brave soldier. "They are going to kill him!" Anasuya cried, at once dismissing a voice inside her which said it was only a movie and there was no one actually dying.

From the moment the young soldier was introduced into the scene a tender emotion had taken hold of Anasuya, and rapidly grew in intensity. In her intimacy with the soldier she had already began to suspect that the gradual building up of his life was only due to one motive in the movie creator's mind, which was to kill him off. She was moved by the young soldier's innocence, and she experienced the same anxiety that the soldier felt, and she knew that the soldier would be killed before she herself, Anasuya, had said everything she wanted to say to him. And she wanted to say so many things to him about herself, about her life; and to ask the soldier about his life, and to listen to him.

None of this happened however, and the young soldier was killed off remorselessly, just as smoothly as he was made to enter into the scene, galloping from far away mist in the rainy evening, his shiny black horse carelessly stepping on mud puddles.

When the scene was concluded, Anasuya whispered, *"Amma...!"* softly to herself; and discovering that she was crying, she laughed, wiping away the tears. An overflowing affection, and a feeling of pity, for her brothers, for her mother, for Vasundhara, and for everything in her world, flowed in her heart.

A FEW DAYS LATER, IN a short and a brief ceremony in the temple, Anasuya was married to Rushi.

The day before her wedding she went into her room and stood near the dressing table, in front of the tall mirror that had flower patterns on its brown frame. Her eyes lowered for a few moments and her fingers, on their own, detached from the whims of her heart that was evidently thinking of something else, pretended to grab hold of something on the table. Then she looked up and stared straight through herself, twisting the red sewing thread round and round her finger, as though she wished to twist it round and round her very heart.

She then opened her black diary, stared at it for a few minutes, and with a heavy sigh tore off the pages from it. But before she threw away the pages, she took one last look at them.

It was a journal entry she had written a few months earlier, when she was carried away by an especially elevated state she was in, and not another soul knew of it.

It happened when a handsome young man, the very same boy who had slipped a note in her school bag years ago, had sent Anasuya a present and Vasundhara had taken it to her discreetly. It was a small, elegant, transparent crystal jar, and in it was a milky white egg. Anasuya lifted the crystal high in front of her eyes, stared at it directly, and saw that the egg, visible in the center, was suspended in mid-air like an Olympic gymnast. Mesmerized, and feeling an inexplicable rush of sensation in her body, Anasuya sat down, unable to control herself from crying. That night she took a long shower, went into the kitchen, boiled the egg and ate it privately all by herself. She then came into her room and wrote the words in these pages.

This long entry, which she was now going to throw away, went like this:

"Strangest thing!" she had written. "I was about to resume my study, but wanted to just sit in the sun for a minute or two, to lose my sleepiness. Though it was bright afternoon, the April sun was just warm. I imagine I drifted into some place, then suddenly was woken up by a soft rubbing sensation. It was near my cheeks, but my eyes were still closed so I could not see what it was. From a distance somewhere, but directly in my field of vision something very bright, very red, very pink, was spinning rapidly. I could sense it was also approaching me because its size kept increasing and increasing. As it got closer, it became visible as a red, round egg spinning like a top with ever increasing speed, emanating in a spraying motion something smooth, not hot, not warm, but just smooth, from all around its circumference. As it got closer the smooth soft rays were brushing off my cheeks. It got closer and closer and suddenly merged into my face and I felt a sensation of having touched that delicate, supple egg, red and pink. I involuntarily opened my lips and nibbled the egg that was already almost in my lips. Suddenly it shuddered, and I took its pink top, that was already quivering a bit, into my mouth; and all through this the smooth rays kept caressing my cheeks, kept brushing against my lips, playing with them, trying to pry them open. I open my mouth wider and suddenly, at once my mouth engulfed the entire thing that was in front of it...or so it seemed, but instead the thing itself engulfed me, sending electric currents of a peculiar joy through my back, my neck and my fingers. "What could this be?" I wondered and was about to open my eyes but no matter how much I tried, I could not open my eyes. Suddenly the spraying intensified, and now I knew what it was...it was a smooth jet of fine, warm, bright sun rays that kept blasting out of this spinning red egg that was entirely inside my mouth. These bright sun rays completely filled my mouth, my throat, my heart, my innards, reaching rapidly into my arms and suddenly my finger tips began to glow brightly intensely, from the excessive overflow of these sun rays that the spinning red egg kept spraying and spraying inside my mouth. I experienced a sensation of being lifted above the ground, far above the ground, but strangely I could still feel the smooth silky sensation of a soft skin on my outer lips. Now I too, like the spinning red egg-top I saw before, was spinning at the distant field of vision of my own self. It was me seeing myself. Then I recalled, "Oho.... I remember closing my eyes...and then I lost consciousness..." and immediately realized that I am simply sitting there, still in the sun and while I experienced all this, only a few minutes passed by. So here my heart, is the story of what happened to me when I nibbled on this warm egg, and imagined all sorts of things under the hot sun."

Many years later, after her children were born, when some unknown feelings elevated her sadness, Anasuya sighed again, thinking of this journal, but dismissed the wail in her heart, chiding herself.

On the fifth day of the wedding ceremony, as the euphoria of the festivities came to an end, towards evening the remaining guests began to leave.

All of a sudden, but still as though she too was waiting dreadfully for it, uncontrollable tears choked Anasuya. She felt that life has now become so different and so overwhelming that only the warmth she felt on her cheeks seemed real to her. Wiping her eyes she imagined the figures of her mother, of her brothers, and of her sisters-in-law also in a similar state.

At the sight of the men who did not hesitate to expose their bare upper bodies during the prayers until the previous day, now coming out in their shirts and trousers, talking with animation, the yellow pasupu marks still at their finger tips; and at the sight of the women talking and laughing in groups, seeing that they had already crossed the front gate, now smiled vigorously at each other before parting at once, Anasuya experienced a terrifying feeling that into the torrent which surrounded her there was about to descend a sudden quietude, and that somehow this quietude would be unbearable.

At times she had a look of surprise on her face. She was surprised that even after such an inexplicable sadness swamped her, even after *such a* separation from her family, there was life around her in her new house; and that such a life still went on and on with a vigor that was as full as it was in her mother's house.

And no matter how self-satisfied Sarangapani was, how joyful everyone in the house felt, and how, like a fresh flower, Anasuya's presence lit the house with bright smiles, she was still only a new bride, still only a daughter-in-law and not the daughter, in that Srivaishnava Brahmana house. As a result, soon it became clear to Anasuya that the new household did not share her dream of continuing her studies.

Rushi left the decision, hence the fate of Anasuya's study plans, in the hands of Sarangapani and Janakamma, where it languished and died.

"What's the use?" they said. "She has already achieved what any woman dreams to achieve, marriage."

From that moment on, a peculiar expression, something resembling a frown, but not quite, began to accompany Anasuya's every movement.

4

"Same, Everyone is the Same!"

IN THE YEARS AFTER THEIR marriage, Rushi graduated with an advanced engineering degree and was appointed at the Roads and Buildings Division.

His service began to flourish. The couple settled in a house of their own – an allotment they were fortunate to receive in the Housing Board Colony in the Old City of Hyderabad.

Everyday Rushi departed for the office early in the morning, leaving to Anasuya the task of attending to everything without which life would come to a standstill.

She would get up early, before it was sunrise, clean under the boiler, push the coals in, run into the kitchen to replace the overflowing brass water-pot under the tap, and rush back to fill up the boiler and light it. Then she would go out, walking briskly to the milk booth, returning within ten minutes, in time to fill up all three waterpots, before the pipe house turned off the water.

Visitors were always arriving from Pillanagrovi, staying on for weeks and months, and even for years sometimes.

Frequently they appeared in the middle of the night, and if Anasuya did not get up to cook for them, there was talk from them. Whenever this happened, Rushi simply stared at his wife with a smiling expression.

One such frequent visitor, Seshu, a brother-in-law of Rushi, arrived one night with his wife Chintamani, as usual without any advance notice. Seshu stayed with them every examination term, having enrolled in the university for the degree course in Literature.

It was well past eleven, approaching midnight, when they arrived.

Young Anasuya came out, saying, "Sit, sit," and hurrying to take the bags from Chintamani. "I myself have been thinking isn't the time for the exams coming up soon, and expecting you should be here today or tomorrow."

"We were thinking to get here yesterday itself, but your sister," Seshu said, referring to Chintamani, "...she was held up by the inspection at her school. Is everything fine here? Rushi hasn't come home yet I see..."

Though he was nearly ten years older than Anasuya, Seshu experienced jealousy at the confidence with which this round-faced, sharp-eyed young girl, with a peculiar derisive twist of her mouth that showed on occasion, assumed a firm place in her house, so that those on Rushi's side checked their natural tendency to issue orders to her.

"All this month he'd been taking on extra inspection work. It's all due to this new director, there's no getting around him. He should be home soon."

After a few minutes of conversation, Anasuya, speaking

to Chintamani, said, "Before lying down you both wash up. Rice is already on the stove. Your brother will arrive any moment," and went into the kitchen.

THE FOLLOWING MORNING THEY SAT in the center room talking loudly, with the usual boisterous jokes, and the two brothers-in-law teasing each other.

Anasuya was in the kitchen.

Having tired themselves, the men abruptly became engrossed in the newspaper. After a few minutes Rushi asked his sister if she intended to apply for the university, now that she had completed five years of teaching at her school.

"Stay with me if you have to, but don't ignore your studies, having come this far," Rushi said in a soft tone. "Or is your husband opposed to it? What do you say Seshayya?" turning to Seshu.

"Why would he oppose? Nothing like that," said Chintamani. "I myself have been thinking, with two little children can I manage...how should I manage," drawing out her thoughts.

"What is there in it? You managed it this far, just two or three more years and you will complete it," said Rushi.

"You say that, and what have you got to lose? For yourself you are a successful engineer," said Seshu, with a sudden animation, pricked by the wish to needle his brother-in-law once more. "...and a wife like Laxmidevi. How can we measure up, no matter how many degrees we pass?"

"Say why don't you make arrangements for Anasuya's study. She is only four years younger than you," Seshu continued.

Rushi smiled self-consciously, as one who was just being asked to take up a thing that was far beyond his simple means, and thereby refusing even the thought of it. "Well, that time for us has passed. Now with the city life and my impending transfer to the new division...," his voice trailed off.

Anasuya, who had come in during this conversation with the coffee glasses, turned a little pale at first, before she brightened her expression and said, "What habits you have, keeping on with mere talk this early in the morning, when he should really be hurrying up for the exam..."

She then left the room to check the boiler for the hot water.

That night Anasuya, dismayed at the sight of her own face in the mirror, seeing the unceasing quiver of her lower lip as she was trying to hold her tears, returned to her bed. Lying sideways with her cheek on the pillow, she kept gazing at the empty space beyond the edge of her bed.

When Anasuya woke up next morning she knew that, for her, everything changed after the marriage.

IN THE TENTH YEAR OF their combined life, during the spring, Rushi was promoted to the position of Assistant Engineer.

Two days after the news arrived his friends gathered at Rushi's house, congratulated him, raised their tea glasses and drank to his success. There was an energetic discussion of what this meant to everyone around the table. The possibility of more contracts was considered while they smoked cigarettes with increased enthusiasm and ordered more tea to be made.

From then on Rushi immersed himself more and more

into work. Even before his government vehicle, an old Jeep, came to a full halt, Rushi would jump out with a special enthusiasm in his feet, follow through with a step or two, and would abruptly stand still, strike a match, light a cigarette and then resume his motion, walking firmly with a purpose.

THIS WAS WHEN A CERTAIN inner agitation entered into young Anasuya's heart, the chief cause of which was a suspicion that took root in her, that her husband Rushi did not belong wholly to her. Someone *else*, whose face she could not quite fully imagine yet, had already encroached into that forbidden place in his heart, forbidden to everyone but her, his wife.

The children were still very young then, still in their primary school years.

After *that* suspicion, though she tried to suppress the awakening of it in her heart, Anasuya knew that Rushi had become one of those intelligent, outgoing and energetic men who led a double life, though not deliberately. Anasuya saw the good in him, but that good did not fulfill her wishes, only his own.

On occasion, when the family set out for a social visit, it was common for the neighbors to hear unusually loud voices outside, near the auto-rickshaw; and see the bright, full-figured Anasuya climb into the auto, heave herself to one side of the back seat, making room for the others, while a healthy-looking Rushi, with a ruddy, youthful complexion, waited by the front wheel. On his face beamed an outward look of joviality aimed at the onlookers, but with a secret, private expression of pinpricking aimed halfheartedly at his wife, he joked with the children, evidently carried away by his own wit.

As these neighbors saw it, at first the wife laughed heartily, thinking nothing of it, but inwardly she was annoyed that he made fun of her even when they were with his friends. When they returned home Rushi, as usual, was meekly apologetic and forgot everything, while the anger and the isolation Anasuya felt continued to ferment in her. These neighbors were very sure that she began to suspect everything in Rushi's words on such occasions.

"He behaves fine with me when we are all at home but out in society, he changes," Anasuya tormented herself with such thoughts. "No doubt, I am convinced, he takes the side of his friends' wives even when they behave as if they are superior to me."

Thus, for Rushi it was such that, though in the years after the marriage and three children he continued to prosper in his job, though he felt especially cheerful when once every month he handed his wife thick folds of hundred rupee notes and asked her to remove the rubber band herself, and though he knew that everyone in his social and friends circle thought of him as a bright and enterprising young officer, he experienced a dull feeling of agitation in himself, but every time he put away that feeling without any resolution.

For Anasuya, *her* inner agitation, emanating from *that* suspicion, not only remained but extended to all nooks and crannies of their combined life, just as water seeping under the mattress slowly soaks the entire bed.

PERHAPS IT IS TO BE expected that when this One Big Thing came into the house and began needling a million little things between the wife and the husband, certain early signs in the little boy Arya went unnoticed. Some people who remembered these early days thought so anyway.

The truth is, during these early days the boy did develop a disturbing tendency. He was barely nine years old then. He would wake up in the middle of the night and walk around in the house while still completely in his sleep. Of course the boy himself was not aware that he was sleepwalking at the time.

All the children slept in the same room. So in the morning, when the boy's sisters began telling Anasuya and Rushi how he suddenly rose from the bed, walked up to the windowsill, grabbed the keys and opened the front door lock, all the while not at all looking at them and not hearing their questions why was he opening the door in the middle of the night, the boy listened and laughed, thinking they were making fun of him. He really did not remember any of it, but Anasuya, listening intently to her daughters, stared at the boy for a minute.

The next morning she woke up the children at six, made sure they bathed in hot water, dressed them in new clothes, and off they went, in an open-top rickshaw, to Srivenkateshwara temple, the early morning cold wind making their noses and cheeks red.

IN THE SAME SIX O'CLOCK hour at the temple, the bald-headed priest, with a thin chest and a wrinkled stomach, had abruptly woken up only a few moments earlier. He then warmed his pale face with his thin, unsteady palms; and putting on his thick spectacles with his long fingers, he stared at the temple gate, and frowned.

For the next few minutes, as he briskly commenced gathering all that he needed for the morning harathi, a chief discomfort the priest experienced was seeing the fear of falsity in the people entering the temple. When they expressed this fear in their prayers, he suspected that they habitually made it as though it was still everything around them that was false and they themselves were true. He winced inwardly with shame, recalling with self-awareness that he had also prayed that way in his life once. That shame still lingered in him, not by reason but by something else in his soul.

And so the priest stared and frowned day after day as the sun rose and came men, women and children, walking along the narrow lane that led up to the temple entrance.

They rushed past the line of beggars, who stopped rattling their tin boxes for a moment or two and stared curiously at them before nudging their young ones to persist in begging. The visitors went in neither looking at the beggars nor at their little children, their expression at once becoming solemn as they stepped over the yellow-red temple threshold.

When Anasuya and her children reached the temple, there were people going in and others coming out. Among them were several of their neighbors who, seeing her, smiled brightly and approached her.

The more they spoke to her, the brighter their mother appeared to her little children; and the feelings of tenderness for her heightened in their hearts. Her white cotton saree, with a bright red-and-golden silk double border, made the boy Arya linger nearer to her. He stood quietly when the neighbors spoke of their sons, daughters and husbands, even though Anasuya did not say much about their father Rushi.

Anasuya prayed on behalf of Arya, the expression on her face solemn, her face tilted to a side, perplexed by her son's habit of sleepwalking.

WHEN THE PRAYERS WERE CONCLUDED the only people remaining in the temple were Anasuya, one or two workmen, and Anjamma: an old woman with grey hair and pale complexion, who was now putting away the thick blue plastic sheet that was lent to the coconut-seller.

After a few quiet moments passed, Anjamma got up to sweep the temple yard. Standing quietly for a second near the marble pillar at the far end, the broom swaying loosely in her hand, she saw Anasuya at a distance, surrounded by three children.

One of the children, the boy, had just gotten up and stood in front of his mother, saying something to her. At once feeling bright at this sight, Anjamma approached them, coming up with enthusiasm at first, but slowing her pace as she came nearer.

The smaller girl, Sita, wearing a bright yellow long skirt and a white blouse on which were small green leafs, stopped her movements and stared at Anjamma.

The older girl, Yashoda, with bright red bangles on her tiny arms, and with two or three roses on her hair, which were at least a day old but she wouldn't let her mother change them, alerted her mother.

"Whatever keeps Amma brooding on and on, only Lord knows. A soul daren't make itself come up and speak," Anjamma said with a smile, her eager eyes looking on with affection toward Anasuya.

Anasuya, who had been sitting there lost in her thoughts,

sharpening her eyes as if trying to comprehend a complex matter, softened her expression, and then raising her eyebrow in a show of a sudden warm feeling, said, "Aaa, what don't you know, what else is there to brood but the house and the children. Come this way, sit here."

"See how like three dolls they are," Anjamma smiled at the children, who stopped their movements and stared at her with a look of curiosity. "Why only three, Amma, couldn't you have more?"

"Yes, yes. Just these three," replied Anasuya. "Handful for me! As it is life is already overwhelming with these three."

A new titillating feeling entered the children, which they always experienced whenever a stranger spoke to their mother.

"What does the master do, Amma?"

"Officer," Anasuya replied. "High officer," she continued. "What does your man do?"

"He drives a rickshaw." Anjamma replied as Anasuya rose to leave.

OUTSIDE THE TEMPLE THE SIDEWALK was still crowded with beggars. Whenever someone from the temple came out, they moved out of the way only a little, and instantly crowded together again, pressing into the gate.

When they saw the small figures of the three children emerge from the gate, the beggars rushed forward and swarmed Anasuya, who came out following the children.

"*E'ey...!* Look now!" cried Anasuya. "What will come of rushing over and over to me like that...!"

She then passed out several coins, "Here!"

Having emptied her hands of everything she had, so that

only a crumpled handkerchief remained when she opened her strong palms for the beggars to see, Anasuya proceeded toward the rickshaw-stand with the children, walking with the usual, slight sway in her right leg.

The beggars, who were charmed by the young woman, and who were filled with an endearing affection for her three bright children who came closer boldly, nearly touching their tin boxes as they dropped the coins into them, by virtue of which there flowed a special feeling among the beggars for the mother, these beggars now abruptly dispersed away from Anasuya, as soon as they knew that there was no more money to be had from her hands. To a young woman beggar, about the same age as Anasuya, all at once Anasuya appeared as just ordinary, and her three children just like her own. On seeing this abrupt change of feeling on the beggars' faces, Anasuya's benevolence too became deflated, which made the beggars ignore her even more.

In Anasuya that old feeling, that same feeling, which she kept turning in her head while she sat on the temple steps, returned.

"Same...everyone is the same!" she said to herself with a rising anger, approaching the rickshaw-stand with the crumpled handkerchief still in her hand.

"Even these despicable beggars are the same...!" she muttered inwardly. "No different from *him!*"

Climbing the rickshaw, seating herself in the middle and watching her children, with the boy Arya sitting near her feet, dangling his shoes and merrily holding onto the round steel hook on the back of the rickshaw driver's seat, Anasuya experienced the dread and despair of one who was trapped in an out-of-control locomotive that kept on hurling forward, always in motion, always on the endless rails of the very time itself.

Those few serene moments she had experienced while she was inside the temple, when she was not conscious of the need for any mastery over life, when she was not even conscious where life was leading her, as a result of which she was less anxious and more free, those moments evaporated and Anasuya at once became her old agitated self again.

5

The Siege

IN THE DAYS LEADING UP to July of the year 1978, the mood in the Old City of Hyderabad was the same as the anxiety that filled Anasuya's heart.

One moment there she was, she who wished always to improve herself, now taking her husband's hands in hers, now her arm around his shoulders, embracing him sideways with a happy gleam in her eyes, suddenly twisting his t-shirt all the way till he closed his eyes in pretended agony.

Then the next moment it came; the formless, cloudy, terrifying monster of *that* suspicion, hauling with it the oppression and the animosity, at once emptying itself into her heart's consciousness, so that in the very next breath all the brightness in her dissipated and she was filled once again with the despise of a woman betrayed by her husband; and the gnarled hands and arms of Rushi now pressed her deeper and deeper into a terrifying condition of isolation.

Over the next three days of that July, a force resembling this formless, cloudy, terrifying monster, perhaps this very thing itself, hissing with a pair of grimy hands and a grimy head, as though it were the very devil itself, roamed the streets of the Old City; and thus began a breakdown of the human relatedness, that is, a breakdown of the very ingredient of love, between men and women of the Muslim and Hindu communities.

On one particularly bright morning in that July, when the tops of the extraordinary mosques of the Old City stuck out serenely, the city of Hyderabad began slipping into an unsettled state, because all of a sudden, without anything that indicated the excitement that led to it, a party of armed rioters marched into an Old City public library, headed directly toward the librarian's office and began attacking the city committee chairman and the secretary who were sitting there.

Though the two communities of this city, the Hindus and the Muslims, had mingled among one another's families freely, sent their children to the school in the same rickshaw, borrowed sugar and milk from each other's kitchens; though their men, at the sight of the other's elders, stood back in respect, turned sideways and hid their cigarettes behind them; though in this manner they lived and shared the same space in the city, they were not particularly conscious of that unity, until now.

Then, on hearing that a riot had broken out somewhere, they emerged out into the open air, saw one another's full face all at once filled with hostility, and began to believe that this hostility was the true nature of the other; and therefore experienced even more suspicion toward one another.

ON THE SECOND DAY OF the riot they found an old woman's

body, her head split open, in the corner house a few blocks from Anasuya's.

When the police arrived at the scene of the death, neighbors were already there, gathered in groups.

Someone was heard saying that it was Kareem Bi, and that a large granite boulder, with blood marks on it, was found lying a few feet away from her pulverized head.

Others were sure that five or six young men in cut banians, with iron rods in their hands, were seen rushing in and out of the house.

These neighbors now stood and stared at the blue police Jeeps, and at the inspectors, as they sealed the house and left.

A complete account of this killing incident, which occurred just a few days before the start of that year's season of the Ganapati puja festival; and which was one of the many such incidents that led to the burning of the Old City of Hyderabad that year, can be truthfully told only by following the trajectory of this formless, cloudy, terrifying monster as it took over the impulses of the city folk, hauled them over to the graveyards, and buried them, and their brotherhood, there.

And it begins upon our acceptance, without further questioning, of this: that as soon as the word of *"Hindu-Muslim clash"* ignited itself in the morning and spread, all of the Old City was in a state in which people of one religion at once came under the sway of only one suspicion: that all those of the other religion had come together to operate under the influence of a common will to attack them, thereby revealing their true malicious colors.

This suspicion, having thus germinated by itself in

one group, grew rapidly of its own accord and compelled everyone to believe that unless they too collaborated and gathered together under the sway of a single emotion and act, their city was bound to be stolen from them.

THUS, SOMETIME IN THE LATE morning of the tenth of July, just as the third period was coming to end, one of the schoolteachers received a message that a riot had broken out in the Old City.

He came out of the staff room and began running towards the Principal's office. Seeing that the doors of one of the classrooms were open, he slowed to a brisk walk as he passed it, and entered the Principal's room in a rush.

After a few moments both men came out of the Principal's office.

A minute or two later more men and women, that is, the teachers, the drill instructor and the main attendant, gathered in one corner of the long corridor, just behind an enormous round pillar, doing as much as they could to stay out of the sight of the curious students.

Then the main attendant, having just received his instructions, nodded his head vigorously, turned around, walked rapidly toward the stairs that led him to the top of the building.

He then opened the top staircase door with his master key, and stepped onto a small platform under the bronze school bell, raising himself so as to reach the rope that was tied to the bell's tongue. He grasped the thick, smooth bell-knot, glistening from continuous usage, paused as if to time himself, and rapidly rang the bell.

Even before he completed the ringing of the long bell

a muffled roar of children's voices erupted from all the classrooms. The doors burst open and that peculiar, high-pitched reverberation, emanating from the swarms of excited school children, who already grasped that school was over for that day, filled the playground.

Seeing that only the small gate was open, and that not only the watchman but one or two teachers also stood on either side of it, the children immediately understood that something out of the ordinary had just happened outside, somewhere in the city.

The seniors, the fourteen and the fifteen year-olds, were already enquiring in anxious tones, as they passed the teachers before stepping out of the gate, if the city buses were still running.

Outside on the street, the rickshaw-men, who were parked near the fruit vendors and puncture-repair shops, glared at the school children as if envious of their unexpected freedom.

From the small gate the lowered heads of the school children emerged in a single file, paused a moment and straightened immediately after running into the street, just in a manner of a bird, which on seeing the cage door open, pauses a bit before it takes off flying.

These same streets, which had not been fully awake when the children went into the school at seven in the morning, had acquired a great deal of movement by this late morning hour.

Two hundred yards from the school, on the far left, the traffic was dense. Presently a giant deluxe double-decker bus went hissing and heaving around the roundabout. Following it on its rear and sides, like small fish with tiny tails hovering near a giant whale, were motorcycles, rickshaws, and auto-rickshaws. Now the same little fish tails, those that emerged on this side of the school street, stared curiously at the untimely sight of so many school children at this hour. Evidently not everyone in this part of the city had yet become aware of the riot, which seemed to have began, as usual, somewhere inside the Old City, on the other side of the Musi river.

"Why are they letting you out like this?" a rickshaw driver, thin, dark-complexioned, asked a group of kids, who passed by him. "Is school over?" his fingers closing the top button of his bright green checkered shirt that he had just put on.

"Curfew! Curfew!" replied a boy, who had his arm around his companion, while he waved his other hand with animation.

"Hindu-Muslim fight in the Old City!" cried another boy.

Shouting, "Riot, riot...! So school is over...!" the boy then suddenly ran, shrieking, "Aahh...You can't catch me!" being chased by another boy from behind.

"Riot?" frowned the rickshaw man, walking back to his rickshaw. "What nonsense? Every year same thing, will this fight ever stop!" he muttered. He anxiously looked in the direction of the city bus stop near the roundabout, towards which the large groups of children were now headed, and began to ponder how far into the Old City he could safely take his fare.

WHILE THIS WAS GOING ON, beyond the roundabout, at the central bus station – an enormous covered terminal for the district buses – the passengers with jute baskets and gunny bags, arriving from districts and villages, filled the streets busily. Evidently they were unaware that in only a few hours this central station, and half the city, would come to an abrupt halt; that the throbbing activity and the life that pressed them from all sides, scowling at them, barking confusing orders at them now to go here and now to go there, would disappear altogether, and that just as rapidly the normalcy would return again.

By one o'clock in the afternoon the machinery of public transportation that moved in and out of the Old City abruptly came to a halt. All those bus drivers whose routes for that day passed through the Old City were at once given orders to avoid it, except the school buses.

So, as soon as they reached a traffic stop, these drivers climbed out of their driving compartments and hurriedly replaced the last-stop signboards overhead with the new one that said, "Afzal Gunj," which was the last station before one entered the Old City.

As a result, throngs of citizens: men, women and school children, got off at Afzal Gunj, and were now seen walking with anxious looks on their faces.

These citizens, who were neither only Hindus nor only Muslims but as the soul and character of the Old City were both Hindu and Muslim people, were now on the Naya Pool bridge, which took them over the Musi river into the inner Old City.

ALL WAS QUIET. THERE WAS no one in the traffic kiosks, not even in the one near "Akbar Shoe Mart."

As these citizens descended the bridge, proceeded down the narrow deserted street toward Madina, and saw a long line of policemen in hard black shoes with brown metal tips, they at once became conscious of each other. The stern look of the policemen heightened their self-consciousness, and it happened to these citizens that which happens to all people who, having entered into a large, thinly lit auditorium, at first laughed, applauded, cried together, felt themselves in union with one another, entirely forgetting their dissimilarities; but upon coming out of the auditorium, saw the faces of the fellow men and women revealed in the full light as strange faces, and suddenly feeling that they had nothing in common, averted their eyes, and began to feel a certain inexplicable hostility toward one another.

A tall man, with a mustache and alert eyes, carrying a pale faded-blue briefcase, looked about him with curiosity, doing utmost to act as if none of this perturbed him, and purposely walked faster than the stout man next to him, passing him with a stern look on his face.

In the half-empty school bus, the school children, who until a moment ago ran from one window to another, shouting and calling at the fruit vendors, now abruptly became quiet, seeing the fearful, dense faces of the citizens on the street. One of the Muslim schoolboys, who earlier spoke to the rickshaw man, began staring at the man with the blue briefcase without taking his eyes off him.

The school bus drove past these citizens on the deserted street, on both sides of which, as far as the eye could see, the old buildings of Madina stood desolate.

Up on the balconies of these old buildings, seeing no movement of people or children who lived there, and no one peering down at the traffic below, and no large sheets of clothes on the clotheslines up there that waved in the wind, scores of blue bar pigeons emerged from under the dark, discolored roofs, and were seen moving freely.

High above these roofs, behind them, against the fading old concrete minarets that rose tall, thick branches of trees were visible in the bright blue sky, swaying lightly, and showing their green lush now and then.

Lower on the street, where the empty road led toward the main Madina Square, the view of the closed shutters of the shops was striking. Not having seen so many closed shops before, the citizens stared at these rows of iron shutters, some yellow, some white, with big brown and red letters on them, with a mix of curiosity and fear.

Not a single rickshaw, nor an auto-rickshaw, nor anyone driving anything, was seen as far as these citizens could see on the road.

Then suddenly a sight, of the motionless figures of two bodies by the roadside, came into their view. The citizens all at once recognized that the two figures, lying next to one another near a toppled fruit-cart, were of a man and a woman, and that they were already dead.

EARLIER THAT MORNING THESE SAME two figures were seen on this same road in an entirely different condition, in which the light of life still burned in them, just as it burned in every living being. The terrible and meaningless end to these two lives happened this way.

"...hurry up...! By the time you are ready the sun will sit on our heads...!"

Saying this the man spat one last time, took hold of the fruit-cart by the handlebar, and paused a moment so the woman, his wife, who was one or two paces behind him, caught up with him. They then, together, began pushing the heavy fruit-cart towards the bus stop.

Before they left their small hut by the Musi river that morning, they had a fight over their six-year-old daughter Ameena. So now, though they walked like this, without speaking to one another, pushing the fruit-cart until they reached the main road, they both were thinking the same thing, of their little girl Ameena.

Meanwhile back in their hut, the young child Ameena, having played around a bit and feeling tired, came into the hut, drank a big glass of water eagerly, and instantly fell asleep on the bare mud floor.

As soon as sleep came over little Ameena, she dreamt that her father was swooping her into his strong forearms, then talking to someone with a quick whisper, and then turning to her again. In her dream little Ameena thought, "My father, he always smiles at me, he always laughs at the sight of me." With her tiny fingers little Ameena reached for her father's nose, and for his face, which now was in her dream clearly, shining even more brightly. "How did he know?" Ameena wondered in her dream, "Exactly when to smile at me…?" While dreaming like this, Ameena did not know that her father and mother were now lying there on the main road, in a pool of blood.

"Is it true?" the man wondered in his dying moments, staring with his motion-less eyes at his dead wife's body that was lying a few feet from him. "Can it be true that I am forever estranged from her?"

In those last few seconds, he had a desperate urge to see his wife's face. From somewhere several voices reached his consciousness, saying all confusing words, "…surely it is a bomb...what else...?" Then a wry smile appeared in his expression, and an abrupt transformation came over his face. "Yes, the sweetness of the flesh. My bloody bloody hands," he muttered to himself, before life evaporated from his body.

THE MEN AND WOMEN WHO now passed these two bodies stared at them with surprise at first, but for only a second, before their movement carried them forward, even before they themselves could comprehend what they were seeing.

As soon as these citizens emerged out of the narrow street into the Madina Square, all at once in front of them stood, on the right, a bus ablaze in the thick black smoke and dense yellow fire.

"Who burnt this?" asked an excited, nervous man, addressing no one in particular. "Our men, or Muslims?"

"What does it matter who burned it?" retorted another voice. "It got burnt so it is burning! What nonsense!"

Away from the blaze, across the street, over on the left, was seen a police vehicle and an assembly of policemen in uniforms.

At a distance, and turned away from this assembly, stood two or three policemen, appearing to be talking among themselves but doing nothing.

Around the Madina Square, at various corners, small crowds could be seen. Here and there isolated people moved about, occasionally staring at the dark smoke, and then resuming their movements.

Beyond the Madina Square, where the main street formed an artery towards Charminar, the city appeared as if a pale, gray gauze enveloped the streets and the sidewalks. It was as though people and vehicles at once became invisible as far as the eye could see on this artery, leaving a striking view of a wide-open empty road and empty sidewalks. At the far end of this artery stood the giant figure of Charminar. Behind it stood the sprawling Mecca Masjid.

Nearer at the Square, next to the Madina Hotel, two or three shop owners in white caps, upon becoming alert, at first hurriedly emptied the cash boxes and began to pull down the shutters, but on seeing two police vehicles arrive, left them slightly open.

Suddenly, out of a narrow lane on the left, just ahead of the citizen's group that slowed the pace a bit, a police vehicle emerged with a roaring engine. It then violently turned and just as it straightened toward the Square, it began emitting a loud police siren and disappeared just as fast into the opposite side street. The two policemen in the vehicle sat straight and didn't look anywhere but ahead, in the direction of their motion.

A few seconds later, from the same narrow lane, speeding just as fast as the police vehicle, came a white-and-blue Enfield motorcycle, and stopped abruptly in the middle of the road. A sub-inspector dismounted and angrily, with animated movements of his baton, walked up to the crowd near the Square, and whistling loudly directed the citizens vigorously into the kaman on the left.

Among the crowd was a schoolboy, not quite nine years of age, who stood back on a step above the pavement, and stared at the sub-inspector through his spectacles. A thick green military-type school bag, heavy with books, was on his shoulder.

Just as quickly as he drove the crowds out of the Square,

the sub-inspector ran back to the Square and, seeing the slightly open door of the Madina Hotel, ran towards it, as if angry once again.

The young schoolboy, meanwhile, had crossed the road quietly, and disappeared into the maze of narrow streets behind the Madina Hotel.

This was Arya.

WHEN ARYA LEFT HOME THAT morning for school, there existed in the house the same morose and dark condition that always existed in that house for as long as the children could remember.

After they had their morning coffee, as Rushi was preparing to go to the office, there was such an expression of enthusiasm and expectation in his eyes that Anasuya once again suspected he might not return home that night.

"Again the same, usual lie that he has to go to the district for the inspection and won't be home until tomorrow morning," thought Anasuya, staring at her two daughters.

That freshness in his face, that smile with which he selected the new silk shirt, that patience with which he tolerated her sarcasm and gave all the money in his wallet to her, that playfully submitting himself to her, belittling himself jokingly, bringing her little things himself for which she was calling the children, all of it informed her of a man who was filled with the foreknowledge that a long respite from her awaits him somewhere else.

Seeing his usual forlorn face, with that expression of self-pity when he folded his empty wallet and put it in his trouser pocket, after showing it with a pitiful look on his face to each of the children, pressed the suspicion in Anasuya that his enthusiasm was not for the work at the office, but for a titillating circumstance after work.

That was in the morning.

And now it was nearly three o'clock in the afternoon.

Anasuya, awaiting the return of Arya and Rushi, sat on the chair near the front door.

Everyone anticipated, with a curious excitement, the curfew announcement on the radio at any moment.

The girls' school bus had already brought home Yashoda, as soon as the riot broke in the morning, so that now the most horrible images of her little Arya filled Anasuya's anxious moods.

Forgetting her usual disappointment at Rushi and at everything else that caused the ruin in her life, she imagined Arya, dressed in handsome school uniform, lost somewhere in the dusty Old City; now at last being found by Rushi; now animated words being exchanged between the father and the son amidst all the confusion that surrounded them; now both heading towards home. But the next moment she imagined Arya caught between the two ends of the street, in the midst of rough men in banians who were lunging forward with menacing eyes, and a terrible anxiety again filled her heart.

From her house a full view of the neighborhood playground was visible. Anasuya kept rising from her chair, going up to the front gate, and staring anxiously at the road behind the playground, and, not seeing whom she expected, sat back with increased despair.

After a few minutes like this, unable to bear the idle anxiety any longer, she made herself busy with afternoon household chores.

When Anasuya asked her to bring the sieve from the kitchen, Parvathi, maid Satyamma's six-year-old daughter, rose and swaying her head merrily from side to side and singing to herself ran into the kitchen and returned with the large sieve in her tiny hands. She then placed it next to Anasuya.

Anasuya, whose fondness for the little girl was growing day by day, looked approvingly at Satyamma. "Look how gently and correctly your daughter does what I ask! Not speaking a single unneeded word, not doing a single unneeded deed," she said, staring affectionately at Parvathi.

The little girl blushed. Emboldened by the mistress's show of affection, she said, "We too have a sieve like this."

"Do you? How small you are and still you know so many things!" Raising her eyebrows playfully, Anasuya asked, "So now tell me, can you count how many are you in your house?"

WHEN ARYA SAW THAT THE sub-inspector nearly hit the stout man who was earlier walking with him on the bridge, he grew angry.

He wanted to go straight to the inspector and tell him that only moments ago he himself had walked with the stout man all along the bridge. He also wanted to tell him that these were the streets he saw everyday while going in the bus, and that all these shop owners and the waiters in the Madina Hotel were familiar to him, and that the inspector should go somewhere else to beat people with his baton. He was convinced that seeing his school uniform and his bus pass the inspector would believe him, and perhaps even be impressed with his English. But as soon as the crowd began running into the kaman, Arya forgot what he was going to say, and instead became afraid, and ran behind the Madina Hotel.

"Perhaps they really are dangerous people," he thought, not fully believing himself, as he walked on the narrow backstreet.

The road was empty and quiet. There were no shops anywhere in sight and Arya did not recognize any of the houses.

It was nearly two o'clock, and the afternoon sun made the day hot.

On the other side of the street, near the window of a house, was a silvery birdcage with a parrot in it. The parrot just stood still, as if it was sleeping.

Arya walked for a few more minutes and reached Chowk.

Laad Bazaar and Chowk, through which Arya's path led to his home, were dense neighborhoods, with small row-houses nearly touching each other and meat shops here and there.

As soon as Arya walked past a meat shop, climbed over a large mound of thick, uneven ground and descended, he saw ahead of him three figures, fully covered in burquas, talking with animation. One of the burquas was black, as though it was new, and the other two were pale, discolored by continuous exposure to the sun and long use.

"Either she bought a new one or it is a fast color," Arya thought, remembering his mother saying "fast color," in reference to her saree. At once becoming conscious of the way he appeared to them, he changed his school bag from one shoulder to another and adjusted his shirt that was all crumpled where the strap was, before they reached him.

But the three women did not look at him, and without even turning towards him they entered a house. Just before they drew back the thick gray curtain, he saw that the woman in the black burqua was animated by something that the other said and removed her head mask with irritation, exposing her thick black hair. At once Arya felt an urge to go through the gray curtain into the room, and be near her. In his imagination he was sure that everyone in that house always smiled at her.

Thinking like this Arya proceeded forward, trying to remember if he should turn left or right at the next intersection, and wondering if his sister Yashoda went home already.

As Arya approached the intersection, which was already crowded with people, he saw, coming out from the narrow lane on the left, a stream of bicycles, rickshaws and auto-rickshaws; evidently all the traffic had been diverted from Charminar.

Across the street, on his right and ahead of him, stood a small mosque and near its entrance stood a group of four or five men, all with their white prayer caps on them. It appeared as though they had just finished their prayer and were standing at the junction talking among themselves.

Arya then saw children, mostly girls, playing in front of the shops, jumping up and down a raised platform. A sudden feeling of nearness towards the children rose in his heart. "Don't you know it is dangerous to let the children out here, into the open like this, at such times?" he was about to ask someone, but instead something else attracted his attention.

In the adjacent meat shop, through the gap between two

large pieces of meat that were hanging by metal hooks, he saw a swinging movement of the shop owner's arm. With a large black meat cleaver in one hand he cut the meat in rhythmic movements as he deftly moved the pieces sideways and around with his other hand, at the same time saying something to the man by the side of the shop. Next to the man there were three or four older men, also with white prayer caps on them, sitting in plastic chairs, talking something.

Arya was transfixed by these views. "Look how they go in and out of the streets, sit on the chairs and stare at the people, as though out here on the street is their living room, while I am afraid," he thought. He kept looking at one side and the other, mesmerized by the boldness, by the indifference, and by the fearlessness in all that he saw around him. Once again, the same intense feeling of kinship with everything in these streets rose in the boy's heart.

He crossed the junction, and going through the traffic that kept on coming from the narrow lane on his left, he turned his head over his shoulder, to see who else was going in his direction.

From the group that was standing in front of the mosque, one of the men stared fixedly at Arya for a few moments, and without taking his eyes off him, spat to his side.

Suddenly Arya became conscious of several eyes staring at him, and an awkward feeling of embarrassment rose in him. He wished to run away, to go near someone or something that was familiar. Still fixing his eyes on Arya, the man removed his cap and, now appearing more menacing, pushed his shirtsleeves up, and spoke to the others, without turning to them.

"He is looking at me thinking if I am a Muslim or a Hindu," thought Arya, now feeling apprehensive at his circumstance, forgetting his earlier pleasant feeling. "They are talking among themselves, planning to come after me from both sides."

At once all the faces on the street appeared the same to him, with the same menacing, calculating, fixated look on him, with the full knowledge of how to cordon him off, and how to frighten him. He looked away from them, and shifting his school bag from one shoulder to another, increased his pace. But the heavy bag kept swaying and kept hitting his thigh with a thud, and when the sound of the tiffin box lid breaking open came from within, he slowed down, perspiring and excited with a feeling of terror and shame. The consciousness that his fear had a terrible hold on him disappeared, and in that place now he felt the whole fear itself. The boy could not be sure if the ground was giving away beneath him or whether something unpleasant had begun to churn in his stomach. He slowed down further, and with a defiant expression on his face, through the spectacles that were becoming all misty and kept slipping down his nose, he looked back.

Contrary to his expectations and fears, he saw nothing that moved toward him. There were no crowds that were violent to be seen. He felt flushed. Becoming aware of the pulsations of blood flowing rapidly into his ears, making them swollen, itchy and tingling, he continued along that road, and was seen turning the corner onto the street that brought him nearer home.

6

The Beastly Hunger

MEANWHILE THE TRAJECTORY OF THIS formless, cloudy monster that crisscrossed so far with Arya's like the grim silver lining of Death's shadow on the vitreous streets of the Old City, now hovered over his mother's house, where several men and women began gathering near the building.

Gopu, a young man with a mustache, was looking up and talking excitedly with a woman who stood at the window of the second floor apartment.

"It seems they've burnt Medha Talkies completely," she shouted in a shaken voice.

"What? They..." cried Gopu, and then turning to the crowd around him, he shouted, "They burned Medha Talkies!"

"What? They burned Medha Talkies?" exclaimed several voices.

"Can you see the smoke?" asked an older man, looking up toward the woman.

"No, not visible for me from here. But go upstairs, climb

on the roof and you will see!"

The crowd at once became quiet. Instead of going up to the roof, the people nervously began to look around them, and talked in low tones among themselves. Women dispersed, suddenly chiding the men for crowding. Some were not speaking but were lost in a daze, their imagination now entranced by a rapid and dramatic vision of all the violence that they now believed would unfold.

Then Gopu placed himself under the window and began to stare intensely at the cross street two hundred yards away. He peered toward it intently for a few moments, and stepped onto the road to get a full view.

The others, suddenly alert to Gopu's excitement, didn't move.

The older man, timidly, but acting naturally, pressed himself closer to the building, hiding from the road.

"What is it? What do you see?"

A young boy, Jitu, stepped forward, saying aggressively, "Are they coming?"

In his roused imagination, Jitu expected a crowd of Muslims with sticks and knives to appear any moment rushing towards them, and he was ready to take on at least two or three of them all by himself.

"No, no. Nothing," Gopu relaxed slightly, and ran his fingers over his mustache, looking about him with suspicion and disdain towards everyone outside his group, his youthful energies now fully aroused.

Seeing the decisive expression on Gopu's face, and feeling the free-flowing frenzy in Gopu that now searched for an object for it, the older man suddenly recalled his own youthful days, forgetting that he was just as timid even then in his youth.

Enlivened by this confused recollection, the older man too experienced the rising tension at once. In that moment he was taken by an extraordinary feeling of might that he saw flowing in the youth around him. This frenzied might, already becoming communal, now stoked the fretful readiness of this youth.

Then, roused by this very same communal might, which he now felt creeping into his own body, the older man believed that he alone possessed the power to re-direct the growing momentum of this might. He, thereby, accepted the submission of Gopu's will to his own elderly, controlling, guiding and harnessing suggestions.

Ignoring everyone else, the older man stared straight into Gopu's eyes, and, in a manner of making public what was before a private understanding, exclusive only to the two of them, he asked, "Are any of our men here?"

Whether Gopu understood these words or not it was hard to say, but feeling the same harness and yielding to it, he replied with a short, quick and a snapping nod of his head.

"Be watchful this time," nodded the old man, in a manner of a final word of instruction. Just then he saw Anasuya emerge from the house across.

Remembering that her son Arya had not yet returned, the older man's expression became soft. He walked up to her, and even before he reached her, began waving his hands, and said, "What could happen to him, he is just a little boy. He will be coming anytime now," addressing Anasuya.

ANASUYA STOOD AT THE GATE listening to the voices and the excitement near the compound wall, and a moment later came back in with the news of Medha Talkies. Taking the things from the front room she went inside and called Suri, the washer man, from the kitchen, "I can see you already rolled up your sack. Well, in a little while they'll start the curfew. Where will you go? Go around to the back and sleep there. What do you say?"

"Did you hear Amma?" asked Yashoda. "Will you stay?"

Suri smiled at her without speaking a word, scratching his head and muttering to himself.

"He will stay. Where will he go? As if there's a house and wife and children that awaits him."

Anasuya returned to the gate, and again began to survey the playground, staring at the road, asking and answering the women in their talk of husbands and children. All she could hear were the increasing noises of the vehicles, of the police sirens, and of the crowds on the streets that surrounded the neighborhood. A terrible fear and a chill rose in her at seeing those rickshaws, those autos and that specially commissioned bus that passed by, none of which brought her little son Arya, nor the office servant Kadir nor Rushi himself.

She turned away from the women's group, and began examining the compound wall that surrounded her house. The sight of broken glass pieces, pressed into the concrete all along its top edge – to ward off thieves and intruders – calmed her senses.

"Now look how thoughtful we were..." Anasuya said to herself, once again reassured that a protective circle that surrounded her world was still impenetrable from outside.

Just then she heard the animated shouts of the people at the gate, and a familiar voice.

Even before her eyes saw what her soul already knew, Arya appeared in front – one leg already inside the gate – with a pale, excited face and disheveled hair, answering the rapid questions that came at him from the crowd.

"Here he is…! Your mother is nearly heartbroken!"

"Did they burn it while you were watching?" came the excited voice of Jitu.

"Go, go, go inside first!" an adult voice dissuaded the crowding neighbors.

"Have you come? We've been waiting since morning. Did you walk?" Anasuya came up to him, taking his school bag.

"Aaah…! I am exhausted. Such a long walk…" Arya sat on the chair.

Anasuya gazed intently toward his eyes, scrutinizing every part of him. After convincing herself that no harm had visited her son, she sat in the chair, putting the newspaper in her lap.

Yashoda took the bag and brought him the water glass.

"Why did you take so long?"

"Oh, I had to go round and round, behind Madina, through Chowk…I walked all the way!"

"All the way from Afzal Gunj!" exclaimed Yashoda.

The sister and brother continued their animated exchange, with Yashoda and Anasuya's surprise matched only by the step-by-step narration by Arya of his brave journey through the Muslim neighborhood.

Having finally emptied the water glass and exhausted his story, Arya grew tired. Remembering something he asked, "Did Kadir come in with any message?"

"No one came. Now who will come to this side of the city, after all this…?" Anasuya replied. "Only he knows if he is coming home or not. Those who really wish to come home will always find a way. Now look at you, didn't you return?"

The mother and the children sat in the front room for sometime like this, immersed in asking one another if they had enough milk for tomorrow and answering among themselves, and guessing how many days the curfew would last.

BY SIX O'CLOCK IN THE evening, Arya, having washed his face and hands, came out. After replying to his mother, who asked him something from her bedroom, he stood in the front room, considering, in a feverish anxiety, how he might safeguard his mother and sisters, should there be any attack on their house.

After that fearful and shame-filled episode near Chowk, no matter how many times he had changed his school bag from one shoulder to another to look like nothing had scared him, it appeared to him, as he neared his home, that in everyone's face there was a hidden smile, as though the news of his being chased had already reached everywhere – wrapped in the cloud of nervous excitement, the boy was now convinced that he really was chased – and that both his mother and father awaited his return with anxiety.

Hence, as he was approaching his home he had prepared to tell them how it happened: how really deep into those Chowk streets he had to go in order to escape the burning that was taking place on the Madina Street. He had imagined that no one, not even the rough men in his neighborhood, had gone into such small and crooked streets before. He had expected that even before he finished his story his father

would ask him just one or two details of how the street
looked like, and then he would recognize immediately what
street that was, what its name was, and may even have had
some water inspection work done there too.

When Arya had imagined this, it became clear to him that
those rough men in white caps threatening him in Chowk
streets, did so only because they did not know who his father
was. He even became angry at them for their forgetfulness
and callousness.

But, when, having returned home, recited the story,
carefully avoiding saying anything about his being chased,
to his mother; and when, still feeling unsatisfied he finally
queried his mother about his father, Arya had not expected
that expression of disdain on her face.

Then slowly, firmly, thoughtfully, quietly and carefully
he had washed his dirty elbows, his knees, his face and his
feet until everything was very clean. With soap stinging his
eyes, cold water making him shiver, he felt agitated at the
rise of one thought that he could no longer suppress. "Why
did father buy *this* corner house, away from everyone!
Anyone can see it is so easy to jump in over the compound
wall from outside!"

Now, coming out of the house, Arya moved toward the
gate with a steady calmness.

The sun had almost set and the twilight sky was bright
orange. The streets were all deserted, but small groups of
crowds were seen standing here and there.

The windows, through which only a few moments ago
people stuck out their heads and spoke with excitement,
staring curiously toward the streets, were all closed, and the
curtains were drawn.

Arya stepped outside and saw that the men standing near
the compound wall were not the same who had waved
at him when he returned home. Instead, Arya saw Malla
and Satti, not talking loudly, not laughing and cursing one
another as he expected them to, but standing around in
tense postures.

Beside them there were four or five strangers.

As he approached them, Arya once again became conscious
of the shame he had experienced earlier that day. "They
nearly got hold of me," he thought, still thinking of rough
men in white caps in Chowk streets. His chin trembled a
bit. He touched his ear, and slid his palms in his trouser
pockets in an effort to hide his quivering fingers, thinking
once again that those thick branches in the backyard of his
house, near his mother's bedroom, would hide any intruder.

But as he came nearer the men, the boy's anxiety subsided,
seeing Malla and Satti, these able-bodied rough youth that
he looked up to, and with whom he proudly wandered the
neighborhood in the evenings, though he was younger than
either of them.

Standing next to Satti was a figure that attracted Arya's
attention. Not only had Arya not seen him before, but also
he was bigger than either Satti or Malla   with dark, big
muscles that pressed out of the tight yellow ribbed banian
he was wearing. Two men, also strangers, stood on his
either side.

Seeing this large man, who ignored him, Arya began to
experience a strange morbidity. That feeling of agitation,
which first showed itself in the shame for his cowardice,
now grew in intensity, and though he did not know this
menacing figure, an irresistible urge to be near him rose in

Arya.

"Is he going to stand here in this group, near my house, until they start the curfew?" he thought, hoping and wishing that those men, who were due to arrive with iron rods, sticks and swords anytime now, should do so now, before this man disappeared.

The men continued to speak among themselves. Then the younger man, who was standing next to the large man, spat, wiped his mouth with the back of his hand, and with bright piercing eyes and an expression that terrified Arya, asked in a deliberate, low voice, "Where do they live?"

"Inside the colony," replied Satti. "Next to the water tank," showing the direction with his head.

"Who?" Arya asked nervously, his voice barely audible, but they all ignored him and the large man continued to exchange glances with Satti.

"It must be done now or else the curfew starts soon," the young man exclaimed.

It then occurred to Arya that they were referring to a Muslim house – there were only two in the neighborhood. He knew that the occupants of one had been away for some time, and that before they left they had shut their house completely, including windows, covering even the ventilator grills with newspaper.

The other family was just an old woman and her unemployed son.

"Could they be talking about Kareem Bi's house?" he wondered, remembering Kareem Bi, the frail old woman who spoke too fast for Arya to comprehend her, and who was frequently seen sitting in her white wicker chair, chewing paan and beckoning the passers-by to come in.

Then the large man in the yellow ribbed banian spoke for the first time.

"Don't rile yourself, whore!" he said in a hoarse voice, addressing the young man, using the feminine form that was common in herdsman families. "Show them what we brought first."

The young man stepped towards the compound wall, and crouched near what appeared like a pale discolored rucksack, bulging as though two or three cricket bats were tightly wrapped in it in a bundle.

He untied the string on the bundle. This at once released several iron rods that were in it, and they rolled to the side with a muffled clanging sound. He then gave one each to everyone, who, with an excited animation stepped back and began to swing them in the air. All at once a rush entered them, and they swung more, testing their strength and their might that was aroused at the sight and the grip of these rods in their hands.

Arya, who did not step forward, stood where he was, in a state of extreme anxiety and nearly shivering with dread.

An intense dark fear rose to peak in him. Though groups of men, similar in appearance to this dark muscled man in yellow ribbed banian, were expected to appear suddenly from everywhere, surprising them, and attack them with iron rods, knives and swords and sticks, Arya did not really think that he, only a school boy, would have anything to do with them, and that someone or something would always be standing between him and the harm that these swords, knives and sticks presented.

Afraid in the way that a she-goat becomes unyielding, filled with fear that makes its legs immovable as she is pulled by the string on her neck, Arya took the iron rod, feeling its rusted, rough, corrugated threads, and swung it in the air once, following the others. At once he heard a swooshing sound it produced, and a strange, soft, silky smooth sensation was transmitted to his muscles. Unexpectedly, his fear lessened and he swung the rod a few more times. He wondered if his aim should be the enemy's face or his body, testing and moving his grip away and toward the middle of the rod.

Just as he was swaying the iron rod this way and that way, a Jeep filled with several men emerged from the cross street.

Arya stopped swinging and followed the others who ran towards it.

Some men, also in banians, muscular, jumped down from the vehicle and swinging their arms aggressively, mingled with Satti, Malla and the large man.

Arya stood back from them, watching their red charred lips, their blood-shot eyes, their dark bodies glistening in the orange sun, while they exchanged quiet words with menacing expressions toward one another.

Several men spat, and stared curiously at this pale-complexioned young schoolboy who did not even come up to their shoulders.

"Where do you live?" someone asked Arya.

Arya turned his head timidly and showed them the house where his sister was standing at the gate, staring in their direction.

"The lad is one of ours," interjected Malla hurriedly, and taking the iron rod from Arya, said, "You go and stay near your house."

By then the men, whose excitement rose and reached

its peak, began to run towards the inside buildings, in the direction of the old woman's house. Their eyes beamed an intense, energetic, manic desire that swayed them, under the spell of which they ran forward, to snatch something in front of them before it disappeared, as if it fully belonged to them, thinking of it only as a prize for which they have already done all that was necessary, that is, identified her as a Muslim, and that this prize must be snatched quickly, now, in the continuity of this very moment. Having thus reached their destination, spotted the object of their frenzy, they effortlessly, and without thinking, lifted the nearby granite boulder, and collectively threw it on the frail creature.

The old woman, when she heard familiar sounds and voices behind her, turned around and stared at them, at first with her usual glowering expression. Her mouth and lips were reddened with the betel-leaf paan she'd been chewing with contentment after her evening meal. Then, as though she just realized something else in what she saw in their faces, she pressed both her hands on the chair, stuck her thin trembling elbows in the air, and nearly put her legs down in order to get up, when the boulder struck her head, collapsing her and the wicker chair.

The men rushed forward and suddenly came to a halt, as if held in check by an unexpected sight.

Then a strange and a peculiar pallor came over these men. For a moment, just after the blood-stained boulder finished rolling onto a side, their eyes, having already seen and become accustomed to the strange, shapeless coagulation of matter and blood in a few seconds, ceased to be surprised, much less moved by it. Instead, a feeling similar to a disappointment passed through the men at the quick, submissive and voiceless manner in which the life, which animated freely only a few seconds ago, became quiet, ceased existing and fulfilled their frenzied wish, and all was over even before they had witnessed the spectacle fully to their contentment.

THIS MUCH WAS CLEAR TO Anasuya, that something in the death of the old woman Kareem Bi unsettled the boy Arya.

Next morning, as the police Jeeps were heard leaving the scene, Anasuya was sitting in the chair near the front door, surrounded by her two daughters. Next to her were the maid Satyamma, who was talking continuously and Parvathi, who sat at the corner looking intently with her merry eyes at Anasuya's face.

Arya, who had just come out, stood in front of his mother saying something to her at first, but at once stepped outside with curiosity.

"It is safer for you in the village anyway," said Anasuya, giving Satyamma two of her old sarees and a few rupees for the child Parvathi. "These rupees are for the girl. Don't spend it on yourself! There is always some trouble or the other in this neighborhood at every festival."

The next day Satyamma and Parvathi departed to their village.

A few days later Old City became steady with normalcy, but Arya developed a high fever and had to be rested on the bed. Seeing that the boy was speaking incoherently in his sleep, obviously due to the high temperature, his bed was moved into Anasuya's room.

7

In the Mosquito Net

EVEN CHILDREN POSSESS, UNDER CERTAIN conditions, a longing to live in this world as an old man lives in a village.

Anasuya's children too were beginning to feel that longing.

But living as they were, that is, resigned to the frowns, orphaned between the passive and the aggressive, pensive from morning until Rushi left for the office, they knew that their lives, in *this* house, would forever remain the same, the same oppressive.

Except that day, when they witnessed something else.

Though the Old City riots subsided ten days earlier and Ganapati puja festival was almost upon them, Arya was still on the bed with fever, as though the specter of the formless and cloudy monster was still hovering about in the house.

Still, that day began with a Sunday-morning-like feeling. All at once the cascade of words between their mother and father had subsided, and their Amma was bright. And soon they got to making coffee and idle banter, disagreeing on

this and that, but agreeing on one thing, that they, she and
he and them, are one, are the same, just like a family.

Later, when it was all over, Anasuya reflected, recalling
this day, "Nothing happened that day to cause any of it...
it had been raining all day... I was only thinking should I
do payasam for the Ganapati puja... but it was true that I
felt a stone in my heart for some reason on that day... and
then..."

EARLIER THAT MORNING THE NEIGHBOR had come in with
her one year-old child.

Saying, "Who is this? A pearl, or a diamond?" Anasuya
came up to her and at once began pleading the child to let
her see just once the red-green wooden rattle, but the little
child kept moving it away from Anasuya's reach. Tears
rushed into Anasuya's eyes as the child kept hitting the
rattle on her open palm.

Bai, the new housemaid, who stopped sweeping the hall
and was trying to catch the child's eyes from behind the
window, saw those damp eyes on her mistress's face.

At noon, as soon as it began raining the neighbor left, and
the same suspicion that gnawed at Anasuya day and night
sank its teeth into her once again.

Rainwater was falling on everything, on the plastic sheets
covering some old bricks in the backyard, on the banana
tree leaves, on the thin iron sheet that was over the water
meters, and everywhere else.

Even though it was still mid-day, the sky became dim,
and a faint brick-red luster filled the horizon to the brim.

Outside the house, in front and by the side, it was all
muddy. A steady muffled roar of rain emanated from

everywhere.

Near the bedroom window the rain fell slower and fat raindrops were blowing into the room by the gust of the wind, making the windowsill wet.

Anasuya stood near the window, in the full sway of her pride that prevented her from confronting her husband fully with her suspicions. She had found out her name through Kadir, the office attendant, who also told her that she was a Christian.

"Some Tara it seems," Kadir had said, lowering his voice.

Kadir's wife had just given birth to the new baby, and since then he had been feeling that everyone else's life was ordinary and uninteresting.

At last Anasuya made up her mind and moved away from the window.

That evening when Kadir came in, she took him into confidence by giving him an old raincoat, some money and plenty of clothes for the new baby and the mother, and persuaded him to keep an eye on Rushi.

The attendant, seeing that determined look of anger on her face, deflected her wrath by saying, "Those little whores are everywhere these days. They think of no one, high or low officers. Don't worry Amma, I'll teach them!" and promised to report back to her.

MEANWHILE THAT SAME EVENING AT the office Rushi felt energetic and looked forward to a session at the pub with his friends.

He was especially satisfied with the exchange he had with the new director of the department, an IAS officer. Seeing the expression of congeniality on the new director's face, and the excited manner of his responses during their discussion, Rushi felt that he had created a favorable impression of himself that afternoon. At last here was someone who understood the enthusiasm in him, and who actually knew about Tacoma Narrows!

At the thought of Tacoma Narrows Rushi remembered another name, Timoshenko, a name his engineering professor invoked often during his university days. At this unexpected recollection of his student days Rushi experienced a familiar longing, which he had nearly forgotten, one mixed with hopes and wishes for that mystery of future itself. At once Rushi recalled the events that led from his university days up to his present moment, and felt as though they happened only yesterday. He thought of his children and blood rushed to his heart. Mixed with all this the image of Anasuya came into his thoughts, bringing with it an unpleasant discord. But Rushi brushed it away and forced his thoughts to settle on the children, and felt lighthearted.

As soon as Rushi walked into the pub and sat at the table with his friends, his attention was shifted to the discussion at the table, and he plunged himself into it fully.

By the time he reached home he was fully drunk.

When the auto-rickshaw reached near his house, Rushi made him stop before the driver went further, paid him off and got out.

While Rushi was thus coming in, opening the front gate and closing it quietly, inside the house in her bedroom Anasuya was just recovering from a dream.

JUST AN HOUR EARLIER ANASUYA had closed the bedroom door, laid down on the bed, covered herself in the thick navy-blue woolen sheet, and tried to erase everything that was flooding her consciousness – the image of Rushi, his very presence in her life – in a resolute wish to make everything that she was, her very being, a stranger to him.

After a few moments a quiet calmness settled over her.

"When was it," she asked inwardly, "that he felt for *her?*"

While Anasuya persisted more and more to freeze Rushi in his guilt, and make him disappear in it, more and more she only saw her husband who still lived, and who only desired to live just as she herself wanted to live. She tried to hold her gaze into their combined past, pecking her memories here and there and willfully recalling what he had done. But in everything that she could remember there was nothing that fulfilled her expectations.

There on her bed, nearly falling asleep but her gaze into him still steady, the more Anasuya wished to see Rushi as a stranger, the more she began to experience a renewed, tender feeling for her husband.

For a few moments a state of dream entered into her.

In her dream Anasuya was carried away into a time in the future, when the children had grown up, and any talk of them by the neighbors and relatives always began with their mother. "Then what else? Have they grown to be who they are because of *him...?*" she said to herself with a sudden impulsive anger.

Still in her dream scene, Rushi had come home, refused to eat dinner, and did not even eat the puffed rice. Here she could not say exactly what ailed her husband, but she knew Rushi came into the house brooding over something. "Why is he like this?" she despaired, looking at his downcast eyes, a soft feeling for him rising in her. She then saw that he was on the bed, turned toward the wall, and that he was crying. Overcome by a feeling, she wanted to say something to him. She already knew what words she would utter. Yes, what she was about to say was really not what was expected of her, but she was propelled by her own willingness to utter these words. In fact the very next moment, forgetting everything and only experiencing the child-like feeling she possessed for him, she said, "See here?" pulling his chin toward her. "No matter all this. Stay here in this house with me, or there, wherever your heart finds peace. I am still here. What if she was a Christian? It still is our life, is it not?"

At that instant Rushi's face disappeared from her dream, and a steady silence filled her heart, making it heavier and heavier.

Anasuya woke up from her dream.

The next moment she remembered her present circumstance. That derisive smile – so often seen on her – came over her face at the thought of her dream.

"If only he would listen to me that easily," she thought. All the softness that she only moments ago experienced in her dream for Rushi disappeared and a vicious rancor filled it.

Then she heard the sound of Rushi's arrival.

Rushi closed the front gate, and, only dimly aware of his unsteady legs in his drunken state, he came near the frontdoor steps, under the dim yellow porch light.

He was about to tap on the metal frame with his ring finger when he heard, from inside, a shuffle and the sound of the keys, as though someone grabbed them in one impatient motion.

Evidently Anasuya heard his steps. "Why is she so loud?

She'll wake up the children," thought Rushi, seeing her figure come out into the front room. A feeling of deflation descended into him.

He looked at her, making an effort to appear cheerful.

Anasuya removed the lock and pulled the door towards her. Stepping backward, she turned her face away from him.

Seeing the disdain on her face Rushi was overcome by a sudden burst of frustration.

"Are the children sleeping? How is Arya's fever?" he asked, and the rising tension in his own voice surprised him by its unintended harshness.

She looked at him with the same disdain.

Suddenly in that look, and at this sight of his wife, Rushi felt as though everything that he was imagining until that moment: the resolutions that had begun to sprout in him, the renewed anticipation for his future and the rejuvenated determination to better himself, all these seemed suddenly unattainable, and he experienced a momentary surge of panic at this loss.

He cried with vexation, "Why do you look at me like that? Am I not a human being?"

She ignored these words and went straight to the kitchen.

In the kitchen she reached for the plate that covered the rice vessel, lifted and placed it, and the water glass, next to the vessel, on the counter, and said dismissively, "There... Now what else is expected of you? Eat then."

The frenzy that merely flickered earlier in Rushi now rose in him feverishly. In this state he saw that all the agitation he was experiencing was somehow rooted in the irrepressible spite he now saw in his wife, and in that virulent defiance he saw on her face.

He lunged forward, swayed sideways due to his drunken state, recovered, seized Anasuya by her hair and pulled her to the floor. While he dragged her into the bedroom the expression on her face was frozen with the same disdain that he saw everywhere around him in that moment. The anger rose in Rushi uncontrollably. With all his strength and will he heaved her onto the bed and beat her with his hands and legs. The body, which only a few moments ago was resting after another long day, even caressed her husband's chin in its dream, now barely felt the unstoppable blows from him before Anasuya's consciousness began to recognize what was happening to her. "Oho, I am being beaten..." she said inwardly to herself, at once terrified at her condition. Another involuntary recollection passed through her, that her fever-struck little boy Arya was asleep in the same room, over toward the far corner in his small bed. She held her moans, concentrating instead on anticipating the blows, in an effort to tighten her lip muscles, so as to suppress the involuntary whimpers that emanated from her own throat. She did not move. Only her arms somehow were flailing in front of her eyes. Blood marks were visible on her wrists where the glass bangles broke. A mix of sensations: of the sight of her own blood; of the violent thud that first struck her body, then her temple and her forehead before receding into a distant muffle; and of a sudden dryness in her mouth, flooded her. Suddenly she remembered her mother and in that instant she heard her own voice calling, *"Amma...!"* She thought, "Am I being beaten? How? *Me...?*" The same instant it occurred to her that the life she possessed, that which was hers, that in which she imagined herself growing to be more glorious than what she was, that life may at last be separated from her, abandoning her and taking away her dreams from her. She experienced a terrible feeling of helplessness and the finality of that helplessness. She was not aware when Rushi ceased beating her and her body slipped into a motionless state of exhaustion.

A FEW HOURS EARLIER ON that very same evening, in that very same room, Arya, in a high fever that had not subsided even after four days, rested in his bed, barely able to make out what was going on around him.

Once or twice he felt the cold touch of the ice-water towel but could not remember who was sitting near his head. Now and then he was awakened by a muffled scraping noise, as cold droplets of water seeped into his ear when the towel was changed with a fresh one.

Gradually his delirium subsided, he opened his eyes and discovered that he was in his mother's bedroom, next to her large bed.

Over his mother's bed frame was a large white mosquito net. Both the windows in the room were closed.

On the small nail next to the cupboard, a dim bed light, flame-shaped and red, flickered steadily, smiling at him.

Through the grill above the window the sky was visible. It was not yet dark. A small end of a tree branch swayed slightly in and out of the view in the window, then disappeared altogether. He heard the birds chirping. Then the tree branch came into view again. The boy tried to make out if it was Jitu who was playing and shouting outside.

Without moving his body he turned his shoulder and saw that the door curtain was drawn. One door was closed and the other was slightly open. He knew his mother set it like that so she could hear if he called. Arya turned back and listened to the sounds from the living room. His mother was saying something to Bai, who had just come in.

"You look like you have finished early today. Sit, sit."

Bai sat at the corner near the door, letting a heavy sigh of relief.

"Just this one day, Amma, I got off easy! Doctor-sahib family is away for two days. How is he? Is he sleeping?"

Arya heard his mother reply in a soft tone, and he knew that she hushed so Bai did not speak loudly, fearing he would wake up.

Whenever his distress became intolerable he turned to his side and stared at his left arm, which was lying motionless on the pillow.

A few moments later he was overcome with sleep.

Sometime in the night Arya woke up. The room was dark but the light from the hallway illuminated the objects dimly. When he opened his eyes he tried to ascertain what his position was and where the door was.

He then saw two bodies in the mosquito net on his mother's large bed. A dim satisfaction began to grow in him. He recalled the weak tone of his mother saying something to Bai, and imagined it happened not a few hours earlier, just before his weariness overcame him, but yesterday or even two or three days ago. Now seeing his father next to his mother the boy felt a rush of longing for her. The thought that now she was not alone, and hence was no longer weakened by the burdens he saw on her, made him think of the sweet rice pudding he liked so much, and he decided to ask his mother to make some tomorrow.

Then he saw that some movement in the mosquito net

made the top of the net quiver. At first he could not make out what it was that moved inside. He thought it was something else besides his mother and father. He heard only voices, faint and clear, and it seemed to him that they were his mother's cries.

He looked up. The dim red light glowed and still flickered faintly as before. Then the movement became clear. Through the mosquito net he saw his mother on her back but her hands were outstretched as though she was trying to stop something that came at her. Then his father's face came into view. Seeing what he held in his hand confused Arya. "What is it?" he thought. "Why is he holding a belt in his hand?"

Then he heard his father's voice, angry, and with that peculiar upward tone, "...every time it is the same...!"

Arya did not hear what his father said next. His eyes were glued to the sight in front of him. He saw his father's hand swing in a confused manner and come down with force on his mother's stomach. At once Arya saw that his father was beating her. He now understood why his mother's hands were outstretched, a sight peculiar to him at first. Then another feeling, of pity for his mother, overcame him. He heard his mother's whispers, hurried and pleading, "No! *No!* I beg you! Stop, please!! Stop!" Blood rushed in Arya and he suddenly became conscious of himself. His whole body felt like a burning wood that would break with a crackling sound at any moment. "Why is he like that, is he my father?" he said to himself inwardly. A peculiar sensation came over the boy and he felt his arms become motionless. A voice inside him was asking him, "Why are they together like this, don't they know I am here? Their son! Why won't he talk to me? Why is she being beaten?"

A sudden thought entered Arya that perhaps that which was occurring in his view was his mother's suffering, and that had to do with him, Arya, causing fever to his own body. Had he been able to control his fever, his mother's suffering would not have occurred.

At once the boy believed that his mother was taking the beating meant for him. She was protecting him. But from whom? This was his father, not anyone else! Simultaneously Arya saw his father's face that terrified him for a moment but then the next moment the boy wanted to reach out to him. He thought if he were to make his father aware that this was Arya and not someone else, then it would surprise his father, make him laugh, and then he would stop and pinch his cheeks instead. It occurred to Arya that his father might have forgotten about him. He was sure that the very moment his father saw him, he would also see his mother, and then he would recognize that it was indeed just them and not some other people, and then that terrifying look on his father's face would disappear, and he would smile at him and at his mother again. But the continuous physical movement, and his mother's muted cries, begging his father to stop, terrified Arya. He remained sunk into his bed, fully riveted to not making any physical movement. After some time like this, the weariness, the increased fever and the terrifying condition tired the little boy, and he lost consciousness and fell into sleep.

8

The Boy

THOUGH THE SAME SMOKE OF the auto-rickshaws, the same blast of hot diesel winds, and the same incessant noise of the burburring lorries would fill it soon, on this early morning hour of the next day the Old City of Hyderabad was still quiet, and like a new bride's still-sleepy eyes, had not awakened fully yet.

But Ganapati puja is Ganapati puja, which meant that the day began in the same manner as it did every year, that is, with the same hesitant, staccato sounds of a coarse voice bellowing, "Hello, hello! One, two, three... One, two three..." out of the loudspeaker perched above the temple.

The streets began to be filled with the sounds of milkmen heaving large aluminum cans from the carriages of their Hercules bicycles for the special festival delivery. Newspapermen, who usually flung the paper into the houses from the outside, on this day, upon seeing the prominent red, white and yellow rangavalli, came in instead; and tiptoeing on the wet earth in the front yards, soaked and made even blacker by the early morning festival sprinkles, they were moved by an unexpected rise of feeling in their souls.

The temple loudspeaker blared once again with a song, and though the noise was excessively loud, in everyone who heard it a festival feeling entered that they were no longer strangers to one another.

With a final burst of, *"Jai Hind...!"* the loudspeaker then became quiet.

Early in the morning a note arrived from Sarangapani, brought from Pillanagrovi village by a young man, a carpenter. The note was addressed to Rushi and urged him to provide the young carpenter a living space for a few months, to help him find his bearings in the city and put his tradecraft to work.

"As long as he stays with you, use him to get any work done. He is a disciplined boy and would do anything you ask him to do," wrote Sarangapani. "By God's grace we are all safe here. We expect and hope the same with you."

They were all sitting in the center room.

"How can he live with us? To support a grown up man, is it just talk?" said Tiruvengalam, a brother of Anasuya, who came in that morning. "What a lot one needs! A body needs to eat at least three times a day, then the clothes, where will he sleep? What work anyway, as such do youngsters even listen to us these days?"

Tiruvengalam was one of those who habitually rejected at once anything they heard, without considering its merits.

Rushi was sitting on the floor in his morning clothes, amidst bunches of fresh mango leaves. He was pointing to one leaf after the other, which then Sita handed him, while he wove a festoon.

"Should we then send him back?" said Rushi with a slight smile. "It appears we ourselves are that poor. Go ask him if he himself can lend us some money on this festive day," he addressed Yashoda with a smile.

Yashoda hushed him. Getting up, she looked at herself in the mirror, ran her fingers in two or three quick sweeps over her hair, and whispered, in an earnest tone, "Should we give him some tea?" referring to the visitor from the village, who sat on the verandah floor with his elbows on his knees, just as someone from village sits.

JUST THEN, INSIDE ANASUYA'S ROOM, Arya woke up without any clear memory of the previous night. He nearly forgot his fever but remembered it when he saw that his shirt was damp. He was not fully awake, but already his mind wandered off to the purple marbles in his cupboard. He turned to his side and opened his eyes, but only a little, and stared at the window.

In the window was the steel vessel, evidently left there with ice cubes in it from the previous night's use for the ice-water pack. On its side, up to halfway from the bottom, were tiny bubbles, which seemed to have grown on the vessel while he was asleep. The white kerchief, which was the wet ice pack on Arya's forehead the previous evening, was now dry, frozen over the rim of the vessel. The water drops under it had nearly disappeared, and were only visible when Arya moved his head closer to see.

He stared at the tiny bubbles, transfixed by something for a long moment, during which someone opened the door into his room slightly, saw the boy sleeping and withdrew, saying, "He is still sleeping. Let him." Then another voice, his father's, spoke in a hushed tone, "Close! Close the door."

After a moment or two, Arya stretched out his hand and touched the vessel with his finger, drawing a sharp line through the tiny bubbles. Next to the steel vessel was a porcelain saucer. On it were the covers of the medicine tablets, with blue letters on them.

Voices, sounds of laughter from the outer rooms, and from somewhere beyond the yard, reached his consciousness.

A few moments later, rising above these voices there emerged a most vivid recollection of his mother in his imagination. Arya saw that his mother was sitting on the bed, her hands resting on the clothes basket she dragged near the pillow, her black eyes sparkling as if someone sprinkled water on them and began shining a bright merry light on them. Then she turned to him suddenly, and catching him completely by surprise tickled his stomach with her face until he kept laughing for a long time.

Carried away by how his mother kept making him laugh, Arya's recollections drifted, now and then interrupted by the abrupt changes in the song that came from the loudspeaker through the window. The sounds from the center room faded in and out, and he felt himself reawakened from sleep and falling back into it. He began to imagine his mother and father abruptly in a new light.

Then the memory of all *that* which the previous night swiftly crept back into him. As he lay on his side, staring at the white cloth and steel vessel, the figure of his mother behind the gauzy mosquito net appeared in his recollection. Blood rushed to his heart, and an intense pain, mixed with pity, aroused in him by her appearance. In that moment he saw his father's image. A sudden urge rose in Arya to go near him, stand in front of him, make him see that he was there. In Arya's little heart there was only one wish: that his father be surprised when he opened his eyes, seeing that it was really Arya and no one else; then his father's face would be bright again, everything would be bright again. His father and he would then take the white cotton and tie the bandage where his mother was hurt, and tighten it just once until she winced jokingly. And he would sit between them on the bed, roll on his back and see that brightened look on their faces.

At once rejuvenated by his feelings, Arya sat up, his recollection broken. But just as rapidly, the same hurtful and angry look on his mother's face reappeared. Disappointed, Arya slipped back and once again tried to summon fresh images in his reflection and tried to mix them, until all that he saw, all that he felt and all that he wished merged into one. But he only succeeded in waking himself completely.

SEEING NO ONE IN THE kitchen, Arya walked into the center room where everyone was gathered. His mother was not there.

Following the voices from the front room, he peered through the window, raising his head just above the curtain spring, and saw her speaking to someone.

Rushi, having just tied a festoon to the doorway, got down from the stool, steadily holding a half-finished festoon and the cotton ball in his hand.

"There, have you woken up? How is it, still feeling fever?"

Arya expected to see in his father's eyes some recognition of the previous night. But contrary to what Arya had imagined, there was no sign of any severity, nor was there any look of doubt on his father's face.

"No, all gone. I was sweating in the morning," replied the boy, looking into his father's eyes that smiled at him.

Not satisfied with his reply, Rushi took his arm, felt his pulse, then put his palm against the boy's forehead.

"Yes, yes. You are sweating a bit, which means it has subsided."

As a last measure Rushi felt the boy's head, and his neck, with the full face of his palm and pronounced once again, "That means it's subsiding. You will still feel a bit tonight," and still not satisfied, said, "Don't stop taking your tablets."

"Who is outside?" asked Arya.

"That's the carpenter from our village."

Arya continued to feel perplexed. He had woken up fully charged with the memory of the previous night, especially the menacing and confusing sight of the belt in his father's hand. Brushing his teeth and washing his face, Arya thought only of his parents, and formulated a notion that the previous night something resembling a murky cloud came in and was blocking the stream of love that otherwise flowed freely between them, darkening their mutual affection.

And now that it is morning, Arya, determined to drive away this murky cloud, kept trying to pull his parents back into that same stream of love and pity that overflowed in him too the previous night.

As a sign, he expected his father to ask him any minute to help with the white bandage for his mother, and he was ready to go to him instantly.

But there was no sign. Neither his mother nor his father appeared to be cross with each other. Arya was confused.

Whenever the boy was near his mother and father, at a

moment it was safe to do so, he looked secretly at their faces. Unconsciously he probed into their expressions toward each other. But no matter what he did, he could not bring them together into that stream flowing in him, because he saw no recognition of the previous night's pain in their faces. Arya began experiencing a new, strange and an unpleasant feeling of being disconnected.

Just then Bai came in to announce Rushi's colleagues, Pathak and Kelkar. Rushi got up and went out hurriedly.

A few moments later Anasuya came into the bedroom and took something out of the almirah. Then she stood just still. In his isolation Arya could not find a way into her heart then either.

Later that afternoon, when his colleagues left after two hours of laughter, cigarette smoking, gossip and six rounds of tea, Rushi came back inside, saying he must go to the office.

BARELY THREE HOURS PASSED AFTER Rushi left the house when Kadir came in with a large gunny bag full of sugarcanes.

Children were playing somewhere in the backyard.

"Sir sent these for home, Amma," Kadir said, untying the bag from the back of his bicycle. "They were going on an urgent inspection trip to Suvarnapuram. You should've seen, Amma, there they had such a bumper crop this year. And here for us in the city it's barely an hour of water and that too they skip a day! What a city life!"

By the manner of the attendant, going on and on about the sugarcanes, Anasuya's suspicion, that Rushi was really going to Tara that evening, heightened. In her imagination a picture of Rushi appeared next to that vile creature, clear with her vile intentions, and a burst of a feverish emotion arose in Anasuya.

"Which Suvarnapuram?" she said angrily, sitting down on the chair. "That god-forsaken place, wherever is it, so far outside the city, as if thrown away. What is he doing there, inspecting cows and buffaloes?"

"Who else was with him?" she lowered her voice, still angry.

At Anasuya's tone and her words, a discomforting feeling passed through Kadir. He knew Anasuya always had *that* suspicion, which he and everyone began to see more and more openly on her face. As a man, Kadir was conscious of that peculiar commonality by which all married men are bound in this familiar suspicion in the eyes of their wives. Still, seeing Rushi, his master, enveloped in that same commonality, continued to surprise him.

"There was Hangal saar, Pathak saar and then two or three contractors. This new project is taking a lot of saar's time, Amma."

Just as he uttered these words Kadir quickly averted his eyes from her and turned to his bicycle, folding the bag and smoothing it. He continued to fix his gaze away from Anasuya while his hands strapped the gunny bag to the back of the bicycle.

Suppressing the rising anger in her voice, Anasuya said, "All this is due to that new director at the office, I don't know what. When did he say he is coming home?"

"Sir didn't say anything, Amma. `Give these to Amma and go home for today,' is all he said."

"Then go. Your wife must be waiting. She, all on her own with the little one, is a new baby such a small thing?"

Even as Anasuya sat there, in a state of extreme moroseness, watching Kadir hold back his bicycle until the throng of school children cleared the front of the gate, she was tormented by what Kadir just conveyed.

She gave her children some orders, but the next moment she once again fell into that involuntary replay of all that her life had become. An intense concentration wrinkled her eyebrows, as if she was straining to hear the faint sounds from her fierce recollection, sounds that barely reached her, of everything that she was, of everything that she wished to become, and of everything that she nearly became but had not, all because *of him*.

MEANWHILE IN THE BACKYARD, ARYA, who had been listening to his mother silently, rose to go inside the house.

Just then one of the kittens approached him with inquiring eyes.

Arya picked it up, wrapped his hands around the velvet smooth fur, and held the kitten close to his cheek, listening to the purr that emerged from somewhere inside the animal.

Then suddenly his hands trembled a bit. Holding the kitten tightly with his one palm round its tiny, warm and quivering stomach, from where the purring sounds emerged, he freed his other hand, took a step back and hurled the kitten against the backyard wall, which was ten feet away.

The kitten struck the wall with a strange, violent sound, fell directly beneath on the ground, and lay there without any movement.

Arya stood there, without approaching it.

The kitten remained motionless.

Seeing there was no blood, Arya wondered if this was how

all kittens die.

Then the creature stirred slowly, lifted its head, and in an abrupt motion, as if it was alerted by a sound, tried to rise on its feet.

Arya wondered, "How could it do that? Didn't it know it might be hurt? Didn't it remember I just threw it at the wall?"

The kitten fell but rose again. It swayed a little but somehow managed to remain on its legs. It didn't move, but stood on its four legs, its eyes half-closed, its face trying to collect itself, trying to decipher where it was. It then uttered a dull whimpering cry and took a step forward but fell sideways, as if its legs were broken. The kitten ceased moving again. Suddenly its hair rose as if it just remembered what horror it had just experienced. A muted sound came out of its mouth. Then, to Arya's surprise, it shook its head and body vigorously and walked on, as though it forgot what just happened.

The next moment, drawn by his mother's increasingly noisy movements, Arya ran into the house and saw that she was already rising from her chair.

Kadir had left.

Anasuya walked slowly into her bedroom, leaning on her hand against the wall, and declared to the children, with a scowl on her face, that she had tired herself with the chores of the day, and she no longer had any energy to prepare dinner "for them," and was going to sleep.

Relieved that it meant an escape from her constant beckoning to fetch that water glass, press her head, close the window, bring her the medicine box, make her ginger tea or run urgently to ask the doctor when he was coming,

her children eagerly reassured her that she need not worry
and that she should indeed go to sleep.

WHETHER OR NOT ANYONE INFORMED Anasuya of Arya's
mauling of the kitten that way, there was one thing that
did escape her attention: that from then on Arya frequently
suffered from uncontrollable bouts of shivers in the middle
of the night, which he suffered alone, and did not tell
anyone.

Two days passed since Rushi had left for the office, and he
still had not returned home.

On the third day Anasuya immersed herself in the
household chores throughout the afternoon, while the
weeks-long Ganapati puja continued to stir expectations in
Arya's heart.

From the moment Anasuya and the girls began making
up the center room, talking to one another in an off-hand
manner about this and that, Arya looked at his mother's
face after every remark others made, and saw that gradually
the forlorn look on it disappeared.

As the day progressed, seeing his mother's countenance
turn brighter, and even cheerful, he felt even more jubilant.
Impulsively he counted his purple marbles once again. He
made sure his books, and that candle-boat, were safely
inside the cupboard, out of sight in the center room, while
they arranged the Ganesha there.

By afternoon the center room was set with their Ganesha
sitting comfortably against the wall, surrounded by bunches
of mango leaves – and shining lamp lights.

Then the main light in the room was turned off, so that the
bright glow of the brass oil lamps, mixed with the shimmer

from the red, yellow and blue alternating bulbs on Gahesha, was the only thing that illuminated the room.

Visitors, themselves in this festive mood, walked in with no hesitation, not even pausing to see who was inside. A neighbor, passing the center room, intimately straightened the green mango leaves on the festoons that glistened in the light of the oil lamps.

Seeing the guests go straight into his mother's bedroom, Arya's mood brightened and he concluded that she would not be alone as long as they stayed. He observed Anasuya's enquiring eyes, her vibrant expression questioning and dismissing in an off-hand manner their self-deprecating remarks, serving them with tea, coffee, showing them her new saree sets, which made them converse with her even more intimately. Once or twice she tactfully sent Arya away to let the guests speak to her in private, to reveal their grownup secrets.

All this enhanced Arya's serene mood even more. It seemed to him that at times like these his mother had forgotten the pain that he knew was in her heart.

A while later, after counting the ripe fruits on the backyard guava tree, he came inside, stood there in the center room for a few moments, and then stepped out of the house.

THE LATE AFTERNOON HOUR WAS not too sunny. There was even a slight dampness in the air. Already the folks at the neighborhood temple were busy making decorations for the evening festivities.

Two rickshaws filled with wicker baskets of flowers, on their way to the temple, came out of the narrow lane next to his house. Three or four boys were running behind one rickshaw that carried two large Ganesha statues, each nearly four feet tall.

Seeing his friends among those boys, a joyous sensation rippled through Arya's body. He instantly forgot the conditions at his home and his plans to be near his mother all day. He ran, bursting out of the house, and became immersed in the shrieks and delights natural to the boys of that age.

A few minutes later this group of happy boys rushed past the bamboo fence of a nearby house and suddenly stopped, seeing what was happening inside the yard.

The figure of Esai, an uncle of one of the boys, was visible from this side of the fence. Seeing him the boys went into the yard, but stopped short abruptly at the sight of a flailing creature – a pale white-winged hen – in his hands.

Esai held the white hen upside down by its legs. It flapped its wilted, dull wings a few times, swaying Esai's arm a little. After a moment or two abruptly the wings ceased in midair and became motionless, making the hen's body look awkwardly larger than it really was.

With a coconut broom in his right hand Esai brushed the ground near him, so the dry leaves, the pebbles and the little stones were cleared. Next he sat down, crouching with his elbows over his knees, laid the hen flat on the ground, firmly pressing its body under his left hand. He then removed the knife from between his teeth, made a quick motion near the creature's neck and cut its throat in one swift movement.

As if a searing metal just touched it, the hen shrieked suddenly and Esai stood up immediately, still holding the hen by its legs, keeping his arm away from his body. The hen furiously flapped its wings with a force and desperation that Arya had not seen before. He knew instantly that Esai's deft hand had cut its throat just as Esai meant to cut it, that is, not fully severing the head, but slicing the neck only half way.

With a satisfied look on his face Esai dropped the flailing body of the hen on the ground where he had just cleared, and with a swift skill set out to gather the tools for the next phase of this act, not even bothering to look at the hen.

Freed from Esai's grip, the hen now jerked and jumped its whole body violently and vigorously. Its thin wrinkled red legs and nose, the feathers on its tail and on its breast, all were now covered in dirt mixed with red blood that seemed to come out of everywhere on its body. Small feathers, hundreds of them it seemed to Arya, flew off the hen and settled all around them. Some even landed on Arya's knees and he jumped back in fear and disgust.

After a few moments the hen stopped moving. But it seemed to Arya, who stared intensely at its breast for a sign of life, that it was still breathing.

Esai returned with a tin pail full of water and two or three rags. He then carelessly held the body of the hen in this way and that way, and began plucking its feathers at a rapid pace. He squeezed the blood from the hen's neck into a small aluminum cup, so that the cup now had a thick blackish-red liquid, motionless and shining with some oil from its earlier contents. Looking up toward the children who gathered around him, Esai smiled, wiping his perspired face with the back of his smeared dark hand.

WHEN ARYA RETURNED HOME AN hour later, Anasuya was in a joyful mood, standing in front of the tall mirror, humming some song. Carefully placing the tip of her forefinger, covered with red kumkuma, in the middle of her forehead, she was saying, "Umm, is it centered? That came out ok?" and, having satisfied herself, "Yes, that looks good."

And as a last measure in making herself ready, she bent her upper back slightly backward, and not taking her eyes off the mirror, cleverly caught the bottom seam of her saree with the back of her heel, and straightened her back in one quick motion. This made sure that her saree did not have that awkward lift exposing her heels.

Just then Parvathi, also getting ready for the evening, came in saying, "Ammagaru, would you put this on me?" handing her the flower bunch, and stood still with her back to Anasuya.

"Look, how beautiful you are!" said Anasuya, "Ey, Satyamma, look now neat your daughter looks. Have you started looking for a school for her yet?" looking at Satyamma, who was standing at the door giggling, covering her mouth with her saree.

Satyamma replied shyly, "She already practices on the slate and can't wait to go to school herself, there's no stopping this girl, even if I want to," at which Anasuya nodded approvingly.

With her deft fingers Anasuya adjusted the flowers lightly on the little girl's head and said, "Now, go."

As the mother and the children stepped outside the house and walked towards the temple, Arya's mood was elevated. Without looking at her face he knew she was smiling, and that she was in high spirits. That knowledge made him feel secure and he forgot about the hen.

9

An Irresistible Enchantment

Two weeks passed following the end of Ganapati Puja festival. Nothing noteworthy happened the next day when, at eight in the morning, Rushi was ready to leave home for an important meeting at work, but everything that happened in their combined life until then still stood between him and Anasuya.

When he was dressed and ready, as usual he first wiped his Vespa seats and handlebar with the damp yellow towel and came inside. Seeing that Anasuya was still sleeping, her heavy body wrapped in three sheets of blankets, Rushi once again became fully conscious of the discord between them, and eagerly waited for her to wake up, for a chance to make amends before going to work.

Every five minutes Rushi came into the bedroom, stood by the door and watched his wife with a despairing look on his face, listening to the faint whimpers she emanated, as one who suffered from a sickness.

Conceding to the state she was in, Rushi tried to make himself believe that it was entirely his fault that she was like this, sick, but among children there was a suspicion. They believed that their mother's attitude this morning was deliberate and measured. They saw that she was not sick but merely pretended, in order to purposely amplify the effects of their father's continued actions.

When at last she woke up, Rushi was sitting at the edge of the bed. As if he concurred with the evil nature of his own actions, and the unfair distress it caused her, Rushi gave quick orders to the elder daughter, "Yashoda! Put on some hot water! Your mother is awake!" Then turning to Anasuya, he timidly asked, "Are you not feeling well? Fever?"

By how Anasuya angrily turned away from him, by her scowl and by the continued frown on her face, Rushi gathered that his suspicions of his own faults had come true. His despair only increased.

Soon Anasuya rose and freshened up but there was still no sign of reconciliation. Besides, her deliberate silence triggered a feeling of self-pity Rushi had always experienced whenever they bickered.

Just before he left home Rushi spoke to the children, making sure to show them his precarious condition – he had already let them know of his important meeting at work that morning – so that their anxiety for him rose, seeing Anasuya's continued passivity.

AT THE OFFICE, THOSE IN his division saw the brooding expression on his face, and thinking that Rushi was already engrossed in compiling the details for the meeting, they curbed their impulses to wink at him, and they too went on to prepare for the meeting.

Rushi could not stop thinking of the morning: one moment recalling the disdain on Anasuya's face, and the very next moment thinking that it was really a smile, which she desired to hide from him in order to torment him.

"Yes, in reality she is not that harsh. She does not harbor those disdainful feelings for me. All this is just an act to claim her territory," he said to himself.

"That means I maybe making more of it than it really is," he tried to convince himself, but he did not believe it.

"She does really think very small of me," he concluded in vexation.

Once again a replay of the series of events in their combined life, of the vulgarity of her expressions, of depression that always seemed to fill the house, directed his mood towards despair.

Then he remembered reading somewhere that women often forgive men. "Could it be that by the time I go home she had forgotten it and forgiven me?"

Unable to resolve such conflicting streams of thoughts, he plunged himself into work, and seeing the attendant carry several cups and two large pots of tea on a large tray into the large meeting room, Rushi hastened his preparation for the session.

It was late in the evening by the time the meeting was concluded. Rushi came out with the director. They waited, talking in a casual manner, while the driver brought his Jeep.

After the vehicle carrying the director left the premises,

he entered his office and saw, from the side window, that
Kelkar and Pathak, from Section C, were already walking
toward the row of scooters parked near the paan shop, under
the shade of the banyan tree, across the road.

"IT'S ALL OVER, DONE WITH," Rushi said to himself. "And
now I am free," recalling the intense, grueling, all-day
session with the director, who never relaxed the austere
expression on his face until the end.

"And they nearly made a mess of it," he thought, staring
at the two figures of Kelkar and Pathak at the paan shop. He
reflected once more with a proud feeling that though they
all worked in the same division, at more or less the same
seniority level, he himself was quite different from them.

Rushi was aware of how everyone at the office spoke
highly of him; how he, though of the orthodox Srivaishnava
Brahmana family, enjoyed smoking and drinking with them.
At this latter thought, his feeling of accomplishment grew.

"This is where everything real is. These people are the
proof of real life," he thought.

Then thinking how others in his orthodoxy were often
seen in white traditional clothes, he said to himself, "What
is the use being so strict and going around talking all that
wisdom in white clothes with these villagers?"

Then that expression on his wife's face this morning
returned to his memory and he despaired, "That means she
still thinks I am inferior to her brothers. Yes, that will never
change. And was she not like this from the start?"

Once again recalling his office life, and the infectious
enthusiasm he felt in the presence of his colleagues, Rushi
thought angrily, "Do these people remember him?" thinking

of Pandurangam, Anasuya's brother. "Does *he* know how to mingle with them?"

Rushi recalled how in the early days of their marriage he was so eager to show Anasuya how he alone, among many high priests on his side of the family, rose to become an engineer. "But all that meant nothing to her! It is always how *her* brother rose to become Chief Accountant of the state," he said to himself. "How did it come to this? How could this happen to me?"

Just then Rameeza, the woman attendant who was finishing up with the cleaning, came up to his desk with a tray that had empty tea cups on it. Her silk saree glistened on her thick smooth shoulders.

"*Are're'*... Are you still here? At this late hour you should not bother with such trifles!" Rushi said, with an excessive earnestness, which appeared in his voice whenever his eyes fell on her, and addressing her formally. "As such it is past closing time already..." He at once stepped away meekly from the metal desk, forgetting, at the sight of Rameeza's shapely figure, the current conditions of his life that only a moment ago seemed desperate.

Rameeza paused chewing her paan for a moment and stared at him intently, with the same look of cheerful softness she had on her face just this morning, when Rushi asked her to fetch the East Hills project papers.

"Should I then leave them here all night? Everyone has already left," she replied, not giving in to the earnestness in his voice. The untamed expression in her eyes, which glanced at him once more before she turned away, seemed to say, "You may have a higher office now, but don't you see, it's all the same to me? I must still collect all tea cups and clean every room as usual."

With the two round pale white cups swaying together on her long fingers that held the tray in one hand, she adjusted her saree with her free hand, and without looking at him left the room, her features made even more round and large by the sedate movements of her silk saree.

AT ROUGHLY THIS SAME HOUR when Rushi, with a feeling of accomplishment, was seeing off the director in his Jeep, Arya returned home from school, and as it often happened on the day he wholeheartedly enjoyed the classes, an entirely different set of conditions that existed at home in the morning rose in the boy's consciousness as he walked in.

The front door was wide open. The stick he was playing with in the morning, watching the shadow while he spun the hat on it against the sun, was still lying in the middle of the center room. There was no one in the kitchen. The small hallway was empty.

He saw that the bedroom doors behind the curtains were half-closed. Arya quietly inserted himself between the curtain and the half-open door and saw his mother sleeping, still the same as in the morning.

Just then the maid Bai, who finished sweeping the garden, and now gathering the steel plates and glasses under the tap, appeared at the back door.

Arya came up to her.

"Is school over? Already?" she asked, looking at him with a smile and pouring, with her wet hands, the blue powder from the damp Rin Surf detergent box onto the steel plate.

When Arya heard the loud sounds Bai was making with

the pails and the buckets he grew angry and wanted to hush her. But seeing her smile he forgot his anger and began to ask her if his mother was sleeping when she came in. What he really wished was to tell his mother urgently how they had moved his fourth-grade class into a new room, and how the new room was upstairs, and how he could see the whole playground from up there.

"Was Amma sleeping when you came in? Did she not get up even once?"

"When did she get up? Just once she got up, ate just very little, not much, just this much," Bai indicated with her fingers. "And from then she was only sleeping? What can she do?"

The maid, who had already gathered bits and pieces of the discord between the husband and wife, maintained a feeling of womanly sympathy towards her mistress.

"Then let her sleep. Don't make loud noises."

The boy then went in, picked up the stick from the center room and slowly tiptoed into the bedroom.

Staring at his mother's sleeping figure Arya noiselessly placed the stick in the narrow gap between the almirah and the wall. Just as he withdrew his hand there was a movement on the bed, at first under the sheets where Anasuya's feet were; then the shapeless mass of cushions, bed-sheets shuffled, and a pair of arms and shoulders and Anasuya's head emerged from within and gazed at him with an alert expression, as though she was not really sleeping.

Arya looked at his mother, relieved that she was already awake and was smiling at him, and that his wish to tell her everything was about to be fulfilled.

The boy came nearer but seeing the change of expression

that came over her face, he asked:

"Should I bring water?"

She shook her head, and in a weary tone uttered something feebly.

Arya leaned on his elbows on the bed, and waving his legs, said, "I just came from school," and began telling her what had been stirring in him until now.

Anasuya gradually became fully awake and began to interrupt him with loving enquiries that brightened and energized Arya even more.

In those moments of elevated state of happiness that her son triggered in her, Anasuya was relieved that the boy did not fully remember that morning's mood in the house. The very sight of her son jerked Anasuya from the brooding mood she'd been in, and she experienced a heightened joy seeing his ruffled hair, the complaining looks in his eyes whenever she interrupted his flow, and his restlessness at her embrace, like nine-year-old boys do when physical expression of parental love becomes unbearable.

Now sitting upright in the middle of the bed next to her, now rushing into kitchen to fetch the water glass, now stretching his plump body to reach the medicine-chest on the air cooler, the boy forgot the displeasure, the disappointment and the anxiety that filled him a few minutes earlier when he recalled this morning's depression at home.

Filled with excitement, he then remembered the most important thing he wanted to do that evening.

"Now I must go and take my shoes to be repaired. Then I am going to fly kites today."

"Well, alright, go!" said Anasuya, playfully raising

her eyebrows and hiding her laughter at the little boy's purposeful tone.

AFTER RAMEEZA LEFT THE ROOM with the empty teacups Rushi stepped out of his office, and proceeded toward the parking area, where Pathak and Kelkar were talking with animation.

Kelkar was chewing paan, sitting sideways on the front seat of his parked scooter.

"I told him it will take a week," Kelkar said, referring to a matter of disagreement with the director. "But he said `Why would it take a week? At Patni Road they did the same work in three days!' So I said, `Here it's a different matter altogether. We don't do the second class work like others do,' ey, cut me a sweet one, put some extra zarda," he ordered the paan shop boy and spat. "Am I right or not?"

He then took a deep inhale from his cigarette, and thought again what he had just said, counting with his fingers. Convinced that he had indeed estimated it right, he continued:

"If he insists then we will do it in three days but what's the use? He himself will come back complaining he cannot approve such sloppy work!"

"Three days! How can it be done?" laughed Pathak, without taking his eyes off Kelkar, with the conviction of one who knew all along that such absurd suggestions always came from directors. "How can it be done in three days? Useless talk, then what else."

It was a common habit of Pathak to laugh at anything that he did not comprehend, which made him an especially preferred company. By his laughing off, with that light-hearted tone of reassurance, anything that was proposed, others experienced a relief from the indecision they felt on the proposal. It was not that Pathak had a special comprehension of such affairs. But Pathak belonged to the kind of men who, while they themselves do not make any decisions, nevertheless argue, with increasing animation, now in favor of one viewpoint and the next moment favoring a contrary viewpoint, so that in the end they made others feel that no decision need be taken at all, relieving them of the burden.

As soon as Rushi joined them, a knowing smile came over Kelkar. With a jerk of his head in a certain direction he said, "Is the evening free? Or..." he and Pathak exchanged winks.

Rushi became red with shame and frowned at the winks. Still he could not hide the excitement he experienced at what they meant. The recollection of *her* face brought Rushi at once into that anxious, vigorous and elevated mood, the same with which he anticipated his evenings these days.

After a few minutes the three men drove towards Tara's house.

EVEN IF WE AGREE THAT the root of the agitation, and of the darkness, in the heart of this family can be traced back to Rushi's association with Tara, we still cannot be certain whether this, "going in the other direction," of her father, as Yashoda put it later, was spurred by a heart-felt affection in Rushi for Tara, or if it was merely the warmth in Rushi's already primed sensual temperament that drove him there.

In any case, when Rushi saw Tara from a distance in her kitchen, standing in front of the stove with her back to him, her firm body quivering slightly as she stirred the batter vigorously, he was overcome with a special brightness in his heart, and recalled his renewed feelings when he first met her.

Now it seemed to him that not only everything between him and Tara was just as before, just as bright and as sensuous as it was the first time, but into that stimulation now entered a new excitement, an ardor of a different kind. He felt that the new state of elevation also allowed him a renewed authority and claim over that figure of her, which was in front of his eyes.

When she served them the delicacies and tea, he allowed himself to meet her in the eyes, and made a special attempt at touching her fingers subtly with his, and satisfied himself that his expectations were not incorrect. In everything he did and expected, she yielded to him with quick softening looks of her eyes after she made a joke about him.

He rose from the chair to leave, and met her eyes one more time, and on their return to Pathak's home, Rushi had risen fully to the possibility that his barely remembered happiness had presented itself once again to him, now with unexpected and irresistible enchantments.

He recalled Tara's smooth and round shoulders, and the heavy bosom that turned prominently, silently, and approvingly toward him.

When he awoke from such recollections, Rushi answered his conscience that somehow this was special, and he did not see any conflict with his present, married, circumstance. He remembered his wife, but Anasuya's face seemed to him as that of a stranger, who had only recently began to be nearer to him, so that not all of his life belonged to her yet.

"Later," he said to himself, thinking of all the future that lay ahead of him and the wife. "After all, it is not as if I am about to abandon her," he muttered, suddenly becoming angry at Anasuya.

WHEN ARYA REACHED THE COBBLER'S shop, which was next to the bicycle store, he was relieved to see that it was still open. The cobbler, a large man with thick forearms, sat on the raised shop floor, with his anvil in front of him. Several black and brown shoes were lying on their sides around him.

Arya gave him his shoes, stood leaning on the edge of the shop floor and watched intently.

The thick, stocky hands of the cobbler drove a nail into the leather shoe, then wiped the anvil surface with a rag, then drove another nail, and wiped the anvil again. Seeing the little black nails that disappeared helplessly at each thud of the mallet, Arya experienced a rush of pity for the three or four black nails that lay waiting next to the anvil. An overwhelming urge to see what happened to the black nail that disappeared under the mallet rose in him. But the bottom of the shoe appeared only briefly. Those thick hands paused for a moment or two while the cobbler leaned on his side and spat. Arya then eagerly saw how the black nail got all squished, got stuck to the sole of the shoe like an ant, but the mallet continued to hit the shoe until the *"Clink, clink"* sound became a soft thud. A smell of the beaten leather emanated. The cobbler's hand tied the finishing knot, snipped it with a quick swipe of the cutter, and threw the shoe to one side.

By the time Arya returned home, put the shoes back in his cupboard, and gathered his charka and the kite from under the bed with his soft hands, it was already approaching six o'clock in the evening.

As soon as the boy came out of the house, holding tightly the zebia kite by its twine in his knuckles, and stepped into a breeze of wind, the kite all at once pulled hard at his fingers, transferring into Arya its desire to be airborne.

He saw that the playground was empty and at once Arya felt calm; the boy did not like seeing crowds of flyers there.

The zebia began to cheer Arya, tugging at his white knuckles and encouraged him to run.

He reached the far-end of the ground. Lowering the kite a little, he released some slack on the twine, then pulled up hard and began running backwards, releasing some more slack and watching the kite climb into the wind. A feeling of confidence entered into him, and flowed in him steadily, as the kite rose in the sky.

Arya felt that everything moved exactly the way he liked, and that everything he experienced in him was so accurately reflected in the kite that flew higher and higher, away from his senses. The higher the kite flew, the more intensely Arya felt that he was attached to it, not just at his fingers, not just in the tug he felt in his arm, but in a rising sensation he felt in his stomach and in his legs.

The kite flew, pulling hard at the twine, taut and strong, begging to break free of the charka. The zebia's confidence was just the same as the coiled-up quietude Arya felt just before he woke up every morning; same as that bright expectation of a cheerful day in his father's eyes; same as that serene face of his mother knowing exactly what she wanted to cook that morning, and same as that joy in his own heart at how irresistible this whole world was with his mother and father in it. Now the kite teased all manner of vague wishes he felt inside him to come out and fly in the blue sky; the blue sky that was so bright that it seemed to engulf him with all its blueness.

ALONE AFTER CHILDREN WENT OUTSIDE the house for play, Anasuya was woken up by maid Bai who came directly into her bedroom. Bai, seeing the condition of Anasuya, instinctively assumed a look of understanding on her face and sat near the door. On her face was a soft smile. It was evident she was overcome with a wish to make visible her sympathy for the special condition of her mistress, so undeserved.

Seeing the look of recognition on the maid's face, Anasuya thought, "How did my life come to *this?*" with vexation, feeling the full extent of the humiliation triggered by the recollection of Tara. An angry frown showed itself on her face.

Anasuya knew that her life was the source of joy and boundless energy of the children, who ran in and out of the house straight from her bedroom. But she also wished that her suffering be known. As she spoke softly to the maid, a desire, that all living consciousness around her must be made aware of this peculiar condition of hers, passed through Anasuya. For a brief moment Anasuya felt an urge to confide in Bai, to tell the maid her innermost fears and wishes.

But this moment lasted only a second or two. As she and Bai talked, a vague feeling of distaste at this unexpected closeness with the maid rose in Anasuya. A familiar fear, which struck her at intervals, that made her lose faith in the only world she had known in all her adult life, the world of her husband and of her family, once again filled her thoughts.

But she suppressed these feelings, ordered Bai to finish up the cleaning but to close the bedroom door first, and covered herself in blankets.

10

In the Dark, A Drunken Body

SOON IT WAS PAST NINE o'clock in the night.

Anasuya could not wait any longer and called Arya. Adjusting his disheveled hair she said, "Do you know where Pathak uncle's house is?"

"I know, I know," Yashoda came running into the room. "We should go like this," showing the direction with a slow sweep of her small hand. "Then first we'll see Jitu's house and then the slope and then Pathak uncle's house!"

"Why is it there? That's Doctor-uncle's house," said Arya. "Pathak-uncle's house is in *our* colony. You don't know anything!"

"E'y, don't quarrel. Yes, Pathak-uncle's house was always in our colony," said Anasuya. "Go slowly, and see if father and his friends are still there talking. Ask him to come home. Tell him `Amma wants to speak to you about something urgent.'"

"Should I call him outside and then tell him?"

"Just go inside and say this only to him quietly. Ask him to come with you," Anasuya said, and seeing the readiness in Yashoda's face, hushed her, "You are not going, Arya will go by himself."

ARYA CAME OUT OF THE front room door, crossed the front yard, stepped out of the gate into the street, and began walking towards Pathak's house.

Directly in front of him, on his left, stood two large apartment buildings, rising into the dark sky with their enormous square-shaped corners. As he passed them he could see, through the large window grills, in the yellow light of the rooms, the faces and movements within.

He nearly missed the turn near the corner of the building because he kept looking at the streetlight, where the bright fluorescent rays near the bulb were swarmed by the fireflies.

Walking through the passageway between the two buildings he emerged into a small open ground, beyond which stood the building where Pathak lived on the ground floor.

Arya approached the building.

On both sides of its outer gate, along the fence, stood a row of trees, small and large.

A yellow porch light revealed small white flowers and overgrown stems here and there that stood erect and swayed a little when Arya opened the gate.

The front room, empty, was lit with white fluorescent tube light. Shoes, slippers and cartons of empty bottles were lying in one corner, near the door to the inner room.

Arya stared at the empty bottles, and the aggressive red-

and-gold-colored labels on them frightened him. He had long ago understood that large brown bottles with red-and-gold-colored labels on them were somehow the cause of that stern, swollen red-eye stare he saw on his father, which he feared the most.

Sounds of laughter, and of voices, came from the inner room.

He grasped the thick red expensive curtain, velvety in his soft hand, and parting it he stepped in, and saw his father. Around the table sat three other men – Pathak, Kelkar, and one other man, a stranger.

At the sight of his father the fear in him disappeared.

Seeing the little boy at the door Pathak erupted into an excited laughter, "What is it kid? Is it `Amma calling' again? Heh, heh…!"

Arya stared at his father.

Rushi looked at him with his blood-red gaze, his eyelids drooping. His eyes were full of brightness and love, but for a moment they lost sight of Arya, and when they looked back, Arya experienced a strange feeling, as if his father did not recognize him.

"Hey kid, say it again, `Amma is calling!' Heh, heh, heh," Pathak continued with his hysterical imitation of Arya, his shoulders jerking up and down with his inebriated laugh.

At once Arya felt pity on his father. It seemed to him that his father's eyes were somehow swollen and perhaps he needed sleep. Arya's pity was just the same as that he often felt towards his pet when it was bruised. But then something else struck the boy as odd. He saw that his father was not injured at all. Instead, he was as though his swollen eyes did not bother him a bit. Moreover, he was nearly laughing, and did not seem to notice that he, Arya, was there, right in front of him.

The red and brown color of the water in his father's glass, the intimidating gold-rimmed bottles that were lying scattered before him, the pale white teeth of Pathak and Kelkar, their hands holding half-filled red glasses, the cigarette between their fingers, all this stirred something terrifying in Arya's physical body, just as that terrifying sensation he had experienced when he became smaller and smaller and heavier and heavier in his dream.

Now it confused him even more that his father's eyes stared at him with this peculiar look, as if he did not know Arya at all. This confusion rose in intensity until it transformed into a feeling of estrangement; and a fear, that something was happening to his father, entered the boy. He looked severely at Pathak and Kelkar but without realizing so.

Rushi, hushing the two to leave the boy alone, and laughing himself at the same time, addressed Arya, "You go home straight and I will be there soon. Tell Amma I'll be home in fifteen minutes."

TURNING BACK ARYA THOUGHT OF only one thing, that something terrible and terrifying was happening to his father.

He was sure that those men, with that awful red and brown water in those hotel glasses, were holding his father against his will, and that they were making him drink it. Now he understood that it was precisely these same men, joined with other such similar men, who held his father against his will all day long at work when he disappeared from home in the morning.

Having thus surmised how scared his father might be to be in the middle of those strangers all day, a myriad emotions entered the boy's soul. An intense mix of pity and love for his father's plight overflowed in his heart.

"Who are these men? Why are they doing this to him?" Arya thought. "And why is Amma not here, helping him?"

Then he remembered that his mother stayed home, that she did not go to work with him. Concluding that as a result she had no knowledge of these men, Arya made up his mind to tell her, and to see in her face the same pity and the same love he now felt for his father.

Rushing forward to reach home and see his mother right this minute, the boy, already near the front gate of his house, ran inside into the bedroom.

Seeing the boy Anasuya closed the book she was reading – a MSCO pocket book – and asked him if he had seen his father.

"What happened? Did you see your father?"

"Yes," Arya nodded his head, paused to take a breath, and without looking at his mother's face climbed on to the bed, and sat at the corner.

"Is he coming?" she asked, her voice angry and stern, as if she knew the answer already.

Arya wanted to tell her everything. In his imagination he wished to hear his mother say, "We'll teach them a lesson. Let him come home and we can all be together." But as soon as he heard her stern voice, and saw the frown in her face, which evidently showed she was angry with his father, Arya's pity and love became mixed with apprehension. Instead, he simply relayed what his father had said.

"Who else was there?"

"Not many, just two or three, Pathak-uncle and Kelkar-uncle," answered the boy.

Arya could not comprehend why his mother always spoke of his father in a strict tone. When his mother was in this mood, with the frown on her face when she spoke of his father, Arya disliked her; it prevented him from seeing the calm and loving expression on her face that brightened him. Now everything became confused for Arya. He decided to wait until that moment when that brightness appeared on her face again. Meanwhile father was still there, in the middle of those people, alone, all by himself. With an agitation that rose in him, but that which he did not speak of, the boy followed his mother as she set the table for dinner.

AFTER THE DINNER ARYA DECIDED that he would sit in the front room with his favorite book and read it for a long time.

As soon as he and Yashoda moved the dining table to a corner and laid the bedspreads, he stepped into the front room, closed the thick light-green curtain behind him and sat in the chair.

Soon everyone was asleep inside.

All was quiet in the house, except for the *"Wroom, wroom"* sound of the Crompton Greaves ceiling fan above his head.

From where the boy sat, he had a full view of the front gate. Night's darkness engulfed the building that was in front, except for a bedroom light that was visible through one of the windows.

On the far side, to the left of his view, was the same bright fluorescent street-lamp he saw earlier, high in the sky. Its large dome, facing down toward the earth, was still swamped with flies. Several flies stuck to the lamp, making it appear as if a thick yellow oilcloth had been wrapped around it.

Occasionally the boy saw a movement of people walking this way and that way in the passageway in front of the gate, and he played a game of guessing from which side in his view the figures would emerge next.

Once or twice a dog walked up to the bush near the fence, sniffed a little, then at once became alert. He looked to one side and not hearing more of what he thought he heard, barked feebly, and ran in the direction of some scent, even though he was convinced there was nothing there.

Arya, in a playful mood during the guessing game and then on seeing the dog, kept smiling inwardly at the brightened faces of his mother and father that were presently in his imagination. After a few minutes, his eyes kept on becoming heavy.

Just then a sound of an approaching motorcycle, which just turned off its engine, reached his ears.

He then heard a shuffle of unbalanced feet, coming from the darkness near the front gate, but he could not see anyone.

He rose from the chair, moved to the left, and from this position saw a movement of two or three men. It appeared to Arya that two of the men were moving something large and incomprehensible, holding it between them, from the back seat of the motorcycle. They were approaching the front gate.

Instantly he recognized one of them to be Pathak.

He then saw, in the faint glow of the dull darkness, that Pathak now crouched at the gate and a distraught expression occupied his face. Evidently he did not see Arya.

"What are they doing?" thought Arya as he approached the gate, conscious of his sleeping mother inside. "Why are they running away from us? Why didn't Pathak-uncle see me?"

At once Arya became aware of who or what that incomprehensible body that they just left in front of the gate.

In a hurry the two men vanished, leaving a lifeless lump of the drunken body on the footsteps.

As Arya approached that which was now in front of him, the boy saw, not the face that pinched his cheeks with his deliberate cold hands in the morning until laughter came out of him, not the head and the nose that tickled him, awakened him and filled his heart with joy and merriment, but still his same father, in the form of a motionless body lying at the foot of the entrance, his white terry-cotton shirt all crumpled and came loose out of the brown pants.

Arya's mind oscillated between the fear that something had gone bad once again with his father, and the comfort of seeing his father's body, with those big brown leather shoes still on him.

"This time I must make sure father gets inside before the neighbor sees him," Arya said to himself inwardly.

He thought of his mother at once. She, who was sleeping in her bedroom, after all that she suffered all day alone, all by herself, need not wake up to see this. Even though he was small he could bring his father inside silently, make him sleep in the center room and tomorrow morning all would be fine.

Just then he heard the sound of the bedroom door being

opened and knew his mother had awakened.

From the dark unlit center room Anasuya emerged into the light, at once folding the curtain and throwing it over the door.

"Who is it? Is it your father?" she asked with a voice filled with despair and disgust, knowing that Rushi came home fully drunk once again.

Arya, who was overcoming his fear and was about to seize his father's shoulders, gazed into his mother's vicious expression. The anxiety in him rose at the sight of her violent movement forward. Suddenly he wished for the morning. "Mornings are much better," he thought wistfully; and the fear that broke the weakening barrier of resolve inside him rushed into his lungs, and a faint jolt of shiver ran through his body. Tears rushed to his eyes.

"Sons of whores! They made him drunk and threw him in front of the house. Wait till I see them tomorrow! I'll skin them alive, sons of whores!" his mother uttered a frenzied cry, and crouching down she took hold of Rushi's shoulders and began pulling him.

"Go that side and grab his legs," she said breathing heavily. "Look how he smells!"

Arya took hold of the shoes and lifted the heavy legs, tightening his lips. At first the lifeless body clung to the ground as if it was stuck and only the shoulders seemed to move. Then little by little, half-dragging and half-lifting they moved it, and pulled and pushed it with all their might, past the door that bumped against Anasuya's retreating back and struck the wall with a thundering clang.

Once inside, they laid Rushi on the floor in the center room, on the far side of which slept Yashoda and Sita;

removed his shoes and socks, and covered him with a bed sheet. Rushi's body descended back into a deep sleep, oblivious to his external conditions.

Anasuya stared at Arya, who, after noiselessly closing the front door, came back and sat kneeling next to her.

"What am I to do?" she looked at the boy, and at the sleeping figures of her two daughters.

"And *he* like this!" she cried inwardly with despair.

11

Convulsions in the Night

IN THE DAYS THAT FOLLOWED after she and her son pulled the drunken body of Rushi from the street into the house, only terrible dreams awakened Anasuya in the mornings. In the end, after several weeks of deliberation she decided to visit Bhadrachalam temple. Children could not go as the schools were still on.

"How long will I be gone anyway? By the time I reach there one day will already be over," said she to Yashoda. "Three or four days at the temple and won't you see me already on the fifth day? It's not as if I am going to Kashi...!"

After asking her ten times if she had enough money and making sure the train tickets were in proper order, Rushi departed for work on his Vespa.

By evening the house was quiet. However, on seeing that the children were alone at home, two or three neighbors came in, sat in the front room, grabbed the newspaper and began talking with them. Their ease was that of those who assume naively that children obeyed them with the same submissive attitude even when parents were not present.

Soon night fell.

Arya, who had been unusually quiet all evening, was sitting on the bedspread on the floor, leaning against the wall in the center room, with a book in his hand.

As the darkness descended on the streets outside, the boy's thoughts began to converge on one thing, the only thing that dominated his alert consciousness during the nights: his fear of his father returning home in a drunken state, and the always-elusive goal of seeing him off quietly into his bedroom without waking up his siblings.

About half an hour after midnight he heard it.

From a distance came the sound of his father's Vespa approaching.

By how Rushi was revving up the engine while holding the clutch, Arya knew he was drunk again.

Arya shut his eyes tightly. An involuntary gurgle, *"Nanna...!"* emanated from his throat. He was seized by a shivering sensation, which gradually began to rise up in his stomach.

The boy rose quickly. "Where are the keys – on the windowsill? Or on the wall?" the question flashed in his mind.

Outside, the scooter had already come to a dead stop in front of the gate. Now the engine emanated its fullest roar, while his father kept his drunken thumb pressed on the horn.

Arya found the keys on the windowsill and wrapped his fist around them. "There is that taste in the mouth again," he said to himself. "Remember to keep your tongue away from the teeth, control the clattering! It'll go away in a while."

"It is only a chill, nothing more," again he reassured himself, as he tiptoed in the narrow passage between his sleeping siblings into the verandah.

When he reached the door what he saw surprised him.

His father's stance on the driver's seat was stooped, and his head was drooping dangerously close to the handlebar, and Arya understood that his father was unable to control himself from the weight of the alcohol.

Behind him, in the backseat, was a figure in a white saree.

At first Arya was perplexed. Then, "she is beautiful," the boy thought.

Trying to balance the scooter, Rushi swayed a little on his feet. She slid down the seat, took a step back and stood silently with her face down.

"Who is she?" Arya said to himself again.

For a moment he wishfully believed that since she, whoever she was, was with him, maybe he was not really drunk today.

Then the same unexpected thing happened, something that Arya often saw when Rushi was drunk. His father, instead of his usual warm smile, stared at Arya for a few moments, as if he did not recognize who Arya was.

Then, with a curt voice Rushi ordered his son, "Go inside, go to sleep."

By then the shivering sensation in Arya's stomach had already reached its peak, and began to take hold of his entire body. Hiding his involuntary tremors with all his strength, the boy returned to his bedspread, and covered himself completely in his black woolen blanket.

A S THE NIGHT'S DARKNESS THICKENED, Arya settled on the
bedspread on the floor, his knees resting against the wall,
his arms folded over his face, and he curled up inside the
black sheet.

Soon the tension in his body eased, as he drifted into
thoughts about everything that had taken place moments
ago.

Once or twice he became motionless, to hear the sounds
from the bedroom. Then his mind drifted to the day before.

He was at the electricity office the previous afternoon,
riding his bicycle. He remembered that lady there, the lady
with the bright orange silk blouse. He liked riding that
hard turn from the main road into the small alley, passing
between the public water-tap and the parked rickshaws,
deftly avoiding the pawn-spit red spots near the municipal
office, a section of which was assigned to the electricity
bills department.

He recalled the orange blouse again, but he could not
remember her face. It seemed to him that this lady was
very kind. His thoughts then drifted. He remembered his
desire to improve himself. Now the orange blouse lady
came back to his imagination, and his desire to improve
himself only intensified. He made a determination that the
very next day he would start reading, with a serious focus,
the "Aztec Civilization," and he would finish it in just a
week. Having set that goal, Arya was content again. The
black woolen sheet was warm on his stomach. Then he saw
a dark forest, but with no clear view of the trees. Instead,
there were only large, dark hills that seemed to emerge on

both sides of the horizon. The horizon itself was black. As
he looked on, the dark hills seemed to move towards him,
slowly first, and then at a rapid pace. He thought, "Someone
is approaching." He began to experience a strange physical
sensation. A sensation of a tug, from somewhere within him,
seemed to pull him into himself. He said to himself, "Oho,
I am rushing towards them," and became aware that he was
rushing towards the center of that blackness at the horizon.
Suddenly the black hills that were on his right, and on his
left, began to converge on his path. He felt as if these black
hills have turned into companions, and were now walking
along with him to wherever he was going. He thought it
was funny. "How can these hills be walking? It must not
be true," he said inwardly. And he looked at them as if to
say, "Come on, you silly." Just then he sensed that these
black hills, and that something that was pulling him hard
into himself, and that toward which he was now falling, all
had rapidly increased in size. It appeared to him that it was
not the dark hills that grew, but it was he himself that was
becoming smaller and smaller. Now instead of being pulled
inward, he was being pushed downward, and he began to
feel incredibly small and incredibly heavy. A terrible and
a terrifying sensation gripped the boy's consciousness. He
forgot everything, except the image of his mother, which
now filled his consciousness completely. He wished to say,
"*Amma!*" but he was afraid. His breathing grew heavier
and heavier. He felt as if his whole body had curled up in
his stomach, and felt everything around him recede faster
and faster, and he himself had become heavier and heavier.
Without being conscious of it, the boy began to cry. His
small body jerked in quick convulsions, causing him to

regain consciousness, and he was immediately distracted by a salty taste he felt on his lips. With a quick motion he wiped the tears off his cheeks, and was swept into a dazed state of being in which he recalled what had just happened to him in great detail. Soon he fell asleep.

When Anasuya returned five days later, he clung close to her and did various chores willingly, without feeling the dreariness.

12

Death

Blackhills or not, like how a restless cat scratching at the night's door rushes in at the slightest opening, life tumbled in as soon as the sun broke. In that awakening children grew up. And in that sameness, months turned into years.

In the middle of it all, a young man who had been brought in from the village the previous night was now on the bed in the center room, unconscious and dying; and the anxiety over the sick man occupied the whole house like the smoke from the woodstove in the kitchen.

The sick man Som was the son of Suvarna, Anasuya's elder sister. It happened that Suvarna, and Komali, her only daughter, and Sarathi, the daughter's husband, were just sitting down after their afternoon meal in their village home when Som complained of a slight ache in his head and a minute later collapsed on the straw mat on the porch.

"We kept saying what should we do to save him but nothing stirred in our heads, so we thought and thought and decided the only thing we can do is to bring him here," said

Komali, her black, sparkling eyes swollen from crying.

"My heart is going to stop any minute. Whatever will happen to him?" cried Suvarna.

"Ey, nothing of any sort is going to happen to him," Anasuya took her sister's tea glass, put it on the windowsill and sat next to her on the bed. "The main thing is what the doctor says."

Anasuya was ashamed to present her house all by herself, without her husband, to the despairing family. Rushi had not returned since leaving for the office two days ago, and in her heart Anasuya knew where he was.

She sat on the corner of the bed speaking softly to Suvarna. Komali was at the other corner, leaning against the wall, staring at the window. Yashoda was on the folding chair, next to the window, her elbows on the windowsill, her eyes on the guava tree in the backyard, but her ears pricked up on the grownup talk. Sarathi was somewhere outside the house, near the corner of the building, far away from the front gate, furtively smoking a cigarette.

Arya had just come into the house with his hands in his military-green trouser pockets, but instead of coming in straight after entering the front green gate, he turned left into the side garden and went into the shadow of the guava tree. There he stood, and began peeling the dry bark of one of the low branches, evidently deep in thoughts. As was his habit, he was brushing back his forelock. His face was red, as though he just had an argument with someone.

THE FACT IS, ARYA, NOW a young man of seventeen years, was passing through that phase which occurs in any young man's life when the playful innocence of boyhood gives in to the restlessness of the youth, but not quite yet. In the case of Arya, owing to his extraordinary sensitivity, a stronger element, of a much more dominant kind, had been holding up the young man's waking hours, and for that matter, sleeping hours too. The shame that his father was in an illicit relationship with another woman, the very conflagration that burned his mother's heart, had already taken a firm hold of the young man's consciousness.

But since Som's arrival the previous day, Arya began wishing the talk of the sick man would go on and on in the house, because even the talk of sickness brings its own diversions, burying every other unpleasant mood that pervaded the house.

When he was walking back to the house from his friends circle, Arya had been involuntarily recalling how Som, during the March holidays earlier that year, had come up with a parrot, and how not only had he let it out of its cage openly in front of everyone, but the parrot did exactly what Som told him to do. It turned out that Som had managed to coax Kesav, the local fortune-teller, into lending him his parrot for an hour or two.

At first Som wanted to act just like Kesav, speaking in a southern tongue only in bits, just as Kesav did. But as soon as the children began grinning at him and kept asking what he fed the parrot and how many times in a day he fed it and did it drink water too, Som forgot his seriousness and began laughing with them.

When he produced small pieces of chopped fruit from his pocket and opened the top of the birdcage, the children screamed in excitement. Som hushed them and inserted his hand into the cage and gently fed the parrot, which caught some pieces deftly with its beak and ignored others, letting them fall by its side.

Arya recalled how, after eating one or two small pieces the parrot ignored the rest, turned its side to them and pecked its beak cheerily at the cage box.

But what Arya recalled most vividly was the following.

During the few days Som was with them the young ones' imagination had become filled with all the ways they would possess the parrot. In everything they, the four of them – Som, Yashoda, Sita and Arya – did, they had imagined the parrot next to it, and the friendly way it looked at Som and spiritedly inserted its beak into the guava fruit. That same night they had talked on and on about how the parrot's tail was bent to its one side as it restlessly moved in the small congested cage. A feeling of pity and love arose among them for the parrot.

"My parrot would have a larger cage, and it would have so much room for not one fruit but two fruits," Sita had said. "One on this side and one on the other."

Som smiled, "Yes, and when it grows we will get even a larger cage so in it he would open its wings wide and fly too."

"But what if he hits the roof of the cage?" Sita asked. At this thought Arya had felt that no matter how large the cage was, it would not be enough for the parrot.

"Why would it hit the roof? Oh, oh I know, I know. We can put the mosquito net over Arya's bed-stand, pull down the covers and leave the parrot in, no?" Som suggested.

"Can we keep it in all night?"

"Yes, and you could keep the bed light on so the parrot could see, no?"

"But where will Arya sleep then?"

"You can sleep on the floor, no?"

"Yes, and you should sleep near the bed so you can see the parrot," Sita instructed Arya.

Arya then recalled how it had occurred to them that even the mosquito net would be small for the parrot's wings. And so no matter what idea they came up with, the image of the parrot, with its confident beak, its friendly eyes, the preoccupied way it lifted its leg and held it in the air just before it poked the card, kept interrupting their thoughts and saddened them.

He recalled what Som had said next. "I will take that parrot away from Kesav, he doesn't know how to make it happy."

"Really?"

"Yes, Kesav has no pity on his parrot. He waved his hand like this, like this, so fast and the parrot was so afraid."

"Yes, I think so, you should take away his parrot. Will you take it back with you?" Sita was asking.

Just then Arya's recollection broke, seeing that he was already near the house.

Becoming conscious of the glares of the neighbors – they were always looking at his house   he remembered the present condition in the house again, and his shame and agitation returned.

At the same time he imagined that the neighbors already saw his grownup full-cotton trousers, and so believing that now they would think of him as a grown man, he steadied his pace like one. But the next moment dissatisfied with himself, Arya stood near the guava tree for a minute, before going into the back room.

The back room, with asbestos roof, was really a store room, long and narrow, where they kept old chests, rice bags and firewood; and almirahs which themselves were stuffed with old clothes and some old rugs.

A small space near the door, with a wooden desk and a chair, with a cotton cushion on it, served as his study.

BESIDES THE SHAME-FILLED STATE HE was in, for many days now Arya had been restless and panicky, because no matter what he did, he could not quite bring himself to concentrate on the preparation for the university entrance exam.

Everyone in the house knew that the seventeen-year-old Arya was bright, and though he did not excel in his academics, he was still striving to enter into one of the Indian Institutes of Technology.

But it was also true that they also believed, without saying it so outwardly, that some students go to the IIT while others who behave the same way do not. And that belief, when it divulged itself to Arya, this hypersensitive, emotional, arrogant but kind young man, prone to frequent rages and moods of depression, it crushed him.

"Leave it there, don't be rankled by it," he muttered to himself at times like these. "Don't look into it, don't look away from it either! Look *above* it!"

A few months earlier, intending to do just that, he began sitting in this cramped space in the back room, making it his private study, and was always seen with his textbooks and notes.

He deliberately arranged the chair near the door so that whenever anyone came in with old clothes to be stored, or for the winnowing basket on the nail, after they left he closed the door shut instantly with a loud noise, muttering to himself, "Not even a minute they leave me in peace," with exasperation. But when his mother appeared at the door with a glass of tea, it was common to see him instantly chat with her, even getting up and following her into the house while he kept on explaining something or the other.

As soon as he came into the backroom, Arya sat on the chair, became immersed in his book and did not notice that quietly a crack opened in the door, and a head stuck itself in.

Feeling disrupted, Arya looked up with an intense frown and saw Sarathi's face smile at him, his curious eyes already going over Arya's head and scrutinizing the storeroom.

"Ah, you *are* here. No, no, I only wanted to see how studious you are, sticking with it day and night," Sarathi said, still with only his head shoved in.

The truth is, Sarathi had been feeling self-conscious that unlike a few other men he knew in the village, who went to the city and returned only during festivals, he himself had remained in the village, under the watchful, and hence embarrassing, eye of his mother-in-law Suvarna. A minute ago, while he stood in the corner smoking his cigarette, he saw Arya, at first in the midst of some youngsters of his age, and then coming away from them. Observing his extraordinarily bright cousin who had a reputation for enjoying rough sports with his friends, a sharp pang stabbed Sarathi inside, making him feel as though he would forever be an outsider to Arya and the likes of such city young men. But the next moment Sarathi experienced a strange kinship with Arya. "He is sure to understand me, if only I just show him I am not afraid of him," thought Sarathi. As though propelled by these very words, he felt emboldened and followed Arya to his back room.

Arya softened his expression, dropped his pen on the desk and leaned back, watching Sarathi push himself further into the room, open the door with his shoulders and cleverly slid into the room entirely.

"How is Som? Did he wake up?"

"When did he? How can he wake up in his condition, mmm?" said Sarathi, still peering into the rice bags.

"Did the doctor sent in the report then?"

"Mmm? Where? Only this evening did he see him, he won't send any report before tomorrow, I think."

Arya returned to his book, turned a few pages, took the pen and made an effort to resume his chemistry exercises.

"Mmm? No telling the manner of people these days, mmm? I see your father did not come home yesterday night, mmm?" said Sarathi, his eyes still wandering, now checking the top of the almirah, now scrutinizing the number of chests.

"Yes, he did not," Arya sighed.

Sarathi softened his voice. Leaning into the table and nearly whispering, he spoke as though prying into a secret, "Well, does he go days and days like this often?"

"Even an unemployed loafer like him is asking about father, what nonsense," thought Arya, his vexation rising at the boldness of Sarathi.

"Only now and then when the work load is excessive," he mumbled and sighed excessively. "Did you eat well at dinner?"

"Mmm? What is there to dinner? One should eat something just for stomach's sake. Mmm? Still, I ate well."

"Then do you want some coffee? It's not that late."

"Mmm? Coffee is what causes all this stomach trouble. Mmm? What is it that I hear, your father bought a new house in the city, mmm…?"

"I cannot bear this!" Arya muttered inwardly. "All these people coming to our house, eating our food, taking our help and then talking like this! What an insult! Look how openly they are talking about him. Look at that germ of curiosity in his head, squirming! Look how he is smiling, how dare he even speak his name! Oh, this is unbearable!"

"Whoever told you this? Even we don't know. What nonsense people spread!" Arya scowled, openly giving Sarathi a once-over.

"Ah, is that so? Is that all there is to it?" Sarathi laughed nervously. "Ah, that must be it, ah, people these days, mmm? Anyway I can see you are studying, mmm, study, study," saying this Sarathi left the room.

SOMETIME AFTER TEN O'CLOCK IN the night Arya stepped out of his room and went into the house.

The kitchen light was turned off, the dining table was clean, the leftover dishes sat together over at one corner of it. The bedroom was dark and he noticed that his mother had fallen asleep. He came away from the door and stepped into the center room quietly.

It was dark in the room but the dim light from the front room showed that the sick man was still motionless on his bed.

Suvarna was lying sideways on the floor, her head resting on her folded arm, and her eyes were fixed intensely on Som, not wishing to miss even a slight movement of her son. Komali was lying similarly on the other corner of the room, along the hallway wall, with some magazine in her hand which she did not even open.

Seeing Arya, Suvarna opened her eyes wider and signaled him to come nearer.

Arya approached her, tiptoeing around Som's bed.

Suvarna, without getting up, extended her hands and clasped Arya's arms. She did not move, but her grip began to tighten around Arya's palms, and her eyes at once became sparkling with tears gushing. She pressed Arya's hands on her chest, which was now heaving with her soft cries.

A soft rustle came from behind Arya and the next moment Komali came nearer, herself choked by the sight of her mother's cries, and sat in the same crawling position, pressing her chin on her mother's shoulders.

Arya whispered, "Don't cry..." himself drawing her shoulders close to his chest, faintly aware of a shiver that began in his own body. "If no one helps here, I myself will take Som to the Main hospital, why do you cry?"

Quiet sobs came out of Komali at these words.

Still sobbing softly, Suvarna made a motion with her hand, "Did you eat?"

Making similar movements himself Arya replied, "Yes, yes... I ate even earlier than you..."

After sitting there for a few more moments, his palm still on her shoulders, Arya got up and came out of the room.

He stepped into the front room, where Yashoda and Sita were sleeping, and stood for a long time at the door, pricking his ears to the sounds of approaching scooters.

After a few minutes of standing like this, Arya put two chairs together, took one of the sheets and a pillow, and reclined in the green wicker chair with his feet on the second chair, his eyes still looking for something in the darkness outside. He then closed his eyes.

Soon it was quiet everywhere.

A moment later a recollection came into Arya all by itself, in which the scene with Som and the parrot again rose in this imagination, as though he was dreaming.

...as soon as a five-rupee note was placed on the card pack, Som opened the cage door. "Ramoo..." he then addressed the parrot. "Her name is Yashoda. Now be a good soul and show us her fortune." With tiny movements of its legs the parrot stepped out of the cage. Everyone sat motionless and still. The parrot then picked a card with its nose, held it high for a moment or two. "Hand it in Ramoo..." Som pushed his palm gently toward the parrot, which then released the card and hurried back into the cage. Som closed the door, and opening the card he went on to recite Yashoda's fortune, hiding his laughter.

This scene disappeared from Arya's dream and in its place was the figure of his mother. She was sitting somewhere behind a mist, her body hardly visible, so that only her voice was heard. "They think I don't need a reason to be this way. As if it was in my nature! When will they grow and realize *his* true nature?" she was despairing silently.

Dreaming like this, Arya went into sleep.

Sometime later both Yashoda and Arya were woken up by the sound of something odd and peculiar, as though a puppy dog somehow got inside one of the inner rooms and was trying to get out. Both the brother and the sister ignored the puppy dog at first but after a few minutes like this they became restless and opened their eyes.

Still in a sleepy state, they saw that the front door was wide open. Cold air was coming in, and they now saw that even the front gate had been opened, and some sort of a figure was in front of it. It was still dark outside but the night was rapidly becoming transparent, as it usually does before the dawn light sets in.

Seeing the light in the center room, they got up and came inside and saw that which they only later understood as the dead body of Som.

IT SO HAPPENED THAT JUST after four o'clock in the morning Anasuya woke up, and feeling uneasy for some reason came into the center room.

Just then, perhaps at the sound of Anasuya's footsteps, Komali too opened her eyes and they both at once saw that Som had stopped breathing. It appeared to have occurred sometime in the night.

Anasuya rushed to Sarathi – who was sleeping near the kitchen – and woke him up. In the minutes that passed, Suvarna's cries became uncontrollable. This was what awoke the children.

Together, Sarathi and Anasuya carried Suvarna and Komali into the bedroom. After half an hour like this Anasuya became alert and saying to herself, "A body shouldn't be left bare like that," she lit a small oil wick lamp and placed it near the head of the deceased young man.

Meanwhile Sarathi came back into the house with his phone book still in his hand – he had rushed to the phone center near Medha Talkies to inform Anasuya's siblings in the city.

An hour later Pandurangam arrived in his apple-green

Ambassador car.

Both Yashoda and Arya stood near the center room door, their eyes fixed at the sight in front of them.

Leaning on Pandurangam's shoulder, Suvarna entered the center room, which appeared strangely bare to her. Only minutes earlier there had been bright brass lamplights, throwing gold-colored shadows on everything in that room, she thought, but now they were nowhere to be seen. The entire floor was bare as though they had removed everything, except for the body of the deceased. On the side, touching the wall, was a small green table. On it was a small oil lamp, which was burning motionless. At first Suvarna thought she was suddenly terribly hungry as her stomach felt very hollow. Then she felt as though someone with a broom was whisking everything in her innards, like whisking cobwebs, making her empty, and she collapsed on her knees, leaning her face into her son. Something pushed against her throat, into her mouth, from somewhere inside her. Everything that she was, and that she became, ever since she remembered holding Som's hands, with his tiny fists, came into her imagination. An inexplicable state of being came into her, in which she had not yet awakened to the fact of her loss, but only to a mysterious intensity of love and recollection that comes before such awareness. Only one feeling she felt, "How alone my child is now!" She saw her little child, alone, crying in the midst of a desert, and her heart broke at the sight of his loneliness. She desperately focused on locating where he was now, but that mysterious place eluded her, eluded her imagination and eluded her consciousness. It occurred to her (this she never forgot all her life) that the little boy Som waited at

this barren place for her – his mother – for so long that his
eyes became swollen, became dry without tears, and finally
he gave up and fell down. Tears finally came to Suvarna's
eyes and she uttered a whimper, *"Somu...!"* before she lost
consciousness.

Struck by what they saw, Yashoda and Arya suddenly
wished their father Rushi were with their mother, who
now appeared to them in a strange light. The brother and
the sister came out and saw, at a distance in the darkness,
sitting on the pile of bricks next to the front gate, just as the
carpenter from the village did once, was Rushi. Unaware
of the goings-on of the past few days, he drove home fully
drunk and was barely able to comprehend his surroundings.
His body was swaying in an awkward manner, and as they
stepped closer, his figure, still in his dress pants and white
shirt, began slipping sideways, his cigarette still clinging to
his lips, and he leaned fully against the mound of bricks,
unable to stay awake anymore.

It then seemed to Arya that several pairs of eyes were
seeing this sight of Rushi, and that these several pairs of
eyes then looked at each other and muttered something,
further intensifying and accumulating Arya's feelings of
shame.

13

Everyone Caring the Same, As One

OUT IN THE WORLD THOSE were still the days when young men and women, as soon as they completed their undergraduate studies, made efforts to "go to America," not fully comprehending the meaning of it.

When they arrived in America, they experienced a heavy heart, and accepted it as a price one pays for not having two bodies. From one body in America to another body away at home, away by millions of heart-beats, away by thousands of miles, they said these things to one another, "Will I see you again? I wish I could see you again," feeling like a pair of fish in a barrel of time. Easy targets they were.

Still, young men like Arya, and women alike, went.

In Arya's case it happened when, as soon as he completed the undergraduate degree in engineering, he found himself spending the days in a manner he had despised in others in the past.

While in the engineering college, Arya frequently experienced disappointment at the ordinariness of his friends but refrained from saying so. But they, suspecting his inner feelings, always smiled at him, read his long handwritten letters, and while he waited eagerly for even a longer, grander reply from them, they continued to smile, and gently changed the subject to the topics that did not interest him.

Soon Arya began to make efforts to go abroad, and just like that the day of his departure arrived.

IN THE AFTERNOON OF THE day he was to leave, after two hours of parting discussion with his friends Arya returned home. Seeing that his mother has become quieter, and did not joke with her usual mischievous raise of her eyebrows at him, he was annoyed at himself for having spent so long with his friends.

The house was filled with guests.

Rushi was sitting on the bed with a newspaper in front of him, but his eyes were fixed at somewhere outside the window. Yashoda and Sita were in the kitchen with a few other women.

Seeing his uncle Seshu, Arya wished that Seshu would, at least now, smile at him, giving in to that secret wish he had always felt for his uncle's affection.

"Though he always had that sarcastic, disdainful look for me, I really believe that is all a façade, because uncle is old-fashioned and he is prone to be stern towards children," Arya thought. "In his heart he actually likes me. And now with my departure today, uncle will look at me with admiration, even love. Oh! How frail he looks...!"

But the expression on his uncle's face remained as it was. Arya sat in the center room chair, peering into the kitchen to see who was in it. He was about to say something, but at once experienced a displeasing feeling that everyone everywhere talked about such accomplishments (Arya thought of his going to America as his "accomplishment") much the same way, and he stopped. Soon all *this*, this house, this center room, that backyard, his cupboard with books in it, would no longer be real for him. The chairs they sat on, the cold wooden cot they slept in, and the smooth cement floor that glistened pleasantly at them...all these will no longer be within his reach.

"Why, just tonight itself it will cease to be real, as soon as I step out of the house to the airport..." he muttered inwardly.

And that look on his uncle's face said what it always said, now with a special disdain, "You are still the same to me, no matter how much your feelings are overwhelming you now. The same you that we are all happy to put up with only because you are one of us."

Arya smiled inwardly, "Just a few more hours."

At once feeling agitated that the presence of so many people in the house was preventing his mother and father from saying what they really wanted to say to him, he rose and went inside.

Just then Anasuya was coming out of the kitchen. Her face was pale, but she was calm.

"Said last goodbyes to your friends?" she said with a smile.

"Yes, yes, all done."

"I will sit in the bedroom for a few minutes. Will you bring some tea for me?" she asked him softly, and saying,

"Wait until I rest a while first," she went into the bedroom.

Anasuya stepped into the bedroom, saw Rushi's forlorn face and lay herself on one side of the bed, next to the newspaper, staring at him.

"Just six more hours," said Rushi.

In both the husband and the wife was the same thought, and the same ache squeezed their hearts.

"What can we do, that's how it is written in his fate. They always said he was born with wheels on his legs."

"Well, it's just you, me and the girls," Anasuya sighed. "One can never be ready for such things."

"Can he live by himself?" Rushi asked his wife, overcome by a feeling. "What will he eat? Will he take care of his health?"

"How could he not?" Anasuya replied with reassurance. "Soon he will immerse himself in studies and the life there..."

Rushi kept staring at the window with the same pale expression on his face.

ARYA WENT BEHIND THE KITCHEN into the backyard, and saw the powder-blue sky and the swaying treetops in the bright afternoon sun.

He reclined on the easy chair, with its green cloth seat and flat wood arms, and moved his head so that the sun had the full view of his face. He then closed his eyes.

Soon the warm rays of sun soaked his face and he fell into that dreamy state, neither fully asleep nor awake.

In this dreamy state Arya saw that he was shouting and chasing someone and ran into the next-door neighbor's bedroom. Wrapped around his knuckles was something like an iron chain or a strong cotton rope – he could not tell which. He was ready to whip it across, or perhaps to strangle himself. Then he stepped out into the open air, and there was a group of three or four fellows, strangers, who were cursing at the madness of it all, and swearing they would beat them all up. As Arya walked by them he heard foul swearing words addressed at him, making him feel taut with fear. Now he glanced sideways at this group. They stopped swearing and began whispering instead. One of the younger fellows showed his teeth at him, and half-smiled at him, and secretly nudged his big companion into silence. Arya relaxed for a moment, knowing he defended himself, but he was also scared at what he had done.

And then there was a window, and outside the window the sky was gray and black all over, as if it was going to rain anytime. "It is a mistake. They will come and beat us up. I am not as strong as them and there was something intimidating about them," Arya was muttering to himself inwardly. Meanwhile his back was aching, as though a huge chain was used to tie his spinal cord to the bed, and whenever he turned he felt the pull of this chain, and heard the sound of it against the metal bed frame.

"If I can just look through the window and enjoy the blue sky, the light blue sky, it would be nice," Arya kept saying to himself. "Surely it is unlikely that anyone would plan to beat me up because I would then be already abroad, in America."

He smiled at himself at this thought, convinced that he played tricks on these intimidating men.

At that moment Arya woke up from the dream.

"What was it that I saw in my dream?" he asked himself,

in a state of incomprehension and near-frenzy. A surge of blankness at once overwhelmed him and slowly gave in to the images and thoughts from the dream that still lingered.

When his dream fully dispelled, Arya saw that people were still talking inside the house and realized that he had been sitting there in the sun only for fifteen minutes.

Soon Arya's bags were packed and moved to the front room.

The newspaper delivery-man, sitting in the front room, waited with a peculiar look of curiosity and brightness on his face. Earlier that year Arya had ordered three dailies but now Anasuya insisted there was no point in it.

"Him too I won't see again," Arya thought as he paid him off, and asked him to stay for a few more minutes while he gave him a glass of tea.

A few minutes later Arya, who was replying to questions with the utmost attention, at once thought he had forgotten something important, suddenly became dissatisfied with the contents of his bag, and unpacked it entirely and repacked it, without really adding or removing anything from it.

Soon the cars arrived.

The family, now in the sway of that heavy feeling that united them as one, carried themselves to the airport, not fully out of their own volition but by that inevitable forward movement of time itself.

When they reached the airport they felt that at any moment the crowd around them would greet them and understand immediately their feelings, but the people were not only indifferent, they were even rude to them, asking them to make way for them, staring at them with impatience.

"Let them go dearie, move aside a bit," Anasuya said, seeing that a large group of people kept pushing through them, nearly shoving Arya's bags aside.

"They too must bid farewell to their children," she smiled at the party.

The girls were silent, as though they were in the midst of a solemn occasion. The indifference of all those around them heightened the solitude of their experience.

"Can't they see what is happening! How can they drink orange juice when I am feeling this way!" they thought inwardly.

Rushi, with a feeling, sat next to Anasuya, replying with a nervous brightness to this and that question, staring at the vast space that surrounded them, filled with strangers and bustle.

At once for some reason Arya broke off from them and went in the direction of the ticket counters. When he turned back, he saw, from this distance, among the crowd, among the pushcarts and darting children, the strikingly pale, uncertain and kind faces of his mother and father. An intense feeling of loneliness and isolation he saw in them, and which he himself had been suppressing in his own heart until now, overwhelmed him with a renewed force.

In that moment a belief reasserted itself in him once again, that the isolation from one another that his parents suffered was the most terrible and terrifying evil in their lives.

"How kind they are to me! How thankful I feel about them now! That is the only thing that matters," Arya thought resolutely. "My only goal should be to lift them up from this isolation."

When the check-in began everyone rose and involuntarily

began to press forward. Struck by the immediate condition in which only one thing, the separation of Arya from them, was in their consciousness, and unable to imagine what the future contained, the family surrounded him, and moved with him as one as far as the security allowed them.

The two airport personnel who stood by the side kept staring at them with a special soft look in their eyes.

As Anasuya, Rushi, the girls and the relatives stood back watching, Arya merged into the maze of the long queue, and then further vanished behind the customs and immigration door.

A few minutes later they caught the last glimpse of Arya as he disappeared into the airplane, and the family returned home.

Part Two

14

"Goodbye Fellows, Take Care of Yourselves, Fellows!"

SOMETIME IN APRIL OF 1996, during a warm northern California spring, five or six volunteers of Leap Forward began to gather early in the morning, around eight o'clock, at a local youth incarceration center. Being in the middle of the woods, it took a visitor a long drive from the city, a good forty-five minutes, on a narrow one-lane winding road through the hills, to get there. Visitors were allowed only into a separate reception room, detached from the main center. The center itself was hidden behind tall sequoia trees, well-secured by a strong fence.

The reception room was a large hall with striking red brick walls. There were large paintings and murals on the walls, wherever the eye could see. At the corners in the hall stood tall black metallic sculptures, curved and bent this way and that way in artistic attitudes; and their smooth, round texture glistened against the lit-up rows of the recessed lights. Many folding chairs were in the hall: some arranged in rows in the center, some lined along the walls, and a few more stacked on top of one another in one of the corners.

By nine o'clock three of the volunteers had already come in. The next one to enter was a handsome young man, dressed simply but well, in jeans and a full-sleeved shirt, looking strikingly like a shy man.

As soon as this young man entered, all the heads sitting in the chairs turned toward him. He sat in one of the chairs. A few moments later, he turned the chair so that now he sat fully facing the others, who ignored him and continued to talk amongst themselves.

A few minutes passed and a burly Afro-haired young man in a shiny black leather jacket; and a slender young girl, in brown boots and light rosy pink in her appearance, came in together.

One of the men, Lawrence, a lean, middle-aged African-American, who a minute earlier was saying something and laughing all by himself, said, "Hello, Miss Chrissy!" to the young girl in boots as she entered. Evidently he was aiming to tease her. He then chuckled at the others and made a playful motion of purposely hiding his face to avoid their recrimination.

"How is it going, Lawrence, Joanie, did you two drive up here together?" asked Christine, putting her bag on the table.

"We did," replied Joanie, the young, beautiful woman sitting next to Lawrence.

"Our fearless leader is already here. Ready to do some

God's work."

All eyes, smiling at once, turned to a man who was sitting with his legs stretched on the chair, his eyes closed.

This man, Curtis, was in his mid-thirties, wearing a pale red-checkered cotton half-shirt and jeans. On his large feet were old brown sandals, out of which two large, somewhat unclean toes stuck out prominently, with their cracked thick nails.

"Hello, Curtis, are you asleep?"

Curtis opened his eyes, and put his feet down. He then began swatting something away from his clothes, now from his knees, now from his back shoulder, as though he was the only one in the room. It was as though Curtis believed that an impression of a certain kind of selflessness can only be created by a certain kind of inattentiveness; and that this was the only suitable way to be a volunteer at an incarceration center. He then rose from the chair, yawned, and with his red sleepy-morning eyes began to acknowledge those in the room.

Anyone who saw Curtis recognized him at once as one who saw himself as a leader and hence would refuse all praise. There were those among the volunteers who felt that by being who he was, that is, a selfless soul, Curtis had already achieved what they were only now beginning to work at.

Joanie, who was wholeheartedly taken in with Curtis, uttered in a feeble voice, "Oh, poor guy," and approached him.

Curtis drank the glass of water Joanie brought him, cleared his throat and began describing the program for the duration of that day.

"Wait, I think first we should introduce the new guy," whispered Christine.

"We can do that. So, before we start, we welcome," Curtis looked at his notes, "Eiraya...? Did I get that right?"

"Yes, Eiraya is good enough, but you can call me Aariya too," smiled the shy young man in full-sleeved shirt.

All eyes turned to Arya and they all said, "Welcome Aariya," and Lawrence winked at him.

"Let me go ahead and introduce the program," said Christine, "Then you can take over."

Curtis didn't say a word but appeared to agree with a condescending look.

"We have a full-day program today," began Christine. "And I want to begin by saying that this is what the Leap Forward movement is all about. This is where the rubber meets the road, and today is the day we make a real contribution and help out the others. You all notice that we are in a beautiful open land, and there's a small lake right next to this hall. That building you see across the lake is the incarceration center. It is a gated, secured location. The organization that runs this center really believes in a progressive vision with openness and inclusivity, did I say that right," she laughed nervously, softly repeating, "inclusivity."

"Anyway," Christine continued. "As a result, the young men here, who are between the ages of fourteen and eighteen, and they are all men, there are no girls or women here, are really treated as family. Putting them up in an open area, in the middle of the woods, with these hills surrounding, really reflects the vision that incarceration should be about rehabilitation, not about the punishment. But please note, and I want to stress this again and again, please do not forget that *every one of these young men have killed.* From what I understand, the young men in this center have killed their fathers, in some cases maybe even mothers, but I was told it was the fathers. We, all of us from Leap Forward, are a part of a non-profit program to provide these young men a connection to the ordinary, day-to-day world, but in a controlled, safe and a mentoring environment, so that these young men, one day a week, get to go out of that building and play and talk with positive influencers such as us, hopefully positive influencers, oh god. That is what we are here for: to provide one full day of play and talk and discussion in a pretty open manner to these young men. There are guards in the premises, but normally you won't see them. If you feel you are in danger, then you use this whistle, which every one of you should have by now, and blow to call attention. So far, in my three years of doing this, there have been just two times someone used the whistle but that too I think one time the guy misunderstood something and freaked out, and the other time one of the young men snatched the whistle from a Leap Forward volunteer and caused a stir, but nothing major, okay?" Christine stopped and looked at Curtis.

"And one last detail," Christine smiled and extended her hand toward Curtis. "Curtis is our group leader. We all know what a dedicated and committed leader Curtis is and we are fortunate to have him lead us. Curtis?"

Curtis stared at everyone silently. It was clear that he wanted everyone to know that he had been doing this for many years, and wanted to say only a few words and desired every word of his to count.

"Well, we all know why we are here," Curtis began. "I

can tell you from my experience that what we do here is noble, but is also very hard. My advice to all of you today is this. Keep it tight. Because, sometimes, as we get closer and closer to these young men, you will be tempted to speak freely to them. We want to say how other great men and women inspired us, and we want to tell them how they too should hold others in high regard. They will listen, oh no doubt they will listen, and they will say things, at first not even conscious of what they are saying, but only totally into what we said to them, and believing that they also have the same virtues as we do. Then you say something that just doesn't cut it, it is just not enough for them. Maybe you didn't praise them enough or didn't acknowledge them enough and they become upset! And then they say that they don't understand you, and that you don't know anything. Yeah, it happens. Then they say you are here only for yourself, to make yourself feel good. And then they are turned off. And you try to recover, but they pull you into guilt. They make you doubt yourself, and they make you wish you'd punish yourself. Then they become cold and withdraw and begin to go away from you. You thought you were going to have a relationship with them, but they are not where you want them to be! So it is important to show who is in control. Let them have their tantrum but make sure you follow the rules. No curse words, no yelling, no pushing and no bodily jousting. Every time I see one of these violations by any of the young men, I will intervene and we stop whatever we are doing and form a circle of prayer. The young man who committed this rule-violation should then say a few words admitting his error, and then we can re-start the activity or talk or whatever it was that we were doing. I hope we all understand this."

Concluding with these words Curtis smiled at Arya. This smile, which seemed especially directed at him, made Arya feel elevated, and his feelings, mixed with a peculiar anxiety, rose in intensity.

"And now we should go outside and sit on the park benches there, the ones in front of the gate. At the right time, in a few minutes, the guards will release the young men and they'll come join us."

THEY ALL STEPPED OUTSIDE THE hall and into the open area.

It was approaching ten o'clock in the morning, and as far as the eye could see there were green hills and green trees everywhere.

Hunter, the young man in black leather jacket, went to the fence and saw the open plains just below them. Not even a few seconds passed and he, with his long fingers curled into the fence, became absent-minded, like a young man at his age often does when his soul takes into flight all by itself, finding the moment among hills, with striking views, irresistible.

Lawrence, who stood a few paces away from the park benches, was saying something to Joanie, pointing with his hand to the adobe tiles on the building to their far right, and they stared at it for a long time.

"Is it that building from which they'll come out?" a voice from behind them asked.

"Yes, that's the one. And there's nothing else out here," replied Lawrence without turning his head.

Another long pause ensued.

"So, Lawrence, how long have you been doing this?"

asked the same voice.

Lawrence turned and saw that it was Arya.

"I was the first to join Christine."

"Is that right, Lawrence? I did not know that, I thought Curtis came earlier," Joanie said.

"Christine started the Leap Forward chapter, I joined first, then Curtis, and then you. But volunteering at this Center was Curtis's idea though," replied Lawrence.

"So have you met any of these people at this center before? How many are they?"

"Oh yeah, I met them. I think this Center has about eight or nine, but we will work with only three guys. They like to keep volunteer to inmates ratio high."

By now a circle began to form itself around Lawrence. "It's a pretty broken bunch and they deserve all the love we can give them," continued Lawrence. "Oh yeah, some of us are old-timers. I think only you and Hunter are new," he said, addressing Arya.

"So you must know a lot then, can you say anything about them?"

"Well, Curtis don't like me to talk about them, so I got to be careful. I have a different perspective on it."

After a moment's pause Lawrence began to speak.

"We'll meet three guys, Morris, Cooper and Colby. They are about fifteen years of age or so. Like I said, each has a heart-breaking story. Each one is a puzzle. It is never that one big thing that strikes you first. You kind of feel there are so many pieces to that puzzle, and you sort of have to work your way with whatever they are willing to throw at you. Never go at the big puzzle directly. They are still raw so just wait for the right moment, if you absolutely have to. I kind of work with this one kid, Cooper. Nice kid. Tells me some things. One time," Lawrence took the handkerchief out of his pocket. "One time Cooper saw a bird with a broken leg, and he caught it. He wanted to mend it so he put it there and was going to get something. But as soon as he moved away the cat suddenly leaped on it and caught it."

"What happened then?"

"He ate it! The cat ate the bird. End of story!"

"I mean did Cooper see it? What did he do?"

"Yeah, Cooper saw it, he saw it with his own very eyes. He didn't say anything though. I guess it kinda hit him hard. He used to walk around in his bedroom in the middle of the night because he couldn't stop listening to the sounds coming from his mom's room. It was like water lapping at the side of the pool. I think the boy was very confused because, I mean, he saw his dad beating her, but then these lapping sounds were like they were doing it, you know? What's this kid going to do? Go in because he wanted to stop the beating or don't go in because he was embarrassed and didn't want to see his mom naked? I think this tormented the kid."

"But, didn't his mom say anything?" someone asked with a voice filled with disbelief. "I mean the kid should know which is which, right? How hard can it be?"

"Kids don't know, Hunter, and it's not that easy, do you think?"

"And his dad, he used to hold little children, infant children, and tickle them on their bellies with his head until they laughed and laughed and pulled at his hair with their little hands. But they didn't realize that he was also putting his hand on their private parts, taking it out and kissing his own fingers. And he would repeat it while the child was still laughing. No one saw it, but Cooper did. At least he was the first one to see it."

At this moment something unexpected began to stir in Arya. No one noticed it but he abruptly took a step toward Lawrence, as though a sudden uncontrollable impulse had struck him. But the next moment he put his hands in his pockets and stood still.

At that very second they heard Christine's voice, and they turned to see that the three boys were already there and Christine was hugging them.

Following the usual practice they introduced each other at first, and then stood in a circle, the six Leap Forward volunteers holding hands, alternating with the three young men: Cooper, Morris and Colby.

For the next two hours they walked in the woods, ran up the hill and stopped at the top, went down the lake and fed the ducks, spotted a deer which stood looking at them for a long time before jumping into the thicket and disappearing in a second, all in an unspoken assumption that one should interact with the worldviews of others and this was a better way to know what people mean when they talk – certainly what these young men meant when *they* talked.

When they returned to the park bench, exhausted, they sat quietly.

A FEW MINUTES PASSED.

"Cooper, do you want to tell them about the game?" Morris said out loud.

"What game?"

"It's just a little game Cooper came up with and we were

going to play with you guys. Cooper, explain the game, man!"

"What kind of game?" Curtis said calmly.

"What kind of a game?" Cooper rose from the park bench. "Let me explain it then," he said and walked over to the fence, where heavy stones were placed along its foot. He then began lifting a stone, a smaller one but still heavy, and another of the same size, and another, until he had his both hands full.

"Wow, wow, wow, whatever you are doing, doesn't feel like we should be doing that," said Curtis in a loud voice, and standing up.

"No, no, no, it's going to be fine, it's just a game."

Curtis walked up to Cooper and stood facing him aggressively, but Cooper swiftly moved past him, walked back to a spot near the bench and dropped the stones there.

"Ok, ok, let me explain it then. But first let me say," Cooper laughed, breathing heavily. "Curtis, man, we really appreciate you, and all of you, that you are so generous with your weekend, and come here to spend time with us. We really do. I mean look at us. We are cooped up in here and sometimes, I don't know, maybe you all think we don't make any sense."

"That's right Cooper, we don't have to do this," Curtis replied without moving, still feeling aggressive at what Cooper had just done with the stones. "It takes a lot from us, it's not easy for us, but we want to help out, do what we can. I mean just this morning I had to wake up at five to get here, but when our hearts are set, we are ready to sacrifice anything to be here for you guys."

Then Curtis walked slowly to the park bench and stood

there with one leg on it, and his hands in his pockets.

When Curtis was speaking like this, Arya, who was standing by the fence, experienced a series of conflicting emotions.

While he was driving up here earlier that morning, Arya was convinced that he had at last begun his long and worthy journey into a selfless community; and he had become fully primed with the feelings of the nobility of the task. As a result, seeing Curtis and others at first he expected a similar sea of emotion in them, into which he would be taken in and be filled.

But now, after these few hours, he saw that not only were the volunteers still strangers to him, but even these incarcerated young men were no one to Curtis.

Still, unperturbed, Arya reassured himself, "I am in America. I can help them. This is what America is all about. Oh, how noble it feels to be useful to them!"

When Curtis finished speaking, Cooper's eyes widened and sparkled with indignation for a brief second. Then, as though he did not really hear Curtis, he continued talking, his eyes glowing every minute when he spoke. "I mean look at us right? What are we pretending here, we are the bad apples here and you've come to put us back on the straight. I mean, we don't say it, we goof around it a lot but don't say it, but I want to say now that when I see you guys, right on the dot at nine-thirty in the morning, a tear comes to my eye, and just that moment everything stops, just stops, and all the doubts are put to sleep in my heart. I mean it's like when you watch baseball on TV. I love baseball, and watching something like a no-hitter, it's like that feeling. I mean watching a no-hitter means in all the nine innings no batter could touch him right? You sit there amazed, with tears in your eyes, and then you feel you are shown life can be this good if you just work at it with focus. I mean you always knew it, and someone somewhere has already proved it, but in your life you got to prove it again, one more time, maybe ten more times, more and more times until you are old enough to lose count, and then you'll start believing it."

For a few moments no one spoke.

Morris and Colby sat unmoving, staring in the direction of Cooper, but not at him directly. It was as though a subdued state had overcome them. They had already spoken like this with one another in private, and were not really surprised that some impulsive force moved Cooper to speak the same in front of these men and women.

Arya was staring intently at Cooper.

Curtis kept playing with two pebbles on the bench. On his face was an evident look of boredom.

"But I thought we were going to play the game!" exclaimed Joanie softly.

"Oh, I am sorry," Cooper said, embarrassed. The contours of his face abruptly changed to an apologetic frown. He recovered a moment later. But then just that very moment an unexpected smile came over his face and his eyes stared at everyone, shifting from one to another, as if he was under a new, urgent impulse. He stopped at Lawrence and began speaking loudly, "Remember, Lawrence, you told us about Luther one time? I began reading up the book you suggested and a funny thing happened. It is an interesting book, Lawrence."

"Is that so?"

"Yes, yes, you see, I learned one thing. I learned about

the only difference between people like us, sinners like me, and the lives of the sinners in earlier times, like in 1400s. Finally I seem to have hit on it, Lawrence."

"Don't say that, Cooper," Lawrence replied, his voice choking. A sudden compassion for the unfortunate young man overwhelmed him. "You are alright, Cooper boy."

"No, no Lawrence, hear me out," Cooper continued to speak, now more and more excited. More and more his eyes appeared intense and glowing, as though they were about to become tear-filled. "One thing is sure, that the only main difference is the objects they, the sinners of the past, dealt with. That's it. In everything else, there is no difference: whatever actions they performed, the feelings they had, the interactions they had, the wishes, the ambitions, the intrigues, the daily concerns, the struggles, the sources of dread, of the anguish, and of the love, all these remain the same even to this day. Hence, to be like a 1400s sinner, a man or a woman, or to live like one, we simply have to throw away all the material stuff that have been improved since then, and even more, throw away the more recent ways of interaction. That's it! When you are done with this throwing away of all this modern stuff, then you are nearly one with all the sinners of those earlier times."

SOMETIME IN THE MIDDLE OF this exchange Joanie left the group at the park bench, went into the hall and sat in the chair, opening her handbag and moving things in it for no clear reason. The fact was that Joanie was bored with all the talk, which she didn't really understand, and which spoiled the expectation she had for "a fun day with the poor boys."

A few minutes later Curtis also came in, and one look at

him and Joanie knew.

"The guys here sure talk a lot," she said, looking into Curtis's face.

"Yea, Cooper likes to talk and Lawrence likes to listen," Curtis sat loudly on the chair. "I can only take so much."

"At least they are getting it off their chest. I am so proud of you!"

"Yeah," Curtis drew on, himself distracted by some thought. "I try to do what I can, but you guys also make a lot of difference."

Meanwhile at the park bench, as soon as Cooper finished speaking, Hunter, as though he could no longer contain himself, began talking at once.

"You know?" he looked at Cooper with an expression of affection. "What you just said is deep, and gets to the core of it. I mean we all try to learn so many things, and we think we are learning this and that, but you know, it seems to me that slowly but surely everything that we experienced when we were young is replaced by what we read in the media when we grow old. See what I mean? I mean everything experience is replaced by everything knowledge; and it just becomes media, media, media, you know. Sure we dream this and dream that, but these days we spend so much of our time in reading up, which is just media. What you just said is taking everything back from media knowledge to real experience, which is how it should be. I get you, I get you Cooper man."

"See the thing is, it is you who are teaching us, whom are we kidding," said Lawrence.

A FEW MINUTES LATER THEY saw Curtis walking briskly up to

them. Joanie was a few paces behind him, walking slowly.

Curtis approached Lawrence. His face was red and stern.

"Lawrence, can I talk to you?"

Then Curtis stepped away from the rest saying, "Excuse us you all, this is a private conversation."

Morris and Colby looked at each other and smiled.

When Curtis and Lawrence were out of the earshot, Colby said, "O. O... He wasn't smiling, he's not happy!"

"We didn't break any rules, did we?"

"We were just talking."

Curtis and Lawrence stood at the far end for a long time. From this distance they could see that Curtis at first spoke for a minute and suddenly Lawrence stood still and had stopped talking.

Arya stood still watching them. He was thinking of the conversation he and Colby had earlier, while walking down the hill near the lake. Colby's words had struck him with a peculiar force. "To live properly you have to develop a really good sense of how much darkness is there in everything around us. We keep walking around in life, but we are not aware of this darkness. Actually this darkness is like the sea. And all the vastness in life is really submerged in this darkness. It hides everything, that's why we know so little of ourselves, so little of our fellow human beings, but most important, we ourselves don't know who we really are as a person – which is entirely a separate darkness," Colby had laughed.

As though it no longer wished to be suppressed, a memory awoke somewhere in Arya's consciousness, grew at once and filled his thoughts.

What he recalled was the bruise on his mother's face.

The truth is that Arya had never forgotten it. It would be true to say that he had not forgotten it even for a few minutes in all these years.

As is common with such recollections, in which one never recalls only a singular memory but a whole series of them that surround it, Arya also remembered his mother standing among her friends; smiling with her bruised eye at the green silk saree on her friend; showing him to her friend at the airport, just before he was to leave Hyderabad, and saying, "My boy," to her and then saying, "My friend," to him, feeling his smile and brushing an unseen speckle from his shoulder.

And he? He had stood there beaming and imagining that this world was a vast playground to which he was shaping the key and he could take his mother's hand and enter it any time he desired.

Arya then recalled another Anasuya, without the bruise. "A boy with two wives," she used to needle him, seeing him on the phone with one girl and then with the other. Arya listened to this memory as though listening to his favorite song, remembering how his mother's body shook as she stood laughing at some joke Rushi made, nearly doubling over, holding their gray rusted bed stand, almost getting up, almost falling over but sitting back again, and, unable to contain her laughter anymore, waving her hands to stop.

"Yes," thought Arya. "Everything that I am, I *must*, must, apply to remove her pain. I am only getting stronger and stronger for *her*. When I return, I will know how to remove the weeds from her life and make her smile again."

He was at once overcome with an overwhelming pity and love for his mother, and for Colby, and Morris and Cooper.

"No, I am not frightened, Amma is with me, I am not frightened," he kept repeating inwardly. He pulled himself together, "I must prepare better, be better, not like this, but better, even better."

He looked at Cooper with that extraordinary affection which was already flowing in him for these three young men.

THERE WAS SOME TALK, THOUGH we have to account for the inevitability that some of it might be just rumor, that when Arya reached America, a change had begun to occur in him.

Externally, Arya's facial expression, the special brightness in his eyes, and the sudden reddening of his face when he became shy, remained nearly the same. But there he was, in the early days of his life in America, plunged into a new state of incomprehension of his own condition. It was as though an intense feeling persisted in him that someone or something very precious had died, and everyone around him either did not notice or did not care. Of particular interest to our story is that for a brief period Arya became meek, somewhat unquestioning and often smiled excessively at others.

On that very first day at the university, walking from his apartment to report to the Graduate Office, Arya was taken in by the sight of so many houses with families in them.

"How is it that he, this person, this family, with the dog barking at the end of the leash, and these children, are here with their lives I did not know?" he thought.

Once inside the building he became instantly confused but only for a second, and then quietly located the dean's office. There he stood, shifting from one leg to the other, and waited.

After what seemed to him that an entire hour had passed, during which it was quiet all around him, a sound erupted in the hallway. At first it was like a snake charmer's hand-drum that he used to hear in Hyderabad, but it was really the sound of several disconnected conversations at once, echoing in the hallway.

Then a group of students in striking blue jackets, undergraduates from the Geology department just returning from a field trip, came through the door. Turning the hallway corner, they saw this shy young man, looking just like a foreign graduate student, who at once straightened his legs and smiled nervously at them. Without stopping their laughter they passed him, and one or two from the group gave him a look.

A young woman with striking golden hair, her nose and cheeks red from the cold September weather, smiled at him and turned her head towards a companion who was asking her something.

Arya had never seen so many people, men and women or boys and girls, with pink skin and freckles on their faces. As they passed, he said, "Hi," in a feeble voice that was barely audible even to himself.

None of them said even a single word to him in response.

Arya's face became red. He became even more self-conscious that he had done a stupid thing.

"Eiraya?" the secretary, with milk-rimmed glasses, called out from her desk.

Then a door opened and the elderly pink face of the dean emerged, with frameless glasses slipping on his nose and his wet pink lips appearing unusually shiny. He stared straight at Arya for a moment and signaled with his forefinger to follow him.

Surprised at the wagging forefinger and feeling offended, Arya entered the office and stood facing the dean, who now had some papers in his hand – evidently Arya's admission sheets.

"Well, what do we have here..."

The dean was not sitting on his chair but was leaning casually on his desk, with a pen that he twirled in his fingers.

"Welcome to our university. Are you all set with housing?"

Arya, still in that confused state of feeling stupid and hence feeling increasingly out of place, said, "Yes, sir," in the same feeble voice.

The dean looked at him but only for a second or two. He then turned his eyes to the papers. He shuffled through them quickly, stopping abruptly at one of the middle sheets and stepped out.

The dean then issued a soft instruction to the secretary, who whispered back something to him. Then, instead of turning and resuming their session, as Arya expected, the dean went out into the hallway and disappeared, ignoring Arya completely.

"I am in their country, that's why," thought Arya, unable to reconcile the conflicting emotions arising in him. "Maybe I would have behaved the same insulting way if all these people were in Hyderabad."

A few moments later, having understood from the secretary's explanation that until a formal advisor was found, he, the dean, would be his default advisor, Arya came out.

"See how insignificant I feel, how I keep behaving as though I am in a stranger's house," a wry smile came over Arya's face. "No one tells you that you will feel this way when you come to America."

The fact is, the vigor with which Arya arrived in America went unnoticed. No one else witnessed how his wish to improve himself was coming true in his new life. All the elevated feelings that were rising in him, the euphoria and the rapture that he was experiencing, were only within him and the external world went on as ordinarily without noticing him.

When he did not see in his external surroundings the same surprise that he was experiencing in his soul, he was curious at first, puzzled inwardly, then became terrified at the same ordinariness, at the same sameness.

Immediately after he graduated with a masters degree from the university, Arya entered into employment, and for the next three years he submitted himself entirely to the work and the life around him.

Around that time two or three companions of Arya, who were his fellow graduate students when he was in the university, and who had known him in his Hyderabad days, came to Anasuya on their yearly visit home. That was when they said they were quite sure of his friendship with two or three women in America, but to what extent he was really attached to them, romantically that is, no one could say emphatically.

It was during this period, driven by some unknown intentions, Arya began volunteering for Leap Forward, a non-governmental organization in California; and now in this gathering at the incarceration center he found himself recalling those remarkable details of his mother's bruises.

JUST THEN LAWRENCE RETURNED. HE exchanged a few words with Christine. Curtis was seen going back to the hall without talking to anyone.

"We're going to have to call it a day, it seems, guys," Lawrence said.

"Oh, why, we still have time!" said Arya, surprised and irked at this decision.

"Something came up and we have to head back," added Christine, grabbing the water bottles.

Arya saw that all three young men felt embarrassed and he was sure that they were thinking it was their fault. "But this is not just a weekend picnic, how can you leave them like that?" he cried inwardly, frowning intensely.

On their way back to the hall Lawrence mumbled words to the effect that Curtis did not approve of so much talk with the young men; and that he said it would raise undesired expectations and violates the emotional distance they must maintain with the inmates.

As soon as they reached inside the hall, Curtis, Joanie and Christine stood near a corner under the mural, and began exchanging words quietly.

"Can I say something?" Arya said suddenly, in a loud voice. "I want to say something." It appeared as though he had been restless during the past few minutes and could no longer control himself.

"Yes, sir!" Curtis smiled at him calmly.

"I think all the rules that I hear are fine, and you are all obviously more experienced in this. But I think the main thing is we have to find a way to relate to their own experiences of these boys. But here I am feeling that we are deliberately placing ourselves outside of their experiences. And that would only hurt them more! I mean can't you see their eyes? Look at their eyes! Actually we should not leave them now!"

"Well, you don't know everything Aaraya, so please wait till you attend a few more sessions and then talk," Curtis said all of a sudden, and turned his face away from Arya.

Arya said not a single word. His face became more and more red; it was evident he was embarrassed.

When they came out of the hall with their bags and empty water bottles, they each shook the hands of the young men, who now stood at an arm's length, as though remembering a formality.

"Goodbye Aaraya," Colby smiled and suddenly Arya's voice choked. "Goodbye Colby!" he replied. "Goodbye Cooper! Goodbye Morris! Goodbye fellows, take care of yourselves, fellows!"

IMMEDIATELY AFTER GETTING EMBARRASSED AT the incarceration center, unable to stand apart from the growing recollections of his mother Anasuya, Arya decided to visit Hyderabad.

"I will go home to her and then everything will be clear," he thought inwardly, once again remembering Cooper and Colby.

"Look how long I left her and *them!*" Arya thought, at once filled with only the thoughts of his family and home, and in a mood that was approaching something similar to frenzy. "But my nerves are stronger now. Home is where I belong. Who are all these strangers?"

When the day finally arrived for Arya to leave for Hyderabad, not only was he flooded with tender feelings for everyone coming into his office cubicle, wishing him well for the journey, but an entirely new set of questions, dilemmas that were suppressed until then, began to resurface in him.

Carried away by an urge to say something nice to someone, he began writing.

After he wrote the letter, intending to give it only to his nearest colleagues, he scratched and rewrote it a few more times, and decided to send it to everyone in the company.

Arya felt particularly satisfied with the tone of the entire letter, and read the phrase, "...we better remember to apply our experience the next day," with a special delight. This phrase came to him while he was writing the note.

"But again, you can't be too emotional," he said to himself.

That evening, after an unending string of meetings, when Arya returned to his cubicle, he found several notes of replies on his desk.

He read all of them attentively. He was surprised at the unexpected personal touch he found in them, and his heart swelled with emotion when he read them again.

"Selfishly though, I'm jealous to see you go on a homecoming trip."

"Thanks for the note! Wow, you have been a big help to us many times – we will miss you! I hope your journey goes well!"

"So beautifully written!! You really are a poet! It's been a "kick" working with you, Arya! Looking forward to lots of stories from your home!"

Arya tried to suppress the tears in his eyes. He leaned back in his chair and became engrossed in thoughts, staring at something above. When he heard someone approach his cube, he quickly hid these notes in embarrassment, as though he had overdone something and didn't want anyone to notice.

UNDER THE INFLUENCE OF SUCH experience, in the early hours of a summer day in the year 1996, after five years of being abroad, Arya left for the San Francisco airport to return home to Hyderabad.

15

An Ominous Feeling

By THE TIME THE PLANE carrying him from San Francisco arrived at the airport in Hyderabad, Arya's excitement and nervousness, which had disappeared during the long journey and gave in to weariness and boredom, returned with a fresh force.

As soon as the wheels of the plane touched the ground, he closed his eyes, and at once several figures rose in his view: Anasuya, Rushi, his sisters, waving to him as he climbed into the plane five years ago. For a moment he completely forgot the years that had passed since. He kept turning their faces in his imagination until they became clearer and clearer, as though he was already in front of them.

After the passengers came out of the plane there was a long wait, during which Arya began to feel a mild agitation at the expressions of familiarity on the faces around him.

At last the line moved forward.

Following the passengers in front of him, he passed through a narrow passageway, lit-up by dull fluorescent flickering tubes, and came out suddenly into a large, expansive hall. It was as though his eyes, still adjusting to the new pulsations, saw a tattered gray curtain, damp and full of holes, and this curtain was just being unveiled, revealing a stage lit all over with dim yellow lights, filled with stationary figures that looked aggressively at him. The more he stared back, the more the stage kept opening in front of him, until the lines proceeded toward the center of the hall, where the customs counters were located. Arya became conscious that he himself was being pressed from behind in the direction of these counters.

Beyond these counters stood young and old men and women in an irregular pattern, clutching the orange nylon rope that sagged as they pressed forward, evidently waiting for the travelers to emerge from the customs and immigration.

For a few moments Arya was confused at what he saw in front of him. "Why is everyone looking the same?" he thought.

Just then a middle-aged man, who had been averting his eyes from Arya since they came out of the plane, rushed forward and embraced an animated older woman.

By habit Arya already began making up his mind what to do in case his receiving party did not appear.

"This is my place. I know it like the back of my palm. I should be able to get home in an auto-rickshaw if they don't show up..." thought he, and then immediately checked himself, "But I just came in."

By then he had already walked past the throng of people and stopped as if he had just come to his senses, not knowing why he was there.

"Everything is the same," he thought, and before he turned to switch the enormous big luggage in his hands, an avalanche of familiar voices surrounded him, jerking him into complete consciousness.

Someone hugged him, and he saw in front of him the faces that resembled those he had been imagining all this while.

Then several hands affectionately embraced his shoulders and eagerly cajoled him to let go of the bag.

He could not see them all at once, though he heard all the voices together.

"We have been calling Arya and Arya so loud, you were looking here and there, but didn't you see us?"

"He kept walking without seeing us. We had to run after him!"

"At last!"

"This way, this way! Ey, what, did you forget where we parked too!"

"He hasn't changed a bit! Look at that walk, as if he is about to hit someone! Ey, do you walk like this in America, they will think you are a goonda!"

"Aaaa...I want to be in front, you take his other hand!"

Sita stood before him with tears in her eyes, and he embraced her with an emotion that overpowered him.

Not having yet seen his parents anywhere, a voice inside him kept asking a question, "Where are they?"

Then Anasuya appeared before him.

"Arya! Have you come, at last!" she said and looked eagerly into Arya's eyes.

At this sight of his mother Arya was instantly flooded with the thought that she led a life in which he himself, Arya, figured most prominently in her imagination. He recognized in her eyes what he himself was experiencing, a disbelief that they are both so near each other at last. See how unchanged she is, not at all recovered from the years of hopelessness and despair! Somehow her faith in him, Arya, was the main thing she clung to, while he, in a despicable act of betrayal, did not think about her, did not feel about her, as intensely as she did of him while he was abroad.

He longed to say, *"Amma...!"* but before he uttered it, at once the voice that kept gnawing in him all this time amplified, and instead he asked in a sunken, shrill voice, "Where is Nanna?"

"Here, here. He is just standing by the side, that's all."

There stood his father – or someone who very strongly resembled his father, Arya thought at first – with an expression that said, with the same brightness and love, "Here I am. Just the same as ever. Nothing else matters, and even if I am standing by the side and not with them, our bond is safe, and it has its own life that will shine as long as I live."

With the same sunken, shrill voice Arya uttered, *"Nanna!"* and embraced his father. A strange, new, disagreeable sensation, such as one feels from someone whose physical frailty would not dawn on us until we embrace them, came over Arya.

"How you are! After this many years... Arya...! My son...!"

In a flash Arya's mind emptied itself of every thought and only retained what was in front of him. His senses increased a thousand-fold, just as one who saw something and was alarmed by the unexpected state it was in.

"Why...why like this? Why standing apart, at a distance?"

Arya said.

Taking his son's words as a disapproval of the way he was, Rushi said, "I am fine. How else should I be?" and smiled. "You are seeing me after these many years, it's natural to feel different," laughed Rushi, and stepped forward with his arm around Arya's shoulders.

Yashoda, who was holding Arya's arm, released him and beckoned her mother to come nearer.

Anasuya, who was standing away with a stern expression, softened, and came closer but still looked angrily at Rushi.

Intermingled feelings of immense contentment and happiness filled Arya, though he too saw his mother's stern expression.

Tiruvengalam, who was standing at a distance, with a deference that was new to Arya, now stepped forward, and affectionately patted his shoulders and his back with a beaming smile.

"We were all waiting so eagerly," he said loudly. "Your mother and father did nothing but wait for you ever since your flight was confirmed. Was that a direct flight? Things have improved tremendously since you left. It has to be a direct flight."

HERE AND THERE PEOPLE RUSHED past one another, moving in and out of the waiting area, stopping abruptly and checking their pockets, bags or purses, before resuming their brisk walk, with their hands still searching.

From a group of crowded men and women, who just received their party, a young boy suddenly burst out and ran for an auto-rickshaw, joyfully skating on his feet, as excited youth were prone to do.

By now Arya began to scan his surroundings steadily. He answered the flurry of questions but several thoughts passed through his head all by themselves. "How is it that they have not yet noticed all my new feelings? Oh, how peaceful and unobtrusive everything is. How pure everything is. How simple it is for them to be happy, even though I have all these new experiences in America!"

Something else struck him, that while he, in his clumsy confusion, did not succeed in transferring his tender feelings to them, did not show how absolutely peaked his love was for them; while he struggled with this confusion, they, by their simplicity, expressed their unfettered love freely, without any self-consciousness, making him feel completely the way they felt, and soaked him in their love. Arya experienced an urge, a special force, to bundle everything new that he had acquired since he left them, make it into a new life and serve it to them, thereby wiping away that pain he imagined they suffered while he was away.

At that instant, watching their faces, walking in the middle of them, and confidently raising a hand to stop an incoming Ambassador car while they crossed the road, as though his absence all these years should mean nothing to the car driver, Arya experienced even stronger harmony with everything around him.

He noticed that people were staring at them, and suddenly he laughed, having just remembered something pleasant he had forgotten long ago.

"Nothing has changed. They have the same sparkling bright eyes," he thought, looking at the enthusiastic auto-rickshaw drivers, whose friendly and fearless eyes acknowledged him, as they met his own eyes with a certain backstage familiarity. The harmony that he began to feel moments ago increased to close the gap between him and everything around him.

Someone asked, "Did Ramulu set the luggage in the car? So, let's go. He must be tired."

They all turned and walked towards the parking lot.

Behind them walked Rushi.

"You did a very good thing by coming here now. We are all so happy," said Yashoda in a low tone, so only Arya could hear. "You should take some rest first and then we'll talk," she said, catching his arm.

Arya was still pondering why his father walked slower, falling behind.

"Why is he so weak, what happened...?" he began, but before he finished the sentence, a sudden suspicion rose in him, that perhaps his father had already separated from them.

The next moment a terrible feeling passed through Arya, that by suspecting his father in this way, he had already admitted the unthinkable distance between them.

He turned to meet Rushi, and saw that Anasuya, discerning his intention to endear himself to Rushi, could not hide a disapproving frown on her face.

"What's the matter!" cried Arya, seeing that look.

"What, what happened?" rushed forward Tiruvengalam, with an affectation of an alarmed expression on his face, at once sensing that the newly-arrived son and the mother were about to exchange emotions, and energized by it.

Arya was bewildered, and became irritated at this reaction from Tiruvengalam. He remembered his uncle's tendency to elevate the family tension with his overreactions.

He ignored his uncle, and addressing his mother, said, "Are you tired? Maybe we should stand here, they can get the car around." Then saying, "I'll stand with you," he stood next to her, his agitation increasing at not being with Rushi at this moment.

"Nothing. I am fine. You go," said Anasuya with determination, and averted her eyes from him.

Seeing that she was about to withdraw into herself, Arya felt a compulsion to draw his mother out of her mood and tried to change the topic.

Anasuya smiled at his remarks, but with an expression that remained on her face from the earlier emotion, she said, "It's no use. These government roads are always this bad. No matter how much money they pour in, it's wasted on those inspector sons of whores! Low class fellows! You go, you go dear, go walk with your father. I will follow slowly. Don't worry about me, I can walk by holding onto this side rail."

At these words the animated conversation among the family abruptly ceased. They all knew that this remark was targeted at Rushi, whose department was responsible for inspecting city roads.

When the moment passed Arya felt his elation was not the same as before. Still, the excitement of coming home kept him in that euphoric mood, and he eagerly stood next to his father, saying *"Nanna!"* unable to hide his hungry desire to express his love for Rushi.

BY THEN THE CARS WERE pulled out of the lot but there was a disagreement between Tiruvengalam and the parking lot attendant about the charge. Embarrassed by the loud voices of Tiruvengalam and Dixit, Yashoda's husband, arguing with the attendant, Arya offered to give whatever the young attendant asked, but his words were quickly dismissed loudly by both men.

At last the cars were pulled in, and there was a long exchange about where Arya should sit.

"You sit here Arya, with your mother. Sit, sit, why should you be standing?" Dixit said, winking at others. "How can we let Americans stand as if they are used to it? We can get by because we don't count."

Laughing at this remark and wondering how three people could fit in the backseat of that small car, Arya opened the door and climbed inside, sliding to the center of the seat.

Through the front glass he saw two auto-rickshaw drivers at a distance, looking wistfully his way at the passing fare, and ready to oblige in an instant in case he called them.

Everything inside the car appeared unusually small to Arya and he laughed at the awkwardness of sitting in something so tiny. A faint musty smell of old leather occupied the interior. A dim yellow light hung overhead in the middle.

"They should clean the cover of that light, then it'd be brighter," he thought, curiously touching and tapping the outer cover of the light. "Plastic," he noted to himself.

Rushi appeared at the window. His face, weary but still not satisfied with Arya, pushed itself into the car through the window. He gently held Arya's head and said, "I will go now," and, unable to contain his emotion, he continued, "You are my son, remember! And I am happy you came after so many years!" Then exhausted by the discomfort of stooping into the car, Rushi withdrew and straightened up, so that only his half-sleeved shirt was visible to Arya.

By now Arya recognized that Anasuya and Rushi no longer lived together, but he did not believe that they could be separated like *that*. Though Arya knew, from Anasuya's letters, that the discord, the same that always existed, still remained between them, he could not allow himself to see that everything has come to *this*.

Once again that oppressive feeling entered Arya, that he had not succeeded in transferring the full extent of his joyous feelings to his father. And it disconcerted him that no one noticed he failed like this, again! A desperation that somehow something had gone incalculably wrong entered him. "Why is everything like this?" he asked himself. "And who is *he* to separate me from my mother and father...?" thinking how Dixit issued orders loudly who should sit in which car, and how his parents did not say anything.

Even though Arya answered all the questions that were put to him during the drive, his thoughts were still at the airport. An ominous feeling that something was about to occur, or had already begun, which he was utterly helpless to prevent, remained in him. The frail figures of his parents, their tired faces, their weary eyes, their receded and thinning hair, the expanded forehead of his father, the suffering anger of his mother, her eager looks toward him, her son, the weak shoulder bones when he embraced them, all this continued to trigger in him a morbid feeling.

"Are you finding all these shops new? Did you forget?" he heard his sister's voice, who saw his face and knew what he was thinking.

"Really, not much changed. Actually I am curious to see how our new home is," said Arya, looking at the passing textile shops.

Then purposely appearing offended, Arya said, "Well. I knew it. You saw that I was away and so you all thought, `Well, let's just buy ourselves a big bungalow. He will turn up whenever he turns up, what have we got to do with him?'" ending each sentence with an upward note, teasing everyone.

"It is evident. Who was trying to hide it? What's wrong in it?" said Anasuya, suppressing her laughter and playing along.

"While some people go abroad should some others just sit doing nothing? How can it be? Where's the justice in it? That is why..."

"Even this, consider yourself fortunate," said Sita. "At least we are taking you home. If it were some other family they'd drop you in some hotel and leave you saying, `If you need anything call us.' "

Ramulu, who contained his laughter until now with great difficulty, was no longer able to hide his impulse to add a comment of his own, and said, "Don't call us, we'll call you," at which the occupants of the car burst out into laughter at Arya's reddening face.

WHEN THEY REACHED HOME ANASUYA stopped Arya at the door and stood facing him. From the silver tray handed to her by the maid, she took out kumkuma, applied it to Arya's forehead, whispered a few short phrases to cast off the evil spirits, and thanked the Lord; and then she said, "Now come in with your right foot first."

"Should I step over?"

"Over it and quickly," said Anasuya. She gave the tray to the maid, making sure she did not step into the house right away after emptying it. "Take this tray and throw away this water somewhere far away. Instantly!"

The family spread out and sat in sofas and chairs, surrounding Arya, and continued their animated conversation.

Ramulu and Dixit came in with Arya's luggage, heaved it through the middle of the room, and stood it upright at the corner. At first Arya was about to stand and take the luggage but realized he was home. Instead he finished the tea in his glass and saw the small picture frame that rested on top of the switchboard. On it were displayed two slanting verses, *Prayers go up, Blessings come down.*

"I still remember that picture! You still have it!" he cried with a child-like excitement.

16

"Am I Really Like That?"

THAT NIGHT WENT BY, BUT Arya was already beginning to feel a heightened state of morbidity, contrary to all the bright expectations and goals with which he had come out of the customs and immigration at the airport.

Still, the next morning the household woke up at the habitual hour of six with a consciousness of something new that had taken place the previous night.

And no matter the night's strangeness, opening his eyes in that very namaaz-filled Hyderabad city morning, Arya saw that every thing in the new house revealed itself irresistibly to him.

All the physical things at once renewed their intimacy with Arya and connected him to something else. The hard bed, the room's thickened plywood doors that wouldn't close fully, the soft sliding of aluminum bolts on the windows, the cold granite stones on the floor, the blue gas stove, the red cylinder, the smeared, sticky green gas lighter, the small dark-brown refrigerator at the corner, the black-stone counter top that his mother liked so much because it cleaned easily, the aluminum cans with handwritten labels, the black wok at the corner with its huge hooks, the steel vessel in which freshly cut potato pieces were clearly visible submersed under water... Arya took in all these sights hungrily.

He boldly went into the kitchen and needlessly turned on the tap. And when his mother asked him to make them tea he complied willingly, all the while smiling inwardly. She often surprised him by asking him to do such domestic chores.

He felt particularly compassionate towards the servants whenever they came in with a newspaper and the milk packets, and toward the watchman of the house. When his mother ordered them to do a chore, he thought she was harsh towards them, forgetting that he himself did the same only a few years ago. He chided her privately for giving them such a small amount of money and asked her to double their wages.

Every once in a while he made a joke imitating his father and his office friends but ceased when Anasuya unpredictably became agitated and mocked Rushi using foul words.

DURING THE NOON HOUR, WHEN Arya stepped out of his bedroom after remembering something, he passed Yashoda in the kitchen.

"Isn't it time for another cup of coffee?"

"Yes, yes. What will you have, tea or coffee?"

"It's nearly afternoon already. Tea?" then remembering his earlier thought, he turned to his sister, "Where is that blue chest, the one we used to store our books in our back room? I had kept all my journals in it. The lock must be all rusty by now…"

"Ask Amma, but don't be hopeful. She threw away a lot of that stuff years ago."

"How can she? She couldn't have," said Arya to himself, not believing Yashoda's words.

He turned and walked into the living room, where Anasuya was on the sofa, talking in a loud voice.

Tiruvengalam and Dixit were there too.

"Son of a whore and a thief! His entire family is like that," he heard his mother's angry voice. An intense displeasure at something that only she could see, and which never left her gaze, occupied her expression.

She spoke addressing no one in particular. Now and then Dixit and Tiruvengalam affirmed her aggressive words by uttering something meekly, and then became quiet. They were silent not only because they were men who were afraid of her tongue, but also because they arrived here on this morning expecting *something to happen,* and were already filled with the anticipation of it.

The driver Ramulu sat quietly on the floor near the door.

"There…!" said Anasuya on seeing Arya. "So are you feeling bored already? Come, sit here," in a voice that had none of the previous harshness, but which nevertheless carried a mocking tone.

"Bored? How can you say that, Amma? American minds! They are always thinking. So sharp. He is not bored, just preoccupied. No, Arya?" cried Dixit, excited on seeing

Arya. Then abruptly softening his voice, he stood up, and offered his chair, "Sit, sit here!"

"No, no, you sit. I'll sit next to Amma, there's place here," smiled Arya and hurriedly sat next to Anasuya.

Then saying, "No, no, not bored at all, too soon to be bored!" Arya turned to his mother and asked, "Remember the blue iron chest? Where is it?"

"What blue chest?" Anasuya at once frowned, her voice filled with rising impatience. "Oh, that blue chest," she then said with disdain, "I threw it out long time ago. I neither have any space to keep that old furniture, nor any energy to keep them cleaned. You know how much maintenance is required to keep these rooms clean?"

"Then all my journals, books and letters? Where did you keep them?"

"I threw them all. I didn't know what was inside. How could I know? There were all insects and cockroaches in the storage of our old house. At least now I have a clean house," said she.

"Did you really throw away all of them?" asked Arya in despair, his exasperated voice low with disbelief.

"Yes, dear, I did throw them out," she said, her voice now no longer aggressive. "Who has time to keep track of all your stuff from years ago?" she said, avoiding his eyes.

Then, as though suppressing an unexpected feeling that arose in her, Anasuya continued, "You all have gone away, your life is yours and I am living mine here! Whether it rains or shines, is anyone asking me what was happening to me?"

Seeing that her agitation had increased, and vexed that she was about to draw others into their conversation, Arya,

in an attempt to terminate the exchange, said, "Yes, it is
true, old furniture does get dirty and that too iron, one must
be careful..."

He rose, and saying, "Keep talking, I'll be back in a
minute," he came out of the room.

Walking back to his sister in the kitchen, Arya said, "She
says she threw them away!" in a weak, sunken voice, not
fully believing his mother.

WITH THE OPPRESSIVE FEELING RISING in him at having lost
his journals – his entire past was in that blue chest – Arya
returned to his room and sat with a pile of newspapers.

Anasuya's voice emanated continuously from the living
room, and the conversation never ceased.

"Why should we not say it out loud? Father and son both!
Some days I cry without sleep all night, how did all men in
this family turn into such sons of whores? How did I end
up in this? My brother, he raised me like a pearl! Didn't let
even a fly touch me. What dignity! What honor! Look at
this family. Men like these should be made to stand in the
middle of the road, and people should lineup, take turns and
spit on them!"

"Oh yamma! What a line that would be! Ah, ah!" yelled
Dixit. "Ey, Ramulu, you can be the line runner, ey? Heh,
heh, heh," winking at the driver who had been staring
intently at Arya a few moments earlier.

"What Ramulu? What can Ramulu do? Ramulu is useless.
One look by him and Ramulu will run away. What they
need is someone strong like me. I myself will stand and run
the line," said Anasuya loudly with contempt.

Continuing with the same intense emotion, as one who

thought her proposed action should've been taken long ago, she shook her head in disdain from side to side.

A moment or two passed. At once exhausted, Anasuya became quiet, as though she was attending to a voice inside her, which alone mattered above all those present.

Not hearing any more voices from the living room, Arya fixed his eyes on the newspaper.

Yashoda came in with tea, met his eyes with a look and said, "See how she speaks like this, in front of everyone. This is what we have to live with while you are away."

Arya, with the newspaper in front of him but unable to make out anything from it, said, "How has it turned to this? Why is she still like this? *Nothing* has changed...I thought..." becoming conscious of his own exasperated voice.

"This is normal for her. Everyday! This is nothing, it is worse when father comes. That's why he wouldn't."

The next moment her face turned pale. Yashoda looked toward his eyes, and in a pleading voice said, "You have to do something before you go, Arya! Do something, but make her calm down! If you can do just this, your entire purpose in visiting India will be fulfilled! Just do this! I know it is unfair to you. You came home to relax after five years, and you should not be expected to deal with these issues. But the situation is out of control! Our lives have turned miserable during the last few years, and we've been waiting for you to come! She sits there with all the outsiders and speaks of father like that..."

Arya, bewildered, stared at his sister, and the brother and sister burst into a weak laughter. "What a joke our family has turned into," Arya said.

Then with the calmness that was familiar and reassuring to Yashoda, he said, "Now that I am here, I'll talk to her," in a tone of confidence. "Don't go into that room. Let them talk themselves tired."

AFTER THIS CONVERSATION, THOUGH ARYA felt a peculiar calmness that comes when one believes to have seen the full extent of what was before unknown, he continued to feel vexed at "all this."

Now "all this" was all around him, revealing a life he knew but one he left years ago.

But, to his helpless amazement, "all this" still had a stranglehold on this house, still filled it, not as a memory from a distant past, not as that which was no longer, but with a still-throbbing force of the very same dreary oppression, making everything in this family remain the same. Against this dark and oppressive force of sameness, his hopes and dreams of the past five years seemed to him were simply a weak cardboard barrier, swept aside as a thing of no power.

Arya did not know how long he sat there with the newspaper. A feeling of estrangement that began in him when he first saw his parents at the airport, now grew stronger.

"What is it?" he asked himself. "Can it be true that she sees me really like that!" recalling the words his mother spoke – he knew they were aimed at him – moments ago.

"Am I really like *that?*"

At once Arya thought that his mother's brightness at the airport was contrived, that she did not feel happiness the way he did, and it crushed him.

Remembering the foul words she used, aiming them at he

and his father, a feeling similar to an insurmountable doubt enveloped him.

"Am I really like that...!" said Arya to himself over and over again, as he sat on his bed later that night.

17

"Such Forgiveness Drama"

NEXT MORNING ARYA WOKE UP with his habitual going-over in his head of everything that energized him. Then he recalled the previous day and at once his brightness evaporated. A feeling of moroseness, mixed with an unpleasant sensation of feverishness, occupied its place.

He stepped into the inner drawing room and saw that one of the servants was arranging something in front of the cupboard. The cupboard door was wide open.

"There, they are at it again," Arya said to himself with a rising nervous energy. "They are everywhere...!"

Ever since Arya arrived, he noticed that one or two male servants, whose names he did not know, not only moved freely all around the house, boldly walking into his own room, opening cupboards and almirahs, but also acted as though they had a part in the family decisions that Anasuya made.

At first Arya took this as the natural enthusiasm in them on account of his arrival, and expected the servants to retreat the next day. Now, seeing this same male servant standing in front of the same cupboard, where Anasuya and Rushi kept their clothes together, Arya was agitated.

"To see these strangers even touch father's clothes... how could she give them a place in the house like...that!" he muttered inwardly, feeling crushed at the thought of Rushi.

Arya was in this agitated state when the servant, instead of attending to Arya, simply looked at him. Arya even saw on the servant's face an impatient expression that stared at him, as though saying, "Now what do you want? Don't you see I have no time for you? See how you are encroaching into my territory. This may once have belonged to you but your mother now belongs to me..."

A sudden feeling of powerlessness overcame Arya.

In that moment, in a flash of imagination he saw his mother sitting on the bed, leaning against the head frame, her stomach and her full body shaking as she tried to control her laughter at something that the servant said. The servant was sitting next to her, near her knees, his face beaming with pleasure, while he, Arya, stood at the bedroom door with a sinking feeling in his stomach.

For a brief moment Arya imagined himself yielding to this new situation of his sudden powerlessness. "Can I accept this?" he asked himself in confusion.

The moment passed. Arya recovered and became conscious of his position as the master, and stared at the servant with a stern expression.

PUSHING ASIDE THESE THOUGHTS OF disarray, Arya dressed

to go to British Library. The prospect of visiting his old favorite after these years titillated him.

Just then he heard Yashoda calling, *"Nanna!* It's Nanna…" as she announced Rushi.

"Did you climb the steps slowly? Look how you are out of breath. Sit down here first," said the voice of Yashoda.

Forgetting his plans, Arya came into the living room.

"Why didn't you come yesterday?"

"When did I get time? Just too much work…" said Rushi, answering his son with a weak voice that became thin between his short breaths.

Arya looked at him attentively, still unable to believe how different and weak the figure before him was, from his memory of a strong, ebullient, and heavy body.

Anasuya was inside. She was sitting on the edge of the bed, in the middle of which were bedsheets and curtains that the maid was sorting. On hearing Rushi's voice all at once an intense anger showed itself in Anasuya. She did not know that she ceased hearing the maid, who was asking her if the sheets were to be washed too.

Then, as one who came to a determination, she rose, and said impatiently, "Everything is for washing. Dirty and filthy as it is!"

The maid, making an effort to ignore her mistress's outburst, said submissively, "Yes, Amma, you go," with a sympathizing look that said, "What a burden you have to put up with."

What the maid really wanted to say was, "When did I not wash as you asked? Is anyone trying to escape work and idling? You just have to tell me clearly only once!" but she simply obeyed her mistress.

Walking softly with a purpose, Anasuya approached the living room.

Through the turquoise sheer curtain the view inside was partially visible.

She stopped and listened for a few moments.

Then abruptly she stepped into the living room, half dragging her right foot. Leaning with her hand on the wall, she looked sternly at everyone in the room except Rushi.

"Come, Amma. Sit here," Arya said. Then, wishing to make the stern expression on her mother's face disappear, he said, "We were just settling on the sofa."

Arya moved the chair to where she stood.

Anasuya stood scowling for a few moments in the middle of the room, giving her right arm a jerk or two, separating the silver bracelet that had become tangled with the fine glass bangles on her wrist. Then she sat.

"So early? Did that whore dismiss you so early?" she mocked Rushi with spite. "Pch, it is understandable. After all, she has to make a living! Allowances have to be made for other clients too, it's not as if it's just you two love birds. In any case how can she live with just one client?"

Rushi looked despairingly at Arya and Yashoda, his exasperated expression pleading, "This is what I have to put up with. Every time it is like this!"

"At least while Arya stays with us, let us keep calm, Amma!" cried Yashoda, with indignation and emphasis.

"You keep quiet! You don't know anything!" replied Anasuya angrily. "How will he know if we shove everything under the rug and pretend everything is proper? He has to know the truth!"

"Everybody knows the truth. Doesn't he know? He is

not a stranger! Why should we make his life miserable by telling him everything you have done!" Yashoda exclaimed.

"What everything? What did I do?" yelled Anasuya. "Father and daughter, they are both united and waiting to get rid of me!" her body shaking with anger. "Arya, he had not come home in over a month! And then how did he come? Dead drunk! In the middle of the night, at 2 am in the middle of the night! As soon as he came, not a word he spoke but took me by my neck, like this, Arya...!" Anasuya bent her own head, and held her own neck with her left hand, and continued, "and threw me out of the house! How will you justify that? Where could I go in that night? I walked up to your sister's house, have you forgotten?" she turned to Yashoda. "And because of all this my sugar complaints have become unbearable. Now they want me to sacrifice my body too," she cried, her voice now raised to a feverish pitch.

"Me! Your own mother! Didn't you come out of here, tearing my stomach apart! Yes, your own mother who gave you birth! Whores! Arya, now I cannot look at him, I am afraid at any moment he will kill me in his drunken rage. And now he has the telephone installed in that whore's house and you know what they do? They both get drunk and he calls me and pleads me to talk to *her* on the phone. He makes her curse me. One day he even brought the whore's children here, showed them the house, telling them `All this is your house,'" – Anasuya imitated Rushi's manner of speaking but in a feverish high-pitch tone – "and when I protested he threatened to kill me in front of the little children. In front of them he threw me out, like this, holding my neck, out of my own house! Where would I go?

Am I an earning person? If your father allowed me to study thirty years ago would I be like this? In all these thirty years he hasn't given me a single cent, how will I live? Sometimes I feel like I should jump in the river and kill myself. My whole life has gone wasted. Because of him!"

Then Anasuya rose abruptly.

With a strange sort of devilish calmness that descended upon her suddenly, she bent forward, stuck her head in front of Rushi, lowered her voice and said viciously, "What did you see in her? Why? Is it because she lets you do it like this, like this?" her flailing hands making wild vulgar gestures. "How many times? Tell me! How many times per day! Is it why you go there?"

Her eyes cast an imploring look toward Rushi. "Is it why you blame me, is it why you and your daughter are trying to kill me?" she cried.

"This is shameful, Amma! Keep quiet!" yelled Yashoda.

"Shameful? Despicable? Why should it be?" cried Anasuya, her delirium now reached a heightened level. "Why, because I wanted to know the truth that you know. Why, because your secret is out! You both, how long do you think you can keep the secret from me!"

Then Anasuya turned back to Rushi (who hasn't stopped growling, "Shameful! Dirty, dirty!"), and as one who was pleading a young child, spoke in a sudden soft tone, "How long? How is it arranged? Does she wait outside while you go in or... " turning to Yashoda, "Do you go inside too?"

Trembling with rage, Anasuya cried, "Tell me! What does Yashoda get for waiting? Do you give her money? Or does she go inside too! Is it why she takes your side!" At this Rushi jumped from the chair, and stepped away as if something disgusting suddenly appeared in his sight.

"How dirty she behaves, what dirty words! Have you gone mad!"

"Dirty! Dirty! I cannot stand it!" Yashoda burst into tears and she looked at Arya with indignation, her face flushed red.

"Yes! yes! I've gone mad! You all made me mad! Look what I've become. Look what you did to me!"

Just as Rushi stood up, he saw Arya rise from his chair, with a strange kind of twitch in his son's body.

Arya approached Anasuya as if transfixed by something that only he could see, as though he recognized something in her for the first time. He held his mother by the arm and made her sit down on her chair. Then he bent down on his knees in front of her, touched his head to her feet and raised his head. With a voice that was choking with a gurgle he said, "Here I am. Punish just me! Instead of making so many lives miserable, so many people who love you, your own daughters and your own son and husband, here, as the elder son I am here!" His voice now rising with tremor and anguish, "Punish me! As an elder son I deserve it for not setting anything right! On everybody's behalf I am asking you for forgiveness. Forgive me, Amma...! Put your curse on me, here, take your hand and curse me!" He then took his mother's hand and placed it on his head, and said, "Curse me, and calm down! Let me be the target of your wrath! Right or wrong, your anger is on me! Only let things be quiet just for an hour, just for a day!"

Anasuya stared at him with a look of disbelief. A sensation, which she had long forgotten, suddenly filled her body. But this lasted only a moment or two and she recovered herself, as if what she heard was nothing compared to what she felt.

With disdain she withdrew her hand, and as one who just touched something unpleasant, she said, "Why are you troubling yourself? He won't change! You will soil your knees and then say, `Amma didn't take care of me.' You are here today, and now have you seen the truth? Get up, get up! If only my troubles could be ended by such forgiveness drama then the world would be so easy!"

Then she rose with the habitual jerk in her right arm, and muttered, "All this tension I can't stand. Whatever you are to talk amongst yourselves, you do. Forgiveness! What forgiveness? As if my problem can be solved so easily! Unless I get my revenge there will be no solution..."

Then at once growing weary, she called the maid servant, who had closed the door, afraid of the goings on.

"Ey, Put on some tea and bring my medicine box here! All this tension is making my sugar and my blood pressure go up! You all create nothing but tension for me."

Then she turned to Arya, as if she wished to say something, but was stopped by the same impulse that made her turn away earlier from the prostrate body of her son in front of her.

Rushi, who until now watched his son with a look of pity and desperation, rushed forward suddenly.

"You brute!" he shouted at Anasuya. At this sudden aggression in Rushi's countenance Anasuya turned her head and stared at him. A terrible fear rose in her, a fear that she was about to be beaten. At the same instant, a helpless resignation, almost a wish to surrender to it, occupied her facial expression, with a blind defiance that arose not in her body but in her soul.

But this lasted only for a second. Rushi was reaching for Arya. Holding him by the arm, kneeling next to him, he cried at Anasuya, "Why do you spurn him! Don't you have an ounce of pity for the boy! He came to you! Such a tender boy, what has he done to you? Animal!"

Arya, whose eyes were transfixed on his mother's face all this time, forgetting completely what she had said earlier, now looked at her with a new disbelief and incredulity. "Why is she so afraid?" a question raised itself involuntarily in him. "What is this? Why is she so meek and why is she appearing so weak and afraid?" He turned to his side, and, through the hazy, warm translucence of his own swirling tears, saw the tired, weary face of his father.

Anasuya, whose gaze was fixed on Rushi, slowly stirred. And in a gesture that indicated to everyone in the room that contrary to their expectation, her anger and vitriol only doubled in intensity, she went into her bedroom and bolted the door from inside.

18

"Police?"

As soon as they had coffee the next morning, Anasuya summoned her son into the bedroom and began speaking to him:

"Listen Arya, as you are my son. And please don't think I don't know you, and how difficult it is for you abroad, you being all alone. You and me, we are fated to be alone. God made that decision. You must now hear from me about your father. They have not offered him any decent work at the office, and since October he has not been going anywhere. He just stays at home. Just last month those whores drove him out of their house two times. Like leeches they stuck to him when he had money but now they wear him out asking for more and more money. When he is emptied of all the money, they will have no use for him. And he, listen to what he did, he cheated and stole our car. Everyone, your sister, your uncle, Dixit, everyone sucks blood from him, and makes his life unbearable, demanding more money. And listen to this. Recently they all attacked me, tortured me, and threatened me that they will drive me out of my own house. Making such demands of me! And you know who comes to my rescue? All these servants and neighbors of this building. They are the ones who come to rescue me and protect me. Your father incited your uncle – my own brother! – and poisoned him with false rumors about me. He sends him to me everyday to pick a fight with me. I had no other recourse but to go to the police station and ask for their protection."

"Police?" cried Arya with disbelief. "Did you really go to the police?"

"What else could I do? Just the other day he asked me to transfer this house to him, and threatened to kill me if I don't give him my gold bangles – I have only four left. And I am all alone, who will give me protection? It is their plan, those whores, to take all this money, house and gold from him and drive him out of their house, and he doesn't realize it. They are all ready to throw him out onto the street! I do not know where to go. Why do you think they were waiting for you to arrive? They all came to the airport, didn't they? Why do you think that was? They wanted to sweet talk you into transferring the house. That is their plan.

"Arya, I am happy to see you, my heart is so relieved. Do not be afraid! I am here, still alive, am I not? We cannot bring him back, that I am convinced. But we all have a responsibility and obligation to protect his assets! As the elder son you must protect his property! As for me, I can neither stay alone nor can I leave him alone. But we – you, me and your sisters – must be strong and survive. He even threatened Yashoda not to come near me. She and Dixit are here only because you are here. Your father is not his old self. He has changed, and you wouldn't recognize him from what all he did to me. In these last six months he has nothing but ill thoughts. This is killing him. Did you see how weak he has become? It is because of those ill thoughts, the work of the devil. Please forgive me for asking you to help me financially, but you must help me. Remember son, everyone I just mentioned will put on some act or another to take you into confidence. Do not believe them a bit! They will spread rumors about me, but what I tell you is the truth!"

Then Anasuya rose from the chair, and avoiding his eyes, said, "And now my duty is over. I wanted to tell you all this because you are here now. However you want to solve it, please solve it. You are the eldest son, you must know your responsibility, I should not have to tell you. Now go. Go meet your friends. I am tired of all this. Some days I feel like killing myself. Go, go." She lowered her eyes, avoided his intense gaze, and angrily turned away.

Arya left the room without speaking a word.

ARYA COULD NOT BE CERTAIN if what he just heard from his mother was true. He walked away from her bedroom door, and for a brief moment he was unable to tell where he was or why he was there. An involuntary mixing of images: of his life abroad, of Cooper and Colby, became juxtaposed with what he had just heard from his mother: the police station, his father's *other* house, and replayed in his consciousness. His heart beat violently, as if something shameful, something dreadful had been going on in his life, which he had come to know only at this moment.

A peculiar feeling came over him. "It was *never* there, my

life," he said to himself with a wistful, bitter and malignant smile. "How childish of me to have thought that this darkness would all go away simply by what I do!"

He began to suspect if there was something dreadful and ill about his mother, despite his own inner voice that dissuaded him from thinking like this.

In that moment the figure of his father flashed before him, and now he thought his mother was not ill at all. To his despair Arya acknowledged that there was nothing false in what she said. He vacillated between these thoughts, unable to resolve them one way or the other.

The house was quiet. Yashoda had departed to her house the previous night after the living room scene, urging him to come to her place for lunch, to set his mind at ease.

Arya went into his room and sat on his bed. His suitcase lay in the corner. The clean sheets, the snug pillows, the smell of the disinfectant – the maid had wiped the granite floor – the closed door of his mother's bedroom, behind which she slept herself into depression, all this plunged him into a state of despair at how incapable he was in his attempt to bring a change around him.

Unable to stay in the room any longer, he stepped out, wondering if he still remembered the streets of the city.

As soon as Arya climbed down the stairs of his mother's house and emerged out of the gate, everything that had been tormenting him receded from his consciousness.

He stepped onto the sidewalk and began walking. Everything on the street was exactly as he had imagined it would be, and there was nothing that made him feel like a stranger.

"People, how safe it is to be in their midst!" he thought hungrily, recalling the days in the past.

He remembered the busy traffic in the streets, and how he drove his Suzuki fast. A tender feeling of kinship with the street, with its blasts of hot city winds, with the smell of the diesel exhausts, and with the smell of the ripe fruits, filled his heart. How he longed for these same smells!

In the past these same smells and winds were morbid and irritable to him. In the past, no matter how fast he drove his Suzuki, no matter how much dust was gathered on his face, no matter how much the hot summer wind made him breathless, he could not stop the oppressive feeling that the world was closing in on him like a vise.

But now he longed to feel himself among the rickshaw-pullers, the pawn-shop owners, the auto-rickshaw drivers. Yes, it is true that only by being with them, he would really see them. When he saw that the men on the streets looked at him with a curious surprise but ignored him only moments later, he felt close to them. He wanted to smoke cigarettes, drink too much, play with their pigeons, sit on the seat sideways, and make himself useful to them. He would have felt unable to talk to them about his life abroad, because he did not want them to think that he had something special that they didn't have. He believed wholeheartedly that he could be just as them, that he could lead a life like theirs.

With these thoughts Arya reached Yashoda's house, a small three-room apartment with a large hall.

19

At Yashoda's

YASHODA MET HIM IN THE hall.

"Did you come in by auto? Come, come, sit here," she spoke anxiously.

"Walked. It has been so long, so I decided to walk," Arya said. "It's not that far at all. Took me no more than a half-hour," and sat on the sofa with hesitation.

He wanted to ask her if Dixit was home. "I won't talk to her much if he is here," he thought. But he did not ask her, and he could not be sure why he hesitated.

From the very first moment at the airport, where he saw Dixit first, a new impression of his sister began to take root in Arya. He began thinking, during his walk here, of his irritation at how she deferred to Dixit on any matter. He felt that his relationship with Yashoda no longer remained the same since Dixit came into the family. He had a suspicion that everything he and his sister talked about, she later discussed with Dixit.

Yashoda brought him water and said, "Drink this first and

sit for some time. Then I'll make tea."

Then, sitting on the sofa in front of him, she lowered her voice and enquired with the same anxious tone, which made her eyes even paler, "How was it this morning? Did she say anything more? Have you at least eaten in the morning?"

"Ah, she didn't say much," he said wearily, then with exasperation, "How did everything turn out like this? She said she had gone to the police. Do you know anything more?"

"I know. If you have the energy to listen to it, I'll tell you everything. This is a long story. A disgraceful story that should never have happened in our Srivaishnava Brahmana family."

Just then Dixit emerged from the bedroom, and seeing Arya, he yelled with excitement, "Look, my famous brother-in-law is here! Ey, my wife, you be careful and don't let him go without feeding him our favorite dish!"

He then sat beside Arya and embraced him sideways. "He is the best! Just as father says, see him, look at him, no matter what everyone says, Arya, you are the top, I tell you!" and with excitement that bordered on buffoonery, he reached with his face, and was about to kiss Arya on his cheek when Yashoda said, "Yes, he is the best, so leave my brother alone," dissuading Dixit.

She continued as one who was about to get into a serious conversation, "Leave him, let him be comfortable. Now we are talking about the family story, the big story. So you sit there," she showed Dixit the chair, "Let us see if he can withstand all these bombshells once he knows the truth."

"Yashoda," Dixit's countenance abruptly turned grim. "Tell everything, yes? Don't hide a single bit. Because let me tell you, there are two reasons why you should tell him everything. First, because he is family, no, no, it must be said clearly, emphatically. He is the family. And it's high time that we, the underlings, those who have lost our way and are ready to give up, offer the facts, complete facts, detail by detail, to him and then see what happens." He turned to Arya with a reverent expression. "Then the expert mind will start to work. He has seen many such problems there in America and solved many such. What is it, didn't we hear you have a certain abode of your own, eh?" he winked at Yashoda. "But we will come to that after this, after we solved the main problem. Yes? The second reason, Yashoda, the second reason is our Arya is such a darling, the most dearest son to both mother and father. To both mother and father. Both...! Didn't I tell you? How father cried at the airport? It's all heart and his nerves are like steel. Even the big ministers are afraid to talk to him, what? And still, he cried and cried. This much I want to say, Yashoda, Arya. You are brother and sister. Arya, she will never tell you, she will never admit to it, but her heart is broken. Broken! Look at her! Every time she sees mother and father, she cries. Not outside, no, outside she is like a rock, but inside, she is so tender. She runs to the kitchen and then cries. I know. I have seen it. She cries for you, her dearest brother. She thinks about you all the time. Every time, Arya, a festival or an occasion comes, she is thinking, `Oh, my brother is not here, how I used to be consoled by him,' I know. So I am here, offering my heart, my soul, my body and even my blood, Arya. Yes, why not, that is more practical, giving blood. But now, I will give the dearest lovely brother and sister some room to talk. I am here listening and from time to time will interject, OK? Just to provide finesse, to provide a more accurate detail to the story. You know how women are, very sensitive, sensual too but that's another story, that's your story," he winked at Arya. "Ok, now I will be quiet."

"Don't tire him with your stories. Be quiet for a minute," Yashoda rebuked her husband. "If he doesn't deserve `sensual' who does? One must go with both `sensitive' and `sensual.'"

"Arya, you know how father was first tempted to go in that direction just for pleasure. I need not tell you that," Yashoda continued. "And while it was pleasure it lasted ok. But now things are out of control. Amma wears him down so much that everyday it is a matter of life and death for him. Her behavior, her language and what she had become, so dirty and despicable, is so unbearable that you won't believe it. Did you see that she stopped addressing him respectfully in public?"

Arya recalled with a feeling of shame the manner in which his mother addressed his father.

"I break down in tears just thinking about it," said Yashoda with despair. "Six months ago what do you think she did? You cannot believe what I will say now but believe me. She went to the police station. They recently opened, after the election of the new chief minister, a `Women's Protection Cell.' There she filed a detailed report claiming he beats her – all lies – and that he abuses her. Now we have a new government, and that police division is new, they are all hard fellows there, women with agendas and political muscle. They are not the type that question what is truth and what is not. A married woman comes to them crying in tattered clothes, moaning and without a clean face, they will automatically register the case and file the husband's name without making any enquiries. And you know what they did? They took him – *our father* – to the station. Asked him foolish questions, treated him like a common thug, and they even beat him. That's the god's truth. Imagine what must be going through my heart. Our own father, getting beaten up by those scoundrels..." – Yashoda motioned to Dixit for water – "Maybe long time ago he was tempted but he never did anything like that now. And she says, `No! I want revenge! I want to see his end!' "

Throughout her talk Yashoda gazed at Arya with intense eyes. Then, as though she could no longer resist the urge, she said, "It seems it was from your words that she got the clue for the women's protection cell. `Arya told me exactly how to deal with it,' she said proudly and went to the police herself. What did you tell her?"

"*I* told her? Who said that?" Arya cried, in a voice vexed with incredulity. "What do I know about these things?" – with the indignation rising in him at this unjust accusation.

Then a faint recollection entered his memory, grew in clarity and identified itself as the source of this accusation. Still he could not believe what he was hearing. "Once," he spoke as if giving an explanation. "Just once, long time ago she wrote me a letter, and in response I merely suggested to her this idea, just to encourage her, make her feel not lonely. But this...?" Arya was at a loss of words, and was unable to speak further.

"What else do you think she did?" Yashoda replied, after drinking the water in a quick gulp. "She calls him at the office twenty times a day, literally twenty times a day!

Imagine how embarrassing it would be for our father. He is a high executive at his office, and shouldn't he worry about his respect? His reputation? One day she walked in to his office and in the middle of everyone's desks she shouted at him. Who will tolerate such behavior, but for our father? And now as a result of all that they won't give him any important projects. He is losing his respect in the office. How glorious he was at one time! Every one heard nothing but venerable stories about him. They used to bow to him at the very sight of him, the minute he walked in. But now..."

"This much is true!" Dixit exclaimed in a high-pitch voice, his hand raised up, with one finger aggressively pointing. "No matter how the office colleagues behave and no matter how much she tried to ruin his reputation, they, the poor folk, they will never think ill of him. They still line up by the side when he gets down the office vehicle. Arya, they have so much respect for him that it cannot be measured. It cannot be!"

Dixit then bent forward in his chair, held Arya's arms with a sudden affection that animated all his movements, and said, "You must do me this one favor. Promise me you will do it?"

"What is it?"

"No, you must first promise. Only when you promise, I will have the relief. You must promise. Put trust in me, because I am not only your sister's husband, but I am also your well-wisher. Ask her! How many times did I not say, Yashoda, that I feel the presence of Arya next to me? Tell him. No, he has to know."

"Doesn't he know? He knows! He and I are all same, we think the same thoughts," said Yashoda.

"You must promise me that you will protect and save our family's great name, his great name. When I see him now tears come continually to my eyes. I cannot see him like this. I cannot. Talk to your mother. Take her somewhere, but no, they cannot live apart. They love each another so much, I am convinced. My heart breaks even more, knowing what a grand family yours was. On both sides! Yes, on her side they are all strong-willed people, and who is she, ah, who is she but the darling of all her brothers! She has that strength, that royal-ness, so how can she adjust to all this? This, all this, you must save, for everyone's sake. What a man your father is! Do you know how poor his family was when he was a boy? What a committed, dedicated man, what education! Do you know he used to walk for ten miles as a schoolboy with nothing but a piece of bread wrapped in a cloth? What am I saying? You know, yes. You are just like your father."

"If he doesn't know who does? He just doesn't show anything, hides it all inside," said Yashoda.

Then Yashoda, as one who was deliberating the issue in a renewed light, mused, "How should this be solved, is the big question, is the main question. We asked them so many times to separate, to legally, completely, separate but she wouldn't consent. And he wouldn't say any word. Should we take her to a mental hospital, show her to a psychiatrist? She lashed out once, `What's wrong with me? You are all trying to make me believe I am crazy. You are the crazy ones.' But the real problem is she wouldn't leave him alone. I tell her every time, `We will arrange for a house, for a monthly income,' – which he was all too glad to arrange – `and stay away from him,' but she wouldn't listen. `Revenge,' she says, `For thirty years he made me suffer, wasted my life and now it is time for my revenge.' How can one deal with such mad craziness? But then, when she is calm she is the most kind and natural person you will ever see! Everyone likes her, treats her with respect and would not believe that she is this way! It is only when *he* comes in front of her, only in his matters that she is like this! We have exhausted all our alternatives."

"*Are're,*' why are you still worrying? He is here, isn't he?" Dixit rushed to her. "Didn't he come all the way from America to here? For whom did he come if not for his sister, right, Arya? Then why do you still doubt him? The more you still worry about this the more you are showing that you lack confidence in his abilities! Come here. My little son," – "She is the son I never had," he addressed Arya – "She is the son, the wife and a daughter to me, your sister. Come, come, don't weep." Then standing close to her, with the bottom end of his terylene shirt he wiped Yashoda's eyes. As if involuntarily spurred by this, Yashoda really began to cry and pressed the end of her saree into her eyes, so that Dixit did not know what to do with his shirt-end, so he patted her back instead, and tried to hold her head close to his stomach, then returned to his chair.

20

Everyone Caring the Same, As One

ALL AT ONCE A DISAGREEABLE awareness, which Arya momentarily forgot, that he was a guest in his own sister's house, came back to him with a stronger intensity. He urgently wanted to go away from there, to go into the street, and to think for himself what all this meant.

In that moment it became clear to Arya that the world he carried in his heart, in his mind and in his soul, has now ceased to be his companion. All the life he had been living on, the friends and the colleagues who filled his world, all his strong memories and happy desires, now appeared disconnected from him. No matter what he thought, he could not escape from the feeling that he had abandoned the most important people in his life in an abyss all these years. Nor could he comprehend the precise nature of this abyss.

Yet he also felt that somewhere in this mix of feelings, thoughts and accusations, was a connection that he sought all along. The darkness that persisted between his mother and his father once again presented itself before him. If only he could somehow pry open the doors that were closed to one another, to reveal to them how they really loved one another, everything would be so clear!

Arya was not aware that he had left his sister's house after muttering something they did not understand, and that he got into an auto-rickshaw.

He began to experience that old sensation, the same terrifying sensation he used to feel when he was a boy. Somehow his whole body had steadily become heavier and heavier and smaller and smaller, so that he was now descending rapidly into himself.

"All that talk of mental hospital is such an exaggeration," he thought.

He recalled Yashoda's words of the police station, of his mother shouting in his father's office, and a feeling of weariness came over him.

"How could she do that? Did it really take place?" he thought, and a feeling of pity for his father again rose in him.

Then a strange thing happened. He became calm but only as though his rapid descent into himself was complete, and outwardly he showed no signs of this sensation.

That was when Arya looked up abruptly and saw, from the backseat of the auto-rickshaw he was in, that the heavy traffic ahead, with lorries, buses and auto-rickshaws, had come to a full stop.

THEN THE AUTO-RICKSHAW SUDDENLY SWERVED and Arya's hand reflexively tightened its hold on the top railing. The rough tarpaulin above the railing scraped his knuckles.

He observed that the auto-driver, in order to avoid the traffic ahead, turned right into a narrow street.

A row of paint shops came into his view and disappeared, leaving the impression of the dark thick-spectacled man at the counter.

"Why is there an urge to label people, people like these, as `low class,' `worthless,' `mediocre,' and such?" he wondered.

A fruit-cart stood near the bus stop, and its owner, a middle-aged man with a weary unshaven face, was adjusting the apples.

"Bad apples," Arya repeated the phrase with which he had become familiar in his life abroad. Impulsively he addressed the bad apple inwardly, imagining it was forcibly plucked out of the rest of the apples. And just as it was being thrown away the bad apple suddenly spoke, and a crying figure peeped out of it, pleading him.

"Who can tell what is a bad apple? Even a bad apple has a soul too, what about that!"

The auto-rickshaw turned left, and at once the road broadened, causing him to feel as if they had slowed down.

A huge furniture store appeared and disappeared from his view on his right, and then what appeared to be a large godown became visible. At the entrance of it stood a bullock-cart, loaded with chairs, one or two sofas and one large gray almirah.

The milky-white bullock stood motionless, not staring at anything.

Seeing this, a strange sort of intensity increased in Arya, and showed itself in joy and happiness in him.

"Happiness," he repeated this phrase, trying to remember

a question about happiness that always puzzled him.

In the past whenever he attempted to answer the question, he was never satisfied with what happiness meant. Now he suspected that life's purpose couldn't be "happiness." It could not be, for that seemed superfluous and even selfish. He imagined himself in the place of the bullock tied to the cart. Instead of the bullock it would be he, pulling people from a deluge, running fast, perspiring, falling over, scraping his bullock knees.

"Is that happiness? No. But I would be happy doing that," he thought, convinced that there are modes of living that are higher than those aimed to achieve happiness.

"What about her happiness, his happiness?"

Instantly that phrase, "the police beat him," which kept gnawing away at him, came back to his consciousness with full intensity.

"The police beat him. Like an ordinary, road-side family, like he is a drunken road-side man!"

Now a new delirious feeling rose in him.

THE ROAD NARROWED AGAIN WITH a jerking motion into a two-lane street.

A few paces ahead, a city bus, packed and already tilted to one side, began to pull out of the bus stop. The last of the foot-boarders clung to the bus as it heaved back onto the road. Seeing the bus gain speed and merge into the road, the traffic dropped back. But the auto-driver, switching to lower gear, accelerated the auto-rickshaw and raced forward to pass the bus. The bus too increased its pace, narrowing the gap with the center divider. Just when the auto-rickshaw was about to be crushed, it cleared the gap between the bus and the center divider, and the bus began to fall behind.

Turning his head around, and passing a quick glance at the bus through the plastic screen on the rear tarp, Arya muttered, feeling aggressive toward the bus-driver, "The fellow was not even looking this way!" to which the auto-driver consented by spitting, and then glowering at the traffic that began to catch up with him.

Arya's earlier thoughts and his mother's face appeared back in his consciousness.

Turning his attention to the street, he observed how life, oblivious to any thought that was in his head, buzzed with excitement around him. These inner-city dwellings, these rows of bone-setter shops, the unruly, incessant arguments and laughter in front of these pawn-shops, all these from which he at one time escaped, with a hope that somehow it would bring resolution for him, how wrong he was!

How little the city had anything to do with his inner struggle!

"Mistaken kinship," he thought wistfully, as if life just opened another corrosive embrace for him and he could not escape it.

Then that strange sensation, as if he was again becoming heavier and heavier and smaller and smaller, began to creep into him. He stared at his forearm, and at the palm that pressed on the edge of the seat.

"Strong muscle," he thought without any feeling or any meaning by this.

WHEN ARYA REACHED HIS MOTHER'S house in this delirious state, he got down from the auto-rickshaw at the corner and saw a small crowd gathered in front of the gate. It was as though that formless, cloudy and terrifying monster, the very Destroyer of the human relatedness that once roamed the hearts of this family and this city, now multiplied and gathered in front of his mother's house, anticipating its triumph at any moment now.

He stared at this crowd, suddenly growing weary of people, and thought, "Why can't they be quiet for a while?"

Anasuya's house was at the end of the narrow lane, on both sides of which stood row houses one after the other. He began walking, passing these row houses.

A little girl, seeing him, stopped her movements, and stared with fixed eyes on him.

He walked past her.

The next second a feeling of terror seized his being when he heard Anasuya's voice. A second passed and he heard her loud voice yelling and cursing.

Through the gap between the people in the crowd he saw his uncle Tiruvengalam and recognized him by his height. Next to him stood Anasuya, her lips parched, her teeth showed as if she was smiling unusually, her saree disheveled, and there stood Rushi, his father, staring silently at her with cold and disdainful eyes, his face swollen, his shirt torn on his shoulder, and both were breathing heavily.

Evidently his uncle was trying to stop his mother.

"What is going on here!" cried Arya, at once seeing that she had been beating his father, and that Rushi had been making effort to hold himself back.

Then, as if she was in another world and did not really see him, Anasuya at once lunged towards Rushi, and with both her hands began throwing blows at him. With every movement of her fists, which she raised as high as she could over her shoulders and head and brought them down on his back with breathless screams, "...destroyed my life...!!... thirty years of...!! my life...," her face contorted more and more.

On Rushi's face, which kept unnaturally jerking and thrusting forward at each heaving thud of her heavy arms, was an expression of a man, who, having submitted his lowered head under the executioner's power, still made an effort to look up at the last moment with his eyes that said, "If this too was required of me, then I submit."

Then with a delirious animation, and a cry that emanated from her throat only as a heavy gasp, Anasuya swayed her leg wildly, tripped, struggled to remain standing, and threw her flailing arms once more, which forcefully landed on Rushi's shoulders, and on his back, in such a way that her glass bangles broke into pieces, and the shards stuck to her wrists, showing blood.

The expression on Rushi's face remained the same, and he continued to yield, "Then, have you finished?"

In that very moment Arya took hold of Anasuya's upper arm, held it tight, and as if he were following a prolonged impulse that emanated from somewhere in his body, he turned her around, and walked her back into the house, and into her bedroom.

"Do you want me to die!" Arya screamed deliriously. He grasped her hand and drew it violently toward him with a shout, *"Kill me!...Kill!!....Me!!...*I will die happily today! Then all this will stop permanently!!"

Anasuya stopped abruptly, stood motionless, and with the same defiant, wrathful look on her face, began to crush, in her palm, the half-broken bangles from her wrist, letting them fall on the floor.

For a brief moment Arya saw what she herself may not have been aware of: the expression on her face that had become entirely, completely devoid of everything, as one who had given up on the very possibility of life.

A strange sensation passed through Arya.

His eyes began to see what was in front of him – the figure of his mother – as if it too had just descended into a special kind of darkness that had overpowered him only a few minutes ago, while he was in the auto-rickshaw. He experienced a sudden release into this power, and felt he ought not to be fearful of this darkness.

With a sudden unexpected force he raised his arms and pummeled Anasuya's body so she fell down on the floor. He kicked her with his feet on her face, and on her folded arms when they came in the way. He felt the heat rising in his own body, and knew his lips were shaking. He wondered if his lips were red with blood. Did he cut himself?

Between the blows there was a deafening silence, except for her muted cries, and his own gasping breath. He began to wonder why no one was trying to stop him. His mind searched for a distraction that didn't materialize. He experienced a surge of cold in his stomach, and became conscious that everyone in the house ran into the inner room.

He noted that a few blows hit her on the temple.

Outside, his father sat crouched on the chair, his head hung low.

"Why does he keep his head down like that, as if he was drunk? I feel so lonely when he is drunk," Arya thought pensively, involuntarily recalling the image of his father's drunken head from his primary school days. As Arya's bare feet flailed furiously against Anasuya's stomach, striking on her ribs and on her face, the strangeness of the touch brought him a new kind of knowledge. His consciousness became filled with new sensations. For the first time he experienced how it must be to feel the skin and flesh of a human body while you strike it, thrash it hard with your bare hands and bare feet.

"Is this how it feels?" he wondered inwardly.

Watching Rushi through the verandah doorway, Arya at once recalled a memory from his childhood. That memory now rose in his consciousness and became mixed with Anasuya's muted cries and labored grunts.

Arya vividly recalled the figure of his mother, seen through the checkered pattern of the mosquito net, struggling to get out of the father's reach – his father used to smoke the same brand – and willingly suffering the blows in silence, because she was afraid the little boy would wake up. He knew she was afraid of waking him. He recalled his wondering as a child what would happen if he were to make a movement. Would his father notice? Would he then rush to him? Would he then stop?

"Why isn't anyone trying to stop me?" Arya wondered. "Are they all afraid of me? But this is *me...!* Arya, not a stranger! Why should they be afraid of *me?* Am I doing a crime? Why won't they stop me? Are all horrors and crimes committed in this uninterrupted way?" his inward questioning persisted.

Suddenly the force that he was already feeling in his body renewed a thousand-fold, as though it broke a barrier, and overpowered him. "Here! Beat me, take revenge on me! Do you want to see revenge? Do you want punishment?" he yelled deliriously at the figure of his mother he was seeing with his own eyes. A fit of rage completely overpowered him and he ran to the kitchen, and as if he knew precisely where it was all along, he pulled the knife from the stand, ran back, past the petrified maid-servant, and stood before Anasuya.

"Do you want revenge!" he repeated.

In that rage a strange feeling drove him. He believed he recognized the hunger for blood in his mother's eyes. In this state of delirium, he experienced a strange power in his hands, as if he could, once for all, give her what she so desired, and once and for all, all this would be over. Even as he rushed, with the knife in his hand, past the screaming body of someone he did not recognize at the kitchen door, he felt, with a clarity and force he never before felt, that he, at last, and only he, had uncovered that hidden clue to his mother's rage. The image of her face bending down when she ignored him, and crushed the bangles instead, reaffirmed it.

A strange sweet sensation, such as of numbness from eating excessive sweet, first reached his mouth. He felt his tongue was swollen and rubbed crudely against his teeth. He felt the same sweetness reach all over his body, into his flesh, into his taut stomach, into his strong legs, and most powerfully into the expansive muscles of his shoulders; and amplify his heart beat that now pulsated through his swollen neck into his hot and numb ears. He experienced an urgent craving to taste that sweetness. In that instant the warm feeling of the knife and the anticipation of the sweetness aroused his craving. "It would be a sweet sensation to run this knife through all this, all this that I am, all this that is hers, and give it to her! Then everything would be alright! This is all it is! Finally, I know what she wants! I have that! I will give what she wants!"

Suddenly a new thought occurred to him that interrupted this rapid flow. "What if this was not enough? What if I don't have enough!" Then the horror of that doubt decreased a bit at the answer that followed, coming from nowhere, "Go slow! Wait and watch for her pain to go down!" In this moment he was in front of his mother, and he thought he heard a faint scream somewhere. "Someone is playing, perhaps children enjoying themselves. Should I go down and watch them?" he thought inwardly.

Then a pair of hands grabbed him and he felt he was being thrown onto the chair, and felt his ears burning, and felt strong hands twisting his wrists and he then realized what had just happened. Someone twisted and tore open his grip and wrested away the knife. He did not struggle but sat staring at the room, as if disoriented, and trying to ascertain if he was still in the same room. Then he saw his father sitting on the floor, his chest heaving, his head plunged low as if he was about to vomit. His mother was where she was, and the same defiant and fixated look stared at him from her face.

Arya wanted to say something, and was about to speak when he felt the dryness in his throat and the hot burning sensation in his lips that were sticking to one another. He became aware of a constant, rapid sensation that something was continually parching his lips, and despite his attempts to hold them steady, he felt them quiver against one another. A feeling of satisfaction, of an inner contentment, entered him, and faded in and out of his consciousness as he looked around the room. Everything appeared so comfortable, so united like a family, feeling the same, caring the same, the same that he always craved for, every thought the same in all of them. Without moving his arm, he ran his fingers on the arm of the wicker chair, and tried to widen the gap between the weaves by his fingernails. "Tough as nails," he thought.

THE NEXT MORNING THE MOOD in that house was what it had always been after a night's violence: that of a dull, oppressive weariness, which habitually dampened their spirits at first, but gradually dissipated its hold on the family as the day progressed.

Though there was nothing but a hush of silence behind the closed bedroom door – the maid was not allowed to go in – the question did not occur to the members of the household whether Anasuya's injuries were fatal. Instead, a familiar dread, imagining Anasuya's behavior in the days to come, pulsated throughout the day.

Whether his mother thought that he was about to kill her, or if some other equally dark possibility had occurred to her, Arya could not be sure. During the following days he repeatedly recalled that strange expression of incredulity he saw on her face, the muddled manner in which she ceased her resistance, became motionless, and how, with her steady, fearful eyes she stared intensely at him with a look of sudden recognition.

He wished to erase *it* – that peculiar recognition – completely from her. He looked for some sign, any sign, in her that *it* somehow no longer existed in her consciousness.

But the more he paused at her bedroom door, looked

into the object in front of him, the more he heard her feet dragging, her arm leaning against the wall, the heaving on the bed and the creaking sound from it, the rustling of the bed-sheets, the sound of the bangles; and saw her frowning expression, the constant scowl on her face, her suspicious looks, the way she withdrew herself from him suddenly in fear while her eyes displayed not fear but disdain, all these confirmed to Arya that *that*, that peculiar recognition, not only existed for her but was here to stay and grow in him and in her.

For two or three days after this incident Arya was not seen in the house. He spent the whole day outside, visiting old friends, and checking into a hotel later.

On the fourth day Arya rushed to the airport and left the country without speaking to Anasuya or Rushi, nor saying a word to anyone, in a state of extreme tiredness and a feverish mood.

Part Three

21

"Why am I So Half-awake?"

During the months, and eventually four years, that passed since Arya went back to America, that billowing locomotive called life, whose endless rails of time plunged Anasuya into that terrible despair at the temple years ago, now avenged her fully by hurling her into a near isolation.

After her son departed, the marks of his assault on her brought a strange deformation on her face. There was a swelling above her right eye, and below it was a greenish dark smear. On occasion she winced inwardly with pain when the fatigue that remained in parts of her body rose abruptly. A strange smile was seen on her face, in her eyes and on her lips, as though she was fighting off a sensation of powerlessness in her soul. Her voice had grown thinner.

Life, the same in which Anasuya once leapt with merriment out of her chair on Deepawali night and, snatching the sparkler sneakily from her children lighted the flowerpot cracker herself, and ran away laughing while they chased her, this very same life, still hers all the same, now wheeled her between two extremes: one, the intense moods that overpowered her during the day, and the other, the terrible dreams that kept her awake in the night, tossing her between dense coruscating mirrors of her memories that opened and closed her eyes against her will.

At least twice a week the two daughters came to see her, but they kept their visits to Rushi and Tara's house secret from her, weary of her wrath.

The maid Bai still came everyday.

THE HOUR BEING NOT YET five in the morning, it was still dark and cold.

Anasuya, still in her bed, abruptly turned, pulled the thick, navy-blue blanket over her head once again, and wondered if it was sunrise already. Neither the sound of suprabhatam from the temple, nor of the namaaz from the mosque was heard yet from anywhere in the city of Hyderabad.

She turned once again on her bed and listened to the creaking sound of the springs.

Still half-asleep, that same, terrible recollection struck her again.

That shrill voice of Arya kept rising once again to the peak of her consciousness, "Always like this! Always the same! I will cut everything to pieces! Why! Living so dirty, filthy! Only foul words...foul, foul, dirty words! Why? You think they are only words!" until finally the very image of Arya, with a contorted face, with his spectacles that broke but still crookedly stuck to his nose, appeared prominently in her recollection.

She turned over once more on her bed.

After a few moments Anasuya saw a vision, not exactly a dream, but something that evoked a mix of fear, longing and a wish in her.

That vision was something like this.

The scene appeared to be the late morning. Arya was in the house with her and they just had their morning meal. Arya went in to his room. Through the open door she saw that he was on his bed, staring at the ceiling. The television was on but the sound was mute. When he heard a movement, he quickly but acting naturally swayed his feet and tapped his fingers on his chest, so that whoever entered the room did not suspect his preoccupied mood. She knew that something was bothering her son, and was asking him what he was thinking. But Arya dismissed her suggestion with a light-hearted remark.

Then the weather all at once turned cold and the sky became red. A few moments later the watchman came in saying it may rain any minute and left on a quick errand. It then became quiet at once in the house. She appeared to have closed her eyes for a few moments. When she opened her eyes, she felt a rush of cold air come in. The front door, which at first yielded to the wind only a little with a slight creaking sound, now opened fully.

Then Arya appeared at his doorway, stopping short of coming near her.

She raised her eyebrows playfully toward him, and was about to say something to pinprick him. But seeing the expression on his face she softened her brow, brightened her face, and with an affectionate gesture said to her son, "What is it dearie? Come here, sit next to me."

But just as Arya was about to speak, she already knew that a terrible fate had befallen her son. She knew that an unfortunate evil had entered into her son. She knew that he had been condemned to stand behind the bars, and that he had come to speak a few parting words to her.

"What is it dearie...?" she spoke to him once again, adjusting the hair on his forehead, fully accepting the fact that her son was now transformed into either a thief or some such evil person; and he now stood before her with the full view of the mark of evil on him visible to her.

All at once an overwhelming pity for him swelled in her heart. Having admitted to herself this evil in him, she began to pour out her love for him. But she was also conscious of her own disappointment.

"He too failed to be good..." she thought with resignation. At once filled with despair, she set out to do what a mother always does, take her son into her arms.

"Yes, she was bound to love him," Anasuya talked to herself, addressing the now fading, now receding and now prominent image of herself that appeared in her vision.

"No matter how often they beat her, abuse her, a mother's love will always strain for her child," a pity-filled voice spoke in this vision, a voice that was of her own, but filled with so much pity that she thought she herself was the target of that pity. "After all, he emerged only after she tore her entrails to make way for him...!"

Such was the vision in which Anasuya saw herself.

A few minutes later she awoke fully, listening to the sounds of namaaz.

AROUND ELEVEN O'CLOCK, SAYING, "WHY is it a year, wasn't

it only two months ago that they raised the auto-rickshaw rates, who knows how they think city folks will survive..." a familiar voice opened the gate, and Yashoda, Sita, and Bai came into the house. Evidently they were engrossed in an animated conversation that entered the house with them.

Anasuya stared with a glowering look at the figures coming into the bedroom.

Bai took the green bag, full of vegetables, into the kitchen while Yashoda and Sita placed their woven bags with thick wooden handles, with their clothes and things, by the side of the kitchen door.

"Have we walked straight in and woken you up?" said Sita, approaching and sitting on the bed.

"Is it fever again?" Yashoda enquired. "Have you been sleeping?"

"When did I get sleep?" Anasuya replied with a wry smile on her face. "My nights are filled with dark dreams and in my days I am alone."

Yashoda and Sita exchanged glances, at once perceiving that their mother was beginning to draw the talk into her morbidity.

"With these heavy bags and three people, rickshaw is the best way to get home from anywhere in the city, is what I'd say," added Sita, and getting up immediately she signaled Bai to bring the large bag into the room. She then began to show Anasuya what they bought at the market.

But Anasuya, already in her own mood, continued, "Tiruvengalam told me that there is no end to his suffering because of them, and how weak his body had become." She really did remember with pity Rushi's wrinkled face, his emaciated body, his always-bent thin shoulders, and that

eager look in his eyes with which he appeared to stare at
the others.

A dull white pallor came over Anasuya's face, and she
repeatedly wet her parched lips between breaths. But an
equally hopeful earnestness sparkled in her eyes, as though
she, knowing that all her fortune was lost, still believed
that she could salvage at least a bit, and was eager to try one
last time with a renewed interest.

"All for what? Because he can no longer bring them
bundles of money? What is more, you must know – and
don't be angry," she said at once in a deliberate, calm voice.
"Allow me to speak completely," she cried, motioning
at them with an open hand, as if stopping the inevitable
interjection she anticipated from them.

"That day Arya eventually did the reprehensible when he
beat me. Let us say for now that the beating is a different
matter."

She stopped and took a deep breath. That she was tired
and had difficulty breathing was evident to Yashoda and
Sita.

"But do you believe it hurts me so much that Arya also
uttered *those* words? Contrary to what he thought I have no
one here for me. Whom do I have?"

While Anasuya was speaking like this, both the daughters
remembered something that they had forgotten altogether;
that Arya had shouted something about another man being
in her house.

"Have you seen any man here in my house, even in front
of my house? Then why should he say all those words to
me?"

All at once the sparkle in Anasuya's eyes thickened as

the tears swirled and began to spill onto her cheeks. She made a quick motion with her hand and wiped them off, and continued:

"Even the phone! If I hear any man's voice I first ask, `Who are you, what was your purpose of calling me, who gave you this number,' if I don't recognize the voice right away. At this age, in these middle years, who would be willing to keep me?" said Anasuya, with a grave voice.

She then at once raised her voice and, addressing both her daughters, said, "Remember that! If my character had been so bad then all of you!" – now with utmost contempt, with her finger pointing at them – "... all of you would have been on the streets like beggars! Begging for food with one pan waving in front of people! That would have been your situation!"

"E'e'e'...y! Amma, why go into all that!" Yashoda interjected. "Just because Arya uttered some words why do you vex yourself? By now he must have even forgotten them. Should we keep all of them in our heart, recount them and agonize over them, why? All these words are not of any use Amma, why, leave them...!"

Anasuya persisted. Then at once becoming quieter, and now directing her attention to the topic of Rushi, Anasuya said, with a change in her voice such that it had none of the wrath and contempt, "Then those children."

Both Yashoda and Sita saw that their mother was preparing herself for a topic that she believed only reluctantly.

At once Anasuya's expression softened. There was even a sign of that old mischievous smile on her face at the mention of the children.

"After all children they are, dears," she said softly. Feeling suddenly weak, but with a renewed force because of it, she stared intensely at her younger daughter.

The next moment, directing her wrath on Arya, she cried, "And after all that, *he too* beats me with no mercy, even after I sacrificed my life all for you...for this...and in exchange for all this sacrifice he beats me and goes away to America."

In both the daughters there was a weary resignation at Anasuya's delirious shifting of moods.

At the same time, a feeling of guilt overpowered them both, "What does it matter that she exhausts us, is it a way for our mother to live?"

Anasuya sighed with a heavy breath.

She then straightened her back with a renewed vigor, and said, "See now look here? All here..." and, with the slightly wrinkled back of her palm she pressed her cheeks, her forehead, the back of her neck, "...all this here... here and here...it always burns...I always feel a constant burning sensation...keeps on twitching. Listen...twitch...twitch..."

Then picturing Arya when he was not even three years old, with his little wrists, fat and tiny, she said, with a weary softness in her voice, "Even as a boy he was heavy and strong, I couldn't straighten my arm for two full hours after I carried him to market."

A sudden shudder ran through her body. She abruptly stopped, then resumed, now forcefully directing their attention to what had just occurred, "Did you see that? Twitch, twitch..."

She moistened her parched lips once more, and reaching her back with her arm over her shoulder, she pressed the flesh just below her neck, and simultaneously, as if straightened by this motion, erected her shoulders and her head.

Then in a strange manner that at first surprised her daughters, before another, a more terrible, feeling passed through them, Anasuya at once lowered her arm, and gesturing with her hands, she grimaced her face, showing them parts of her body, and said:

"Pch. It is to be expected. Like this, like this, he used his bare hands and legs, isn't it? Do any of you remember? For that reason...human bare hands have enormous strength and weight, for that reason what I have is the flesh that had all become lumpy. Here is a lump, here is another lump..."

She continued, "Until this lump melts the pain will persist," as though she were a doctor, who, while diagnosing the patient's body, was herself surprised at first at the extreme state of it; then the next moment reassuring those surrounding the patient's body, before again herself staring at it with disbelief.

"Pch," she nodded her head up and down, as if agreeing to a voice that only she could hear. "Who knows dearie, my poor child, whatever might have happened in his life, poor child, that wrought up so much anger in him?" she continued, speaking to herself on and on, as though this inner voice rose unfettered in her and emerged through her words.

Distressed by some other thought that now swamped her consciousness, her voice trailed off, faltering, "Living in a country that was not ours, all alone, such an adult man..."

"'Why did it happen like that?' is the question," she continued, with an almost naïve expression on her face of someone who distressed to know the answer to a riddle that confronted her endlessly.

"Don't remind yourself of that, Amma! Again and again like that!" said Yashoda, with a choking voice.

AT THE SOUND OF HER sister's voice, Sita, who was conscious only of sitting at the edge of the bed and without knowing when had moved to the center, so that she now sat leaned against the wall with a pillow in her lap, experienced a terrible feeling.

In her sister's voice, not weary or angry at their mother's delirium, but an unexpectedly weak voice, Sita saw that the self-image that Yashoda had built up, of the noble manner with which she suffered her mother, has now suddenly revealed itself to be insignificant, false and untruthful against the blackness of the horrible misfortune that befell their mother.

But that recognition lasted only for a moment, and once again the always bemoaning, the always intense voice of Anasuya interrupted, penetrated and dominated everything that these two young women experienced.

"Then why?" Anasuya persisted, seeming to grow more and more determined to revisit and continue where she left off.

"Why is it necessary to go into all that?" Sita cried, and was about to get up from the bed in a rash of anger, but Yashoda interjected her.

"Be still, Sita. Let yourself be still?" she motioned with her hand at her sister. "Let Amma speak!" she said, staring intently toward Sita.

"What do you know dearie?" Anasuya turned toward Sita, and with a sardonic blurt that heaved her entire body, she looked victoriously at her elder daughter, as if Yashoda alone really understood her. Still addressing Sita she continued, "You are still a little girl. You haven't seen anything. Had you only experienced what your sister and I had with these wretches."

Having thus established, in their present circumstance, that peculiar harmony which exists between an elder daughter and mother, Anasuya pressed on, still addressing Sita.

"Even so, you must get to know the fullness of it, don't you realize that?" she continued in the tone of a mother reasoning with an already tamed child. "If I don't educate you, inform you, then who will? After all I am your mother. Have you grown up to this age without my help?"

Anasuya then looked away from them and began straightening the wrinkles on the bed-sheet while she shook her head, as if saying something else only to herself.

"Now see how it just turned on me? Now I have decided, under these circumstances it is not proper for me to stay here. I understand now that none of you are capable of giving me shelter."

She suddenly raised her voice, her intense gaze looking at them, "But I am not going to plunge myself to death, like all the others do! Until now I lived for you. Now, and from now on, I have to live for myself. I know when I am telling you all this you will be angry, but we have no choice. I have already made a decision what to do. You are my children and for that unfortunate fate you must suffer. Even then your suffering is much less than what I suffer, as your mother and as your father's wife."

"What decision have you made?" Yashoda asked in a hysterical tone, with a heavy frown on her face.

"No, I made my decision," Anasuya refused to elaborate. "Something must be done."

The next moment, with a resolute voice, as if she was going to suspend all her thoughts on this topic as soon as she spoke these words, Anasuya resumed, "Listen, you children, be very careful and see that you don't become like your father. Tell your brother in America this."

Her voice increasingly choking, she continued, "In this lonely phase of my life all you children, your childhood, your plays, your songs come to me. Is my life just a recollection from now on? Tell me! I cannot convince my own conscience whether all you people, your father, are good or evil. But why am I still expecting you to be good or bad? Why such things happen? Pch, pch, then like this my life should go on...see, I will say one last thing and I will sleep after this...see, within your father, within you and you, there is another father, another you and another you, but I cannot seem to reach that another you. Even after all such life you seem lonely. I seem to be standing as an obstacle in your path of happiness. It seems I am in your way. What must I do? Killing myself will only eliminate my physical being and put even greater barrier of grief in your path. How did all this happen? Why am I so half-awake? Why am I as if I am drunk? What is it that I must do, to be completely awake, to be completely, completely awake, awake, to something that is so simple and clear to see? The only way to clear the path is take the role of the janitor and serve. Is that what you all want of me, in the end?"

Plunged into a dazed and a shell-shocked state by her words, the two daughters sat motionless until their mother rose and disappeared into the washroom.

22

"What if Christ was... Just Like Me?"

THE TRUTH IS, AN EQUALLY strange transformation had been occurring in Arya, who, within a few days after he returned to his apartment in America, had begun to imagine that sometime soon there would be a trial.

All sorts of things, strange and new transformations that neither Anasuya nor Rushi were aware of, were taking place in their son's tormented soul. The very day he landed at the San Francisco airport, after a long and tedious journey on the plane, Arya experienced an intense and involuntary replay of all that had taken place until the previous day. At once Arya remembered his mother, his father and his sisters, but mostly Anasuya, not as how they were during the previous few days but only as blurry images, as though he had not seen them for a few years, momentarily forgetting all that had occurred only a few days earlier.

Strangely, he began to notice all sorts of new things in the people around him. All of a sudden he would become alert and look into their faces surreptitiously, to see if they too felt the same intense strangeness he was feeling.

"It is their home," he said to himself. "When will it be my home? When will I feel what they are feeling?"

As the days, weeks and months passed, inwardly in his recollection Arya began to refer to the incident with the knife and his mother as *that ghastly act*. It was as though some psychological inner workings of his mind schemed up an idea, following which he could unstick this morbid memory from his brain, so as to destroy it, but also to give it an identity and a separate existence outside of him, by naming it, so he could nurse it.

"I certainly cannot speak of it to anyone here," he thought, with a shameful feeling. "Then everything they had always suspected of me, and of people like me, would be proven true."

Whenever he slept, not even two hours would pass and he would be brought back to consciousness by a sensation of slow pounding that came from somewhere in his body. It was only his own heartbeat, which for no apparent reason would go louder and louder.

One such night, an image of a bruise mark, bluish in color, on a woman's face, rose in front of his closed eyes. Blood rushed to his heart. At first he could not say who this woman was, and what this mark on her face was, but then strange discolorations began to form in a slow motion on her face, on her forehead, near her eyes; and for no reason her face suddenly became swollen with blue and dark impressions.

He then saw himself next to her.

Out of nowhere he then, as though all this was really new to him, wondered *whose* assaults on her were more severe.

His or his father's?

Arya wished silently that the latter were the case.

He hoped that anytime she would rise up from her sleep, and reassure him that it did not hurt her all that much.

In any case, what he had done to her was nothing extraordinary, was it? In some habitual way everyone in the family had already inflicted the same degree of injury on her, whether by deeds or by words, did they not? How was it, then, that only *his* violence was the cause of her aggravated injuries?

He wanted to believe that due to this fact alone, that others in the family also had struck blows on her, by this very obvious fact, she did not have any special claim on what *he* had done. He wanted someone to acknowledge that it was unjust of her to cause him anguish by suffering so much *only* from his violence.

"Yes, we've all become used to her allegations of the pain she suffered in her life," he thought. "Why should we say *this* pain is any special this time?"

But the next moment he felt strange that such a thought existed in him at all.

"Because I know what I did," he thought. He listened silently to his own heart, pleading her to forget and think nothing much of *that*.

Then, as though he was replying to a theoretical question, he said to himself, "The enormity of these crimes committed against her was larger than anything I had ever known," satisfied by the way he phrased it.

"Still I have always known," he cried with a whisper.

He then rose on the bed to a complete silence around him. He became aware of the neighbors and of the woman who had just parked her car below his bedroom window. He heard her voice. He saw the light that was in the room across the street and turned his head towards the window. A TV was visible in a far away room and he at once imagined the people in that room watching it quietly, sitting still, and not making any movement. He then realized that it was evening and everyone who had gone off to work had begun to return.

Suddenly he experienced the loneliness of his condition.

"She is a thousand miles away...!" he said to himself in anguish. *"Amma...!"* he kept whispering inwardly without stopping.

After a few moments like this Arya felt agitated at these thoughts, rose from the bed quickly, went in to wash his face, came out, and at once became engrossed in the sights and sounds on the street.

GRADUALLY ARYA IMMERSED HIMSELF SEVERELY in his work, became dependent on it, and without quite realizing had become attached to the group at the office.

Eagerly he busied himself with the preoccupations of life at work. He now believed stronger than ever that those gruesome days were over, and he desired nothing more than starting his life afresh and building a life there in America.

"Forward movement," he said to himself frequently.

After four years of living like this, in July 2000, when he was promoted to the senior manager, he felt a renewal in the zest for his life again. In the following month, carried forward by this zeal, he began a new project for the Japan office, the first to be entirely under his management.

Throughout that morning he thought endlessly in search of an appropriate codename for the project. A young engineer suggested "Chalice" to which Arya said, "Well, I think you should drop this. Some religious minded people may not like it because it is also a cup used to hold wine for Eucharist," and then waving his hand with impatience he said, "Some Christian thing."

In the end they chose "Sunrise" and even though Arya did not like it, he was conscious of his new role and allowed it. He felt a pleasant moment of pride, "Yes, everything is coming together."

On occasion the memory of *that*, that ghastly act, would resurface.

To break away from it he would go up to his book-shelf, pick out a book not caring whether he had already read it, open it but then would resume thinking about *that*, as if willed by a force that he could not control, before breaking away from it again.

He recalled his home, his family, but the accompanying morbid feeling only renewed his zealous immersion in his present life. He turned away from that part of him which continued to be tormented by this unbearable memory.

Then something completely unexpected happened.

UPON THE COMPLETION OF THE "Sunrise" project, Arya traveled to Japan to present the prototype to Dr. Eguchi, and after three days of meetings, feeling a pleasant sense of accomplishment, he returned.

At the airport, having checked in his luggage, he sat in the chair with a newspaper, and as was his habit, he at once

began an involuntary journey into his thoughts of recollections and resolutions.

After some time that passed like this, an elderly woman
entered the waiting area, pushing a wheelchair. An old man
was sitting in the chair, with his head lowered as though he
was sleeping.

Arya looked toward him, anxious to see if the old man
could hear and speak.

"Is her life good?" he wondered, staring at the elderly
woman.

A few minutes passed.

The words, "Right now the balance of suffering in this
room is uneven," passed through Arya.

Seeing the elderly woman help her wheel-chaired
companion settle down, and stretch his arms, Arya observed,
"Such meticulous care!"

The elderly woman adjusted the old man's arms on his lap
to a certain position, and pulled the Velcro straps loosely to
the wheelchair arms.

"She is kind to him," thought Arya.

He at once wished to speak to her. "She certainly would
forgive me," he muttered inwardly. "Anyway, it would be
odd to ask Amma forgiveness."

Arya reflected that the special tender feeling, which the
term "forgiveness" evoked, existed only among Christian
societies, such as America.

"It's not in our culture, and I can't bear that discomfort,
she would not believe me," Arya continued talking to
himself, reflecting that it would be awkward to share with
his mother this special feeling.

The next moment a new suspicion about himself began

to grow in him, as though *that*, that ghastly act, had now revealed his true nature in a new light.

"Why do I feel different from the others? Is this what they mean when they say evil exists and is manifest through men? Can men be the carriers of evil? *Am I* a carrier of evil?"

Then with an unnatural, almost malicious smile, he muttered, "Ah, but thoughts are like flies. We probably don't know where they come from, but like that fly that keeps hitting our face in spite of us swatting it, these thoughts never really go away, sticking to us, finding something sweetly aromatic, decadent in us. It is only when you get up and walk away and clear your mind that you forget about the fly and it forgets you."

He then recalled the words of a woman colleague at work, who went on and on about suffering.

"Is this what she means when she speaks of suffering and pain?" he wondered.

Then he dismissed this last thought. "No, what she talks about is her religion, Christianity and all that. I understand that she is a Christian, but I don't understand all that suffering, that divine suffering..."

All at once Arya thought, "But what if Christ was a person, just like me, with thoughts like me, and a life story like mine?"

At once a tender feeling for the figure of Christ rose in him, imagining that this figure too suffered like him, and this figure too carried the secret of *that*, that ghastly act, in him.

DURING THE DAYS THAT FOLLOWED, there remained one thing and only one thing that continued to gnaw at Arya's

waking hours. He could no longer suppress the visceral desire to expose the full extent of the raw emotions churning
in him, and to submit to the compelling power to express
these emotions, so others may experience his feelings.

This new desire, to transfer his feelings to his fellow
women and men, took hold of him with so much power
that nothing else mattered to him. He cried for no reason.
Even a sight of a bird that was just flying triggered in him
waves and waves of recollections. It was as though he saw
Anasuya in that bird and that broke his heart.

It occurred to him that time did not occur in their – his,
Anasuya's and Rushi's – lives in a linear, now present,
now past, manner but that everything, all the past, all the
present and even all the future, was right in front of him,
all mingled up like flakes in a breakfast bowl. He recalled
a similar revelation, which he had confided to Colby years
ago, that his childhood sleepwalking habit had, "killed his
illusion of time." He cried because these millions of feelings
visited him all at once, and he took this as a sign that there
was still a hope of forgiveness for him.

It was under these circumstances that he made an utterly
strange resolution, entirely contrary to his nature. Arya
decided to study the Christian Bible, and with that decision
a new agitation entered into him.

23

Doubt and Hope

FROM THE MOMENT ARYA MADE up his mind to read the Christian scriptures, several thoughts and feelings flooded his consciousness, making him exhilarated, apprehensive and even afraid.

More than anything he became resolute that he would not become a Christian.

"After all *that*," he muttered inwardly, recalling Tara, and that she was a Christian.

"I know what I am and I would not stoop down to *this* level," Arya uttered inwardly, giving in to the impulse that any association with Christians was a betrayal of his love for his mother and for his siblings.

He wished to keep his new resolution a secret. "I am only going there because I have to know. If *that* hadn't happened, I wouldn't be so weak, homeless, oppressive...now I have no choice! But what if I am caught? What then?"

Exactly what it was that he had to know, he could not be certain. But his innermost wish was to reveal to himself the full extent of his own evil nature, and in the singularity of that evil seek forgiveness, which he secretly wished would not be granted to him.

At the office on the first day of the Bible class, Arya waited all afternoon with a heightened anxiety, feeling thin. He once again experienced a surprise that his inner perplexity went unnoticed by his colleagues.

At last the evening arrived, and Arya drove in his car directly from work to the class.

As soon as Arya turned left at the traffic light and fell behind a line of slow moving cars on Del Mar Street, his eyes were alert for any signs of a church-like building.

He had been on this street before but now he felt as though it was new.

Everyone, those in the cars driving in front of him, the people who came in and out of the stores on the side walk, and those that crossed the street, appeared to him as though they too possessed similar thoughts and feelings towards church like his. His concern was not whether they were pious, but he experienced a sudden kinship with them.

At once he felt an urge to slow down. Just then he saw several cars in front of him turning right, into an entrance marked "OPBCC."

He drove forward, following the line of cars. He felt uneasy, as though he was transgressing. As he pulled into the complex, he thought, "If this too turns out to be trivial, then I have nowhere else to go."

His anxiety rose as he parked the car.

He took his old notebook from the backseat, got out of the car, and stood looking around with irritation, "What is this?

Now where do I go? Why can't they put up a sign?"

He then saw, a few paces ahead of him to the right, beyond the parked cars, a group of halls. Seeing that the others were heading in that direction, he followed them.

Walking among them as they entered the hall, Arya came near a large, tall man in a dress suit, who stood at the entrance and smiled at everyone, welcoming them.

Attracted by the man's kindly smile, Arya shook his hand, forgetting for a moment his earlier anxiety.

Just as he walked past the large tall man into the hall, Arya looked back, carried away by an elevated impulse to see his smiling face again. At that moment Arya was instantly met with another man, in a similar dress suit, who smiled with the same kindness at him. Arya energetically shook his hands, and introduced himself vigorously.

"Hi, I am Arya. How are you today?"

"Ariya? How are you Ariya, I am David. Welcome to the fellowship. Have you been here before?"

"Not really. First time!" said Arya, his face red with embarrassment. The pleasant expression on David's face suddenly brightened, and he looked toward Arya with a special smile in his eyes.

"Oh good. We like first-timers!"

Feeling that this man understood his unease, Arya turned to his side and stepped backward, his hand still in David's. With an unexpected confidence Arya said, "Lots of people," scanning around him as if he was a regular. "On a week day, that too. I like this already!"

"Praise the Lord!"

At this Arya became confused. For reasons unknown to him, Arya felt this gesture to be unnatural. Suddenly his confidence dampened. Suppressing a feeling of falsity that rose in him, Arya enquired, "Have you seen Mel today? Mel Jackson? I spoke to him yesterday. I think I am in his group."

David reassured him that the pastor would make announcements of the groups, and of the halls in which each group was to meet, and that Arya would know where to go then.

Arya looked around.

The large church hall was filled with wooden benches. Except for a visit to a Mission, Arya had never been inside a church hall.

He sat, at once thinking that people were watching him, conscious that he did not look Caucasian. With a heightened sense and an intent look toward the center of the stage, Arya directed his full attention on the speaker's movements.

Though he continued to experience discomfort at seeing so many white men in the hall, though he kept suppressing the ambiguity he saw in the effusive gestures of "Praise the Lord!" and though he felt it unnatural that people could be so joyous at just seeing him, expressing it in equally unnatural and suspiciously warm embraces, Arya told himself that the source of all that discomfort lay within him. After all what did he know what churchgoers considered normal? Perhaps they all really felt the warmth inside them at the sight of him, a complete stranger.

But Arya knew he did not believe that. No matter how much he ignored it, that old, familiar feeling of being intimidated persisted in him.

It was not the fear of the language. "That would be silly," he thought, reflecting that he took pride in his mastery of the English language. It was a bond that he believed existed among all Caucasian men; a bond, entirely incomprehensible to him, that stared at him with no expression at first, then glowered at him aggressively.

What perplexed Arya was that he did not experience this glower in the society outside of this church hall. Though he too experienced that alienating feeling when he first arrived in this country, he believed he had already overcome that. Now, once again, in this sprawling brownish church hall, he was overwhelmed with a depressing feeling of someone who did not belong, and who was outside.

Without realizing it, he became self-conscious. He looked around the hall, and whenever he saw a face of anyone who was not a Caucasian, who did not have that reddish nose and cheeks, who did not have that pink skin, he felt less intimidated.

FOLLOWING THE SPEAKER'S DIRECTIONS ARYA proceeded out of the rear door, picked out the room he was to go in among the several in a row, and upon entering it introduced himself once again with vigorous handshakes, to the seven men there, old and young.

The chairs were arranged in a circle.

The study group consisted of eight men, including Mel, their group leader, who introduced Arya as a first-timer to the others.

The reading itself was organized like any other such weekly group discussion that Arya was familiar with. Every week Mel would hand out the next week's lesson in printed sheets before they discussed the current week's lesson.

Having received the current lesson sheets a week earlier

in the mail, and having already studied the lesson, the men brought the two-page question sheet to the class.

As soon as Mel finished going over these details, everyone raised their heads from the pages, stopped writing, and looked toward him with a measured calmness.

Mel made a quick glance at Arya, and his expression said, "Are you comfortable? This is how easy it is."

Arya smiled, leaned back, sat erect in his chair, took a deep breath, and looked around the circle at all of them.

"Andrew, why don't you start us off, what did you find interesting in the lesson?" asked Mel in a firm voice and an encouraging tone.

Andrew, a young man with a heavy-built, muscular body, and blood-shot red eyes, lowered his gaze into the sheet of paper in his lap, and at once uttered something to himself, as if in preparation to speak.

Everyone smiled pleasingly at Andrew, as if the young man's fluster was in keeping with the purpose and the tone of the meeting. Their looks relayed to Andrew that his submission to the hesitation was already fulfilling the purpose of the meeting.

Arya gazed at Andrew with a feeling of embarrassment, saw Andrew's thick, short fingers quiver as they turned the sheets back and forth, and he lowered his eyes. Once again that feeling of unnaturalness rose in Arya.

Then Andrew looked at everyone and spoke in a hoarse and loud voice:

"I learned that God's will acts on you everyday, not just at certain times. It doesn't matter what you are doing, where you are going and how messed up you are, God is always looking out for you," Andrew swallowed, and continued to

speak without any earnest expression on his face so that
what he said appeared grim to Arya.

"I certainly don't believe in God," said Arya inwardly,
reassuring himself, and listened intently to Andrew,
yielding to an unexpected interest that rose in him.

"I mean our society is so messed up that everyone is doing
their own thing and no one really talks to each other any
more," Andrew's voice became steady.

Andrew stared nervously at everyone, animated by his
own words. He continued, "They shoot each other first
before talking, that is what our culture has turned into. This
lesson really reminded me that it is still a daily struggle, it
reminded me that God is there looking out for you, day in
and day out, you know."

"Thank you Andrew for sharing your thoughts with us.
It is a daily struggle," said Mel looking intensely toward
Andrew.

Then Marty, an older man who sat next to Andrew, spoke.

Arya listened intently to all this. He at first felt ambivalent
when he heard phrases like, "God's will," "joy and love at
Christ's arrival," and "God's plan for you," and so on, but
he persisted until the ambivalence no longer disturbed him.

When the participant next to him spoke, Arya became
fraught with nervousness, waiting anxiously for his turn,
and submitting with a force of will to it. But when his
turn eventually came, he spoke clearly, remembering the
interesting literary questions that surrounded him when he
read the lesson.

"The overview of `Acts' in the lesson was short and
concise, I thought," he said. "It provided me with a good
introduction before I actually read the chapter from the

Book."

He paused, as if agreeing with his own words before he felt a rush of confidence. "The immediate challenge I felt was not to feel threatened by the Christian faith. I am not a Christian. At the same time I am drawn towards the idea of "indwelling." I am hoping that I will understand the difference between "dwelling in" and "dwelling with" because I feel it is the key to understand the Acts."

There was a silence, and when Arya finished, several eyes that were staring at him averted their gaze. A whole set of questions that he did not think of earlier came rushing at him. He wanted to speak more but restrained himself with an awkward consciousness that he had spoken too much already. He had a sudden urge to sit near Andrew.

Though Arya believed, when Mel approached him at the conclusion of the session and told him that he was extremely interested in what Arya had said, and spoke to Arya with animation about how the informal organization of the study group encourages such probing questions, and reassured Arya that, "we are all at various stages of recognizing what God's plan is for each of us and not all of us are Christians really," that nagging feeling of discomfort continued to peck at Arya's conscience.

It is true that Arya had read much more than the lesson handout in preparation for the first session. The more he read the more he felt a strange and unexpected recognition at the arrangement and the selection of the words in the `Acts,' and the more he experienced an aching in his heart.

Arya thought he understood the word "Holy Spirit," which he took it to mean the general, religious, uplifting feeling one commonly expects to find in religious scriptures.

But listening to the words of the participants, and to their varied responses to the same words at the session, he was no longer sure.

He began driving back home, carrying with him a swarm of new, incomprehensible feelings and questions that now arose in him.

"No doubt I am also a sinner," Arya said inwardly to himself.

"Maybe even a criminal, in fact," spoke a voice inside him.

"But was *that* really like a crime, as everyone in the society understood crime?" he uttered inwardly with rising agitation, not believing his own words.

Still, just as it happened before, even after such reflections, after every recollection of how *that* was, of how he was in *that*, of how everyone were before and after *that*, he could not penetrate *that* itself when he tried to view that incident in his imagination.

"But maybe this is what constitutes a crime, maybe this is how a crime is committed by people the world over...," said he to himself. "Why did no one stop me?" he muttered to himself with vexation. Still he clung to the hope that he may not be evil.

WHEN ARYA REACHED HOME, HE found a letter from Yashoda in his mailbox. As soon as he saw the pale apple-green envelope, smeared with black stamp grease, and his address written by hand in blue ink on the thick cover, a whole series of images appeared before him.

"This is it," he thought, his heart pounding heavily. "They are calling me for the trial. All that you were able to suppress until now, living in the luxury of a new life, is over. You have to pay the price and now this letter has that," he said to himself, forgetting for a moment that the letter was from his sister.

"Rightly so. At least they let me alone peacefully until now, that was kind of them," he thought, imagining that someone who had been keeping score on him until now had run out of time and sent this letter.

Without removing his shoes he sat on his desk chair, put his feet on the large dictionary on the table, and began to read the letter.

Dear Arya,

I want to convey a few thoughts of mine, for the coming new year for you. This is only a personal opinion of mine, and not at all an advice but an elderly suggestion to my younger brother.

I feel you have stayed long time abroad [Arya smiled at her language]. So many things passed away in the ocean of the time. A day passes away means a day nearer to the end of the individual, everyday we have to spend with the grace of God. The God really bestowed His total grace on you. You have to thank the Almighty for the excellent opportunity given by him to you, to spend the glorious time abroad. Why I am so much particular about all this – is because my endeavor and interest is only to see my brother to flourish in his life, which you already proved with your enormous strength and ability, so I am proud of you.

When we spoke here, you have been saying certain points regarding the life over there – I agree, but the time and age are not under your control. We have only two possibilities, to either go according to the time and age or go beyond the time and age. We can't go beyond the time and age, but I feel personally you are going very fast and crossing the barriers of the time. It's good but the age is the factor! Why, this is happening everywhere around the globe – when you talked to me last November I feel personally my faith in the God really proved that at last my Arya is so graciously talking to me. This indicates the total faith and trust in my God.

But just expressing my views to you is not sufficient; there should be some kind of activity between you and us. My ideas are simply those, i.e., the ideas of an elder sister or a responsible mother. Talking to you or lecturing the things is not sufficient; applying it with a real adherence is important. My ambition is to see you on the top, which is fulfilled by the grace of God.

But there is some kind of misfortune that haunts us, i.e., you know pretty well the sufferings of father, of course mother. Nobody except you can resolve the stalemate prevailing in the affairs of mother and father.

In the coming year you have to formally get married, so that you will also become the fruitful father of a young heir. This enables you to become more and highly matured personality ever produced by our family. The fact is our own father is traveling in this life in his own wandering manner, which is correct to him but in reality, as you and we know, is not correct. But in what capacity you and me are going to persuade him? No, we can't. We can only request and beg him but definitely this is not going to bring any fruitful result. He doesn't want to come out of his poisonous circle. But still we have to look after him and his interest because of the blood relations. The Hindu Dharma that is embodied in our minds will make us to help him in some form or other, which is really already carried out by you. This indicates your good inclination towards the father. I thank you that at least you have become some kind of help to him.

Oh! I didn't tell you about our mother. As we all know pretty well she has become a kind of psycho. Maybe the reasons, as per her statements, are true. But the activity, which had been taken up by her is spoiling the minds of innocent people. You may say that seeing her deeds nobody will believe her words but she is a mother, at least somebody who is new to the family may believe her and see only her side. This will bring unnecessary turbulence around us.

O.K. Anyhow she is a mother. I don't know what ultimately the next venture she is going to take up to ruin the innocent minds of our people.

Do you really have time to read all such things in my letter? Of course, you have to read it at least in the installment basis. See Arya, I am not bothered about problems in my living, but I am definitely expecting a call from my loving young brother. I may not be physically, mentally, financially helping you, but I have lots of love, affection towards you. I really pray the God for your prosperous life. I don't expect anything from you or anybody including mother and father. But still I expect a sweet call from my sweet younger brother. Why because, I love my brother, since my childhood. Still I recollect the old and golden days of our childhood.

You have been there for so many years. Still I feel you have only just left, because of the attachment towards you.

I hope and pray everyday the Superior God to help you in your prosperous life.

All the best in the new year to you,

With Blessings and Love – Yashoda

FOR A LONG TIME ARYA sat in his chair, unable to believe the ordinary details he read in the letter.

"How can they forget *that* like that?" he uttered with exasperation. "Here I am, having done *that* to Amma and she still calls *her* psycho?"

Strangely, a renewed belief rose in him once again that only he loved his mother more than any other. A fresh, hopeful brightness entered his heart. His feelings were that of one, who, upon seeing how tall the ladder was, experiences dread and wishes to avoid climbing it, but on strengthening his will reaches the top, and feels not only devoid of his earlier fears, but is moved to gently guide the petrified one below, gradually transmitting his elevated feelings to the other, until they rejoice at the top.

In that moment, Arya believed not only that he wanted to reach the top of the ladder and live, but also to do all that he could to pull up that petrified part of his own being up that ladder; and together they would make his mother experience the joy he felt. He wanted to submit to all that he had wrought on her and bring both of them, her and him, out of it.

"What do they know?" he thought. "As soon as I go there Amma will forgive me, and she will forget about it."

24

"You Silly, I am Always Here"

MEANWHILE IN HYDERABAD, IN AUGUST of 2000, that is, a month after Arya began attending the Bible sessions in America, Tara, suffering from a prolonged illness, which at first appeared to have left her body, died.

Rushi, after two months of waiting for any word of resolution in regard to his situation at the office, gave up his hopes of reinstatement. He knew his poor health prevented him from working as before, but the desire for the continuity in work still held its sway over his life, though the work itself was now oppressive to him.

Ten days earlier Yashoda brought the news that Sarangapani had retired from his sarpanch position in Pillanagrovi.

"It is just the right time for him to retire, but there is still time for me," said Rushi to Yashoda.

Amidst these circumstances Rushi's health deteriorated

rapidly. Due to the incessant cough that tormented him a constant expression of exasperation occupied his face. He could no longer walk or stand erect. He spent his waking hours on the bed. Even sitting erect on the bed became unbearable to him, and after only a few minutes he buried his head in the pillow, which he always kept in his lap.

On his instruction his bed was moved closer to the washroom.

The agitation in him grew. When everyone left the room he took one more pillow from the side of the bed, put it under his face, and did not get up for hours and hours.

For the visitors his torment was a common sight, ever visible in his heaving chest, and in his quivering shoulders whenever he tried to hide his cough in the pillow.

Rushi wept silently. When he asked his relations to come and see his two children – the girl, barely ten years of age and the boy two years younger – all he saw in their eyes was the look of a stranger, and that look said, "You should be content that we are still in your life, but these children? They are no relation to us, so don't press your luck in this matter. How can we talk to them in the same way?"

Once or twice he thought of going back to Pillanagrovi, but picturing Sarangapani and Janakamma, and unable to imagine them with his children, a weary dejection came over him, and he dismissed this thought.

That Sunday afternoon, after watching the continuous comings and goings of all sorts of relations on Tara's side: men and women speaking loudly, standing here and there in the house, spitting into the washroom while standing near it, walking past him with a hostile look on their faces and spitting by the side of the house, Rushi suddenly sat erect. With a breathless animation in his voice he ordered the two children to be taken away, for the time being, to one of their aunts' place. Then he began to set in motion his wish to move his residence and live all by himself with the children, away from all this.

AS SOON AS HE MOVED into the new place, a two-bedroom row house about three kilometers from Anasuya's, with sprightly movements Rushi freshened and ordered the maid to clean the house once more entirely, making sure his bed was by the window.

Later that evening Rushi sat on the bed, looking outside his bedroom window. The evening sun was so red, and its orange rays were so striking that an old feeling from his youth revived in his memory.

It was the time when Rushi was returning from Pillanagrovi in a district bus. None of the children were born yet. The evening express bus departed the village bus-stand, proceeded through the narrow gap between the huts, emerged into the lush green fields, and suddenly the horizon, with the bright red ball of the descending sun, came into the view. Sitting by the window seat he saw, in the deep orange rays of the setting sun, one or two old cowhands returning in the evening. One of them, a middle-aged man with a thin, strong frame, shielded his eyes from the sun with his palm, and kept peering at the receding bus, standing there motionless. Rushi watched him from the window until he became smaller and smaller but never fully disappeared. "Why is he alone? Why am I going away from him? It must be very hard to live alone like them," a voice inside Rushi said. Then at a far distance he saw a hill, on top of which was a huge boulder, shining in the orange silver light of the sky. It seemed to say to him, "I am always here. Strong, no matter how many people climb on me. I am their shelter. With me they are not alone." The hill appeared to make fun of the intense emotion he had just felt, whispering "You silly!" as it passed him.

All at once Rushi broke from the spell of his recollection, but it still kept lingering: he remembered how, by the time the bus reached the outskirts of the city, the tall trees on both sides of the road gradually disappeared and turned into tall factory chimneys, out of which the black smoke emerged in slow motion.

A dull trepidation filled Rushi. He kept on looking outside through his bedroom window at the evening's bright sky as it deepened in color more and more. His eyes searched for the huge orange silver boulder across the horizon.

A few minutes later Rushi rose, replaced his bed sheets with new ones, took out his new clothes that he had tucked away in the almirah, and began making phone calls to his old colleagues, rejuvenating them with several ideas related to the various water works projects they had discussed in the past.

At once Rushi became his previous self who had, as a young officer, firmly and with purpose dismounted from his office Jeep with a cigarette between his fingers. He now felt there was little time to waste, and began to feel continuously bright, as though something mysterious had re-ignited into motion the locomotive engine of life in him.

25

"The Kind Who...
Gain Control Over
Weak-willed Women"

THE EVENING OF THE FOLLOWING Tuesday Arya arrived an hour earlier at the Church premises, sat in the car and began reading the lesson sheets, but he was continually distracted by his own thoughts.

He closed his eyes, and feeling tired, he let his head lean back on the seat and rested for some time. A flurry of images rose in his imagination. He focused first on an image of the Threepenny Opera poster that he saw in Max Mueller Bhavan in Hyderabad, then on a Bertolt Brecht book, then back to the poster.

Someone parked a car somewhere behind him. And then all was quiet again.

The Threepenny Opera poster came back. He experienced a sensation of expansion and that felt better. Then it contracted and collapsed, and he saw busy streets, cement platforms, two-wheelers, a temple in the corner and his old bicycle. A frightful sensation came over him, and he felt a sudden urge to go back home to Hyderabad.

He opened his eyes.

"It's twilight, that's why..." he muttered, giving in to that familiar, dreadful inevitability that overcame him during these hours. "Why is it that even after so many years, twilights are so difficult to pass when I am alone?" A distant memory of his mother on the temple steps rose in his view. That cold and misty air in the morning as their rickshaw drove them to the temple. Those trees, their clear outlines against bright red and dark blue skies. *Still* trees, silent, fearsome, lonely. Tears filled his eyes. "If you don't pay attention to trees at this time of the hour, they act on you," he recited inwardly. He felt slightly relieved.

"It's getting better," he thought, reaching and touching his notebook.

He opened the book, began flipping the pages. On one page, scribbled in his own handwriting, were the words, "Because we are all made in God's image. That's how it is written."

Startled all at once at these words, Arya looked at them, quickly arresting his reflexive frown.

He continued to stare but he was not reading.

Instead, he recognized something in those words. Blood rushed into his heart, which beat faster, and with a pale face he looked away.

At first the words, "...we are all made in God's image," seemed nothing. But he had never read these words before like this, not in a way that *exposed* him so clearly and so openly.

Still, he felt a strange power, a new happiness, as though he had just discovered in these words that which cannot be told, that which cannot be taught, and that which was not even knowledge.

"This is simply an experience of truth!" he thought. All along he had been suppressing this truth from himself, and how wrong he was!

Then a new feeling, wholly different from his present condition, struck him, as though he saw something else, something he did not see before.

"Could it be that I am like *him?*" he frowned.

But he did not wish to answer this question. Still, in his soul he knew that, having himself beaten his mother, he was just as his father Rushi, and that these words have now exposed him.

"If I admit that, then what else is left for me?" a feeble voice spoke from somewhere within a sunken part of him.

He put away the notebook. He did not wish this question to go away, but, instead of having to utter the words of admission to this question, he wished that this whole thing would somehow transform him, so that the question would not exist.

"I don't want to answer questions. I want to change!" he thought weakly to himself, feeling that the strength to change was somewhere near him.

He grabbed the notebook again, continued to read, staring with steady eyes at the pages, not really registering anything he read, but drifting in and out just enough so he understood the stream of the words, and the solemnity and the pity they evoked in him.

"I know I cannot change a thing. But how should I live, how should it all end? Why did I do it? If only someone just stopped me!" he repeated with an inner vexation. "It's all very well to say `it takes courage and wisdom to believe in what you don't see,' but what is all that if not just an arrangement of words!"

But he did not really believe these last words. On the contrary, a desire to resolve this question, which had been seeping steadily into his soul, and filling him with clouds of doubt, rose in him intensely again. Unable to find any words to express what it was that he should do next, he laughed at himself with increased disdain.

He noticed the time, got out of the car, and saw, over at a distance, in the orange twilight sun, the brick red houses with adobe-colored roofs, and the enormous trees swaying behind them.

THE CHAIRS WERE ALREADY ARRANGED in the usual circular manner when Arya entered the room. He was struck by the sight of Andrew, who was laughing at something that was said among a small group of men. Andrew held four chairs in his hands, and with his muscular arms raised high, he was walking to the corner of the room.

They turned at once to Arya and greeted him with the same uninterrupted smile.

Casey, a tall man who stood erect in jeans, a white tee shirt and bright white sports shoes that showed prominently when he walked, was describing an encounter he had.

"So he was like, `Oh, how can Jesus Christ be a person and God at the same time. I don't understand it,' and I thought, `That's exactly right! You don't understand it. Because you have a different system.' I didn't say anything to the guy but it really comes down to that, I said to myself. I mean you have like hundreds of gods, in these other religions, what is it, the Hindoo, the African religions, they have like a god for rain, a god for monsoon, a god if you buy a house and a god if you found fresh cucumbers in your back yard..."

"False gods, the Book says so, ain't it?" someone replied.

"Exactly, that's what I thought, Amen," said Casey.

Arya stood among them, listening. Though he was not himself for a brief moment, he stared toward Casey with steady eyes and smiled with them.

"Did he know I am a Hindoo?" Arya wondered, smiling at the manner of Casey's pronunciation. "What does it matter? My aim is different. I am above all this."

Just then Casey and Eugene suddenly turned and were drawn toward another group, leaving Andrew alone with Arya.

Andrew, in contrast to the mirthful mood he was in when Arya walked in, stood with an uneasy and stern expression before Arya, suddenly feeling restless. Seeing the urge in Andrew to withdraw from him, Arya too felt awkward and said, "Well, it's time to start, I suppose. Why don't we sit down?"

Then nodding at Andrew, he joined others who were getting ready too.

"Today we want to accomplish two things that I am really excited about," started Mel. "First, we are going to read aloud and share our thoughts on a passage from the Book. Did you all get a chance to pick your passage and think about the message?"

Everybody nodded confidently at first, and then glanced at

one another, as if in doubt.

"We really want to try and be very open, and feel free, and not feel like we are on the spot with this. If you want to simply read the passage, and you are not really sure what the message is, that's okay. And if you really feel the power to preach so that others would feel the word of God, that's okay too!" he smiled at Casey, who mouthed "Aleluah!" and grinned at everyone with his school-boyish smile in his eyes.

"Second, I've been meaning to schedule a time for the prayer list but couldn't get to it until now, so I apologize for that. The prayer list has a list of prayers that you all sent me over the last few days. I made a few copies, I think enough for all of us, and I'd like us to take a moment, go over the list silently and keep the prayers in your thoughts."

Mel got up and handed the stack of stapled, handwritten white sheets, which was then passed around. He then sat down, gazed around the room in his good-natured, kindly manner, his steady eyes rousing eagerness in everyone in the room.

SOME OF THE MEN, INCLUDING Marty, drove for over an hour through heavy highway traffic to reach the church in time. At first they believed that after a long day's work and an arduous, sometimes tedious drive, they could not be expected to carry solemn thoughts expressing their inward life.

Thinking like this, upon entering the church and meeting one another, they shook one another's hands vigorously, and laughed loudly. But now seeing Mel sit down, and seeing one or two faces with severe expressions, they were reminded once again of their inward life, and they too became quiet and severe after a few moments of exchanging meek glances. And as usually happens in such moments, all manner of questions, doubts, insights and memories rose in their thoughts when they opened their Books and stared at the passages they had marked the day before.

Not only the meaning of the words in the passages seemed infinitely more clear to them now, prompting a powerful feeling of obedience in them, but they also now no longer viewed this evening endeavor as monotonous, as they had felt on their way here. As each turned the pages of the prayer list that was just handed to them, they were once more overcome with their struggles with the Christian way of life.

The passing out of the prayer list, the habitual casualness with which everyone at first took the sheet and placed it on their lap, the unspoken familiarity with which they all revisited it, and considered the contents with the same heightened seriousness as Arya had seen in them over and again in these sessions, all this had an entirely unexpected effect on Arya.

"Not for me are these day-to-day, ordinary things," he thought and scowled at them inwardly. An old habit, which roused a feeling of ridicule at the summoning of God into such mundane day-to-day activities, came over him.

"This is just like a church gathering, not what I signed up for," he said to himself, suppressing a strong urge that rose instantly in him to avoid any conversation.

He read the list: Marty – Feeling like being tested in my faith, hoping my resolution will not weaken; Alan – Conflicts in business seem endless and hoping to see light at the end of the tunnel; Tim – Pray to the Lord that He make me win in my struggle with daily sin, and so on, the list ran.

Arya turned the pages and read the same again. "What is all this!" he said to himself in bewilderment. "Prayer to recover from a bad flu? Prayer to plead God so you may find a rental apartment? Prayer because you separated from your wife? Prayer because you have breathing problems?"

A terrible feeling of being worn-out, and of an insurmountable disappointment, came over him. All at once he felt that his wish, that he be led into the singularity of his evil and be spurned of forgiveness, would not be fulfilled, leaving him empty.

A momentary feeling, as if he recognized something, as if he saw a clue, passed through him.

Setting aside these volatile feelings, he saw that they started taking turns to read a passage from the Book. He opened his Book on his lap and waited for his turn, intently listening to what was being read by others.

When his turn came he made a motion to read, then took the Book in his both hands and sat erect. Then his face flushed, he placed the Book in his lap again.

Seeing the wholeheartedness, the complete willingness, and the attention with which they opened the Book and settled their eyes on the said page to follow him, Arya felt a sudden surge of emotion.

He thought he felt the glorious, ennobling state into which they had been nudged by their collective conviction; and he thought he felt their belief; and he thought he understood this belief to cause a sudden showing of a "higher intensity." He could not be sure if this was the intensity of love or of the forgiveness. Though he himself did not really feel the intensity, the mere imagination of it made him believe that he had indeed seen it, felt it and was moved to speak by it. He gathered courage from the word "intensity," and deduced correctly that no one around him would stop him, and that they would not even detect any suspicion in the emotion, and in the sincerity, with which he was about to bare himself.

Strangely, he also felt another emotion that came to him from nowhere. He felt secure that even the Word would condone him if he was not speaking wholly and truthfully. He knew his feelings were not entirely a result of his wholehearted giving himself to God. He knew that he had first imagined how the innocuous words in the Book would make him feel, without actually feeling.

With a trembling heart, fully conscious that the quiet, densely printed words on the onion pages were watching his every move, feeling secure that as long as he spoke what was in his heart his words would not betray him and that even his unfelt intensity would be forgiven, he began to speak, but paused from a habitual blankness that momentarily cleared his mind. He opened 2 Timothy and read Chapter 3: *"They are the kind who worm their way into homes and gain control over weak-willed women... always learning but never able to acknowledge the truth."*

As the session progressed Arya recognized everyone and without knowing that that was the cause, felt reassured by the look on their faces that they too recognized him.

"Yes, I know him. How he struggles, like me, to hide those expressions and feelings! I feel as if I can trace the root of his or his or his every feeling to the precise day, to the precise circumstance that germinated them. How closely I feel with them now! Are they not the same as me, and I as them? What if he was born here and I wasn't, we are all the same!" he thought.

Walking back to his car, a myriad thoughts came to Arya.

"The essence lies in looking half-way into a human being, half-way from the top by which you go beyond the facial diversity, beyond the prejudice it brings, and half-way from bottom, above the morass of all that confusion and conflict and where things are really in an unresolved state. Yes, the half-way point of the human soul is a place to look at..."

Thinking like this Arya headed toward home.

SHORTLY AFTERWARDS, AFTER ONLY TWO more sessions, without giving any explanation to anyone, Arya stopped going to the class and avoided speaking about it with anyone.

"Whether it is in our culture or not, I should be the one," Arya thought, "to ask her forgiveness. I must, I cannot live without it."

On his face was a frown, as though he saw, for the first time, a terrible pyre in his mother's heart, and was surprised that he was the cause of it.

IN SEPTEMBER, A MONTH AFTER Rushi had moved into the new residence with the two children, Arya came to Hyderabad, and stayed at Anasuya's.

In him that inner agitation, which at first subsided after he stopped going to the bible study classes, returned soon with a renewed force.

A few days after he arrived he drove to visit Rushi.

26

Rushi

At the sound of his son's car, Rushi, with a pale expression, peered through the window, and saw Arya approaching the gate. Two or three people from the neighborhood were staring at this new face.

"They know who he is," Rushi thought, with a meek sense of himself that abruptly overpowered him.

A moment later there was the sound of the green iron gate's latch being slid open. Rushi's heart began to beat faster, and a nervous excitement rose in him. A few more sounds, and he heard his son's voice at the front door.

As soon as he opened the door Arya saw his father, dimly at first, in a thick cloud of cigarette smoke that filled the room. Rushi's warm embrace held him by the bones, as he rested his head briefly on Arya's shoulders.

"Sit, sit down here. You must be tired!" Rushi cried with a weak excitement. At once he was overcome with a long and strenuous cough. "Bring a glass of water! Make some tea! Strong tea! You still drink tea? He likes strong tea.

Everything must be so new for you all over again!"

At the sight of his father's ill health, the same meek sense of himself that overwhelmed Rushi earlier, now entered Arya. While Rushi and his son spoke, observing now and then on the matters of the maid's coming and going, of the children's schools, of the apartment rent and such, the children, unable to suppress their curiosity any longer, appeared from behind the doorway, and stood at a distance.

"Look who's there! Ey, were you both hiding from me?" Arya cried with an unexpected surge of excitement. "Do you know who I am? Come nearer. Don't be shy!"

"Children...! Do you remember them?" Rushi said, but was interrupted by a sudden attack of his cough. "Come nearer children, why be shy like that?" he resumed with a cleared throat. "Do you remember them?" Rushi persisted, his eyes now brightly shining, and mixed with that emaciated expression.

"They think about you all the time. Just yesterday she was asking `Where is my elder brother? When is he coming?' Didn't you?" Rushi said, addressing the girl, "Yes you did! You forgot but I remember."

Rushi turned to Arya once more, "Have you remembered them? Everyday remembering would be a difficult thing, but you may have at least recalled them once a week. Yes, once a week is possible."

There was a small gathering of people outside, mainly servant maids and watchmen. Several voices were heard.

"Who is he? Is he the eldest? What a fortunate father, he came to see him!" a watchman from a neighboring residence was whispering to the maidservant.

Saying, "Tea would've boiled already!" the girl rushed

into kitchen.

"Yes, yes, tea would have boiled by now. Sit, sit, Arya you sit!" Rushi paused, and coughed some more.

HALF AN HOUR PASSED. CHILDREN disappeared into their room, and soon became quiet, immersed with the toys and books Arya had brought them, and seemed to notice very little of the external world.

Rushi wished to speak of many things to his son: of his anguish and his worries about the two children, of his health and their fate in the future, and of his gratitude to Arya for visiting him. He even wished to express his willingness to accept Arya's financial help, which he had steadfastly refused earlier.

But Rushi did not say any of this. Instead, he was carried away by one emotion that choked him. "I know you are all alone there, and you struggle," said he, in a feeble voice addressing his son.

Rushi remembered Arya's tendency to hide the hardships he suffered abroad. At once the loneliness, the suffering because of it, and every other trouble his son had experienced, became amplified to its full magnitude in Rushi's imagination. At that instant Rushi did not believe that four years had passed since his son's last visit. All at once Rushi experienced a rush of strength. A surge of an uncontrollable sadness, of love and pride for his son, filled him. He wished to say many things to his son, but realized that Arya was no longer the young toddler whom he had tossed on his knees. A new recognition passed through Rushi: that he was now a stranger to the life that now pervaded his son's world. Unable to find any recent memories through which he could express the overwhelming affection that flowed in him, Rushi simply repeated what he had just said, eagerly embracing Arya's large shoulders, and patting heavily, energetically and strongly his son's back.

While Rushi was thus being overwhelmed in the corrosive embrace of estrangement from his son, Arya experienced an entirely disconnected sway of emotions.

On his father's face he saw an expression of someone who was like a lion, trapped and subdued, which said, "Yes, I am like this today, but I am still my own. You have lived so long under my protection. And now, at this stage, do you expect me to put out my hand and seek your good graces? I didn't love you by making you feel dependent on me, nor did I ever pity you. Now what is it that I see in your eyes? Do you wish to enumerate my faults? Have you learned only that? Why do you make me feel as if I am lower, as if I have become weaker, as if I have fallen so that you can relax your hold on what is important in your life?"

In his father's eyes Arya saw an unusual, and a new look, a look that turned itself inward, not from anger or reproach at him, his son, but from a recognition of something disgusting. Something that only roused weariness in Rushi when he tried to express it, a feeling of terror at his own isolation and mortality.

THE NEXT MORNING RUSHI WOKE up, at once feeling the self he once was.

His son's visit the previous day, and the affection he saw in his eyes at the sight of the children, sparked a belief in Rushi that Arya had forgiven him wholeheartedly.

In the evening, without fully intending to, Rushi went to

Anasuya's house.

Climbing the stairs all by himself slowly and quietly, and after pausing at the front-door curtain for a few minutes to regain his breath, he stepped in and sat on the chair.

All was quiet in the house. Arya was not there, having gone to meet his friends.

Anasuya came out, frowned at the sight of him, and sat on the sofa. She did not speak. After a few minutes she went into her bedroom, closing the door behind her.

Sitting there on the sofa, Rushi experienced a sudden weakening. A strange, painful sensation began to overpower him. When the maid had left, and the room was empty, he at last felt free to release the groans and whimpers of his pain and anguish. Like a young girl who buries her face in the pillow after a restless evening, he stretched himself on the couch, lying on his stomach, his face buried in the folds of his arms, summoning with all his will the strength to feel the desire for life. He could not distinguish between the crushing, twisting sensation in his stomach that made him cold, made him shiver, brought dryness to his lips, and another, a much more fearful and unstoppable urge he felt rising in his whole being, that of a terrible urge to live. In a show of greed to fulfill this urge, he wished that someone, *anyone*, put before him a soul so he may forgive it, so as to relieve his burden, and be forgiven himself.

To no one in particular he pleaded everything to go away, wishing only that he be released. He was no longer conscious that any moment Anasuya might come out again, and say something unpleasant. It was as though he was no longer within the earshot of his own pounding heart, which felt as though it no longer beat ordinarily, but was like a mortar that shook vigorously when trundled with a pestle. He heard a voice that spoke within him saying, "Forgive me..." faintly at first, and then rose clearly above the choke of the pain. Blood suddenly rushed to his face, and he began to breathe rapidly. All at once his son Arya appeared to him. Tears gushed into his eyes, and he tightly pressed his eyelids, and opened them immediately in order to see clearly. But except for a strange white blankness that filled him, he was not aware of anything else. He suddenly became conscious of a warm, tingling sensation all over his face; and his eyes and his cheeks and his jaws ached. He then realized that he had been crying, stretched just like that, with the image of his son in his view, and it was well past midnight.

He remained still, in that state, and in that position for some time.

An hour later Rushi awoke to a sudden burst of a loud sound. He opened his eyes. The next moment the fluorescent tube flickered aggressively and a bright white light suddenly filled the room, with the faint hum that accompanied it.

"Get up, get up," Anasuya stood at the door.

When she too was awakened in the bedroom Anasuya experienced a feeling of revulsion, realizing that she had once again slackened in her resolve and allowed Rushi to stay.

Rushi rose upright and stared at the wall clock. But before he was about to say something, that rush of heavy pounding returned to his head.

"It is only two o'clock..." he said in a weary voice.

"Two o'clock or six o'clock, you should leave now," came Anasuya's terse voice, which began to rise in intensity as if already intolerant to any more exchange.

As he gazed into Anasuya's glowing eyes, and listened to her stern, desperate and brusque voice, a strange sensation passed through Rushi.

His eyes, which once were bright, which peered once with heavy kindness into the external world, which once laughed merrily as he purposely lowered himself on the floor while their children climbed on his back and playfully buried him further, now those very same eyes stared at her, not with an earnest helplessness of a weak soul, not with the tired look of a suffering man, but with the piercing glow of two burning coals that crackled impatiently, before retreating beneath the protruded bone of his forehead.

"How everything appears so close to one another!" he thought. "How little their differences matter to me now!"

He recalled with surprise, and disappointment, how uninteresting everything was now, and how interesting everything was then, when he was young.

Before he said anything, Anasuya left the room.

Rushi stood there silently, leaning on the wall, without any expression on his face, for a few moments.

He looked for his shirt. Having found it on the back of the wicker chair where he had placed it, he opened the door, stepped out into the hallway, and stood with his hand on the cold, blue banister that glistened smoothly in the dull white hallway light.

THE NEXT MORNING WHEN ANASUYA opened her eyes, she instantly remembered the previous night, rose from the bed and stepped into the living room.

She stared at the couch where Rushi had slept the previous night.

Anasuya stood like that, silent, and motionless, for a few minutes.

Out of nowhere, she recalled a memory. Years ago on some street, in some restaurant, she and Rushi struggled to keep their grocery bags standing straight by the side of their legs, while they gobbled the milky sweet, giggling at each other. She had suddenly held out her spoon, reaching for Rushi's bowl and he stared back aghast, "What's this?" and her body had laughed all over at how he hid his bowl from her.

As though she reached a resolution, Anasuya went into Arya's room and woke him up to accompany her to the temple, which was about half a kilometer away from her house. Arya had been with his friends until very late hour the previous night, as a result of which he was not aware of Rushi's coming and going.

AN HOUR LATER, BOTH ARYA and Anasuya were seen climbing down the stairs.

Though it was only nine in the morning, the September weather was already warm. After a few minutes of walking, Anasuya and Arya stepped away from the main road and proceeded slowly towards the temple gate.

There was no one within the sight until they reached the tea stall near the corner.

"Oho, a tea stall here," Arya smiled. "I didn't see this before, when did they start this?"

Near the tea stall one or two coconut trees that rose tall

swayed silently.

Everywhere there was a thin transparent screen of light from the morning sun.

Occasionally one heard the lazy whoosh of the wind from up in the sky, where the sharp, elongated leaves of the coconut trees rustled and reflected the sun.

Passing the tea stall, both Anasuya and Arya abruptly turned and looked back, as if they both heard someone calling them.

At a distance, about three hundred meters in front of them, Anasuya saw a figure of someone moving in the middle of the road and flailing its arms. Thinking they had made a mistake, the mother and the son muttered something to one another, and were about to resume their motion, but at once they turned back and stared at this figure again.

With a steady eye on the far-away figure, Arya and Anasuya stepped away from the road into the shade, avoiding the cockspur thorns on the branches jutting into the road.

By the side of the path, a few paces ahead of them, they noticed a rusted iron-sheet awning near the cement-wall of the temple. "Afternoons will be cooler under there," thought Arya.

The approaching figure now became recognizable, and they both at once understood that it was indeed running to say something to them urgently.

"Whatever is the matter that couldn't wait until we get back home...?" muttered Anasuya softly, but as soon as she recognized that it was Yadagiri, the watchman, she thought, feeling impatient, "What is taking him so long?"

Someone, a sower in thick black cowhide sandals, who was emerging from the temple, on seeing Anasuya and Arya, slowed his pace, and was bowing slightly, when Yadagiri came up to them.

Anasuya stopped and questioned, "Yadagiri, whatever are you running like that for? Has anything happened?"

"Aaa…Amma!" Yadagiri's mouth contorted strangely.

This reply alarmed Anasuya.

But as she was about to raise her voice and press Yadagiri further, she saw, out of Yadagiri's seventy-five year-old face, thin, with even more thinning, gray, peppery beard, a weak wail come out. In that outburst, incoherent and breathless at first, Anasuya and Arya heard the words that he had, only five minutes ago, received the news, through the phone call, that Rushi had died.

What had happened was this.

When Rushi had stepped out of Anasuya's living room the previous night, he stood at the top of the stairs silently for a few minutes, holding the blue banister.

From where he stood he saw that the stairway descended into the dimly lit landing.

At first everything was silent in the hallway. Then from behind him came the sudden clang of the bolt that was shut loudly, and there was no more sound.

The terrible pounding in his head became louder and louder, but his attention was on the landing, which seemed so far away from him. He edged closer to the banister on his left, and stepped down the stairway, swaying a little with disorientation. On reaching the mid point of his descent, a memory at once appeared in his recollection. He remembered Yashoda when she was a child and how, when she saw a toy that was just out of her reach, she furrowed

her brow impatiently and broke out into a cry. Forgetting
entirely that Yashoda was a grown-up woman now, Rushi
experienced a joyous feeling. He recalled when he too was
such a little boy.

"What does it matter that I just felt discarded, thrown out
like a dog," he thought, and submitted himself to the flood
of recollections of all his children.

Except for the dim lights over landings, everything was
dark when he came down the stairs.

Rushi turned left at the last landing, emerged out into the
open, and stood breathless near the wall that was lined with
bronze letter boxes, one of which was left carelessly open.

He reached the gate, near which was a lone fluorescent
lamp.

He stood peering at the latch with his hand on it. He held
the gate at his arm's length, as if he was seeing it for the first
time, but also to stop the disorientation in him.

Seeing the smooth cement slab he would have to step
on if he opened the latch, he turned his eyes away from it.
Instead, he moved sideways, and came out onto the street
through the narrow opening.

Sometime ago Rushi had made a resolution, not for the
first, but for the hundredth time, that when Anasuya spoke
with rancor, he would try to comprehend the sequence
of her thoughts, believing that the trigger for the volatile
memories and the vitriolic reactions of his wife were in that
sequence.

Now he wondered why, even on this occasion, he could
not succeed in locating that sequence in Anasuya. He wanted
to say so many things to her, and this urge had increased
in him especially today. Seeing that he had lost the hope

of reaching her, he wished desperately that someone else, anyone, any voice, would speak to her his words.

Abruptly he felt a rough hand on his upper arm, and heard someone shouting, "To the children, sir? Come, sit in my auto-rickshaw," and a gaunt, dark face pushed itself closer to his ear.

"No, no, this way sir..."

Rushi became conscious that he just sat in the auto-rickshaw, and that everything was now in motion.

A few moments later he imagined that he was in a bus, and that somehow the bus had stopped, and that he had already reached his destination, and instead of arguing with the conductor, he should get down from the bus.

"Your journey is over," a voice spoke from within him.

"But all the pain I inflicted on her, what about that?" he heard another voice. But the next moment he no longer felt that anything would be resolved by asking this same question again.

Thinking like this, he stepped out of the auto-rickshaw but was not conscious of what the auto driver was saying. Having stared with a puzzled and a strange look on his face toward the still-sleepy girl who opened the door – his daughter had just been woken up by the sound of her father at the gate – Rushi sat on the chair that was in his path.

The girl disappeared into the inner room.

Seeing her briefly behind the curtain Rushi experienced an intense flow of pity. A rapid series of complex, confusing thoughts entered his consciousness. Rushi wondered if she, this ten-year-old daughter of his, thought that her life was lacking something vital.

"With whom is she going to share the joy, the happiness

and love that comes naturally and forcefully in girls at her age?" he wondered.

"Can I be granted a wish," he spoke inwardly, "To *be* everyone I love? How strange we are, that we cannot experience the life of others, but only moments..." he thought. "Is our own sense, of ourselves, of our own experience so strong that we cannot feel everyone else's experience? Why should this be?"

A scene, a recollection, from the days of his childhood flashed in his consciousness: one morning, when he was still a little boy, he came out of the washroom, still wet and shivering, and his mother made him stand before her, calling him, "My little Krishna...hold still...!" She then attentively applied, with long sweeping motions of her fingers, the red namam on his forehead, all the while speaking to herself. When she released his cheeks, Krishanveni, his elder sister, affectionately smiled at his forehead.

Still remaining sitting in his chair, Rushi smiled back.

He felt a sensation as though he was lifted up by someone with a kind face, and at once saw that this being who lifted him up was his mother. She swooped him up in one swift motion, in a sudden flood of affection, and kissed him endlessly, talking to him in questions and answering them herself, and she stopped only when the intoxication that flooded her soul overflowed and infected her entire being, fully satisfying her need.

Rushi was flooded with the overwhelming feeling of joy, of pity, of affection, of love and of something much more simple, all of which became mixed in him. All at once he was not aware of either the past or of the future, but a myriad sensations filled him. The earth was everywhere wet, with the smell of it. He was so joyous at everything around him, especially at the wet grass and at two or three birds that were quarreling softly on it, that he would have met his death gladly. But still he felt drawn into the folds of life, as he eagerly embraced everything, the earth, the ground, and the grass around him. He was so overcome with heavy and light feelings of life in him that he suddenly had an urge to let go of something. He would not have hesitated releasing his life right at that minute. He forgot the mortal nature of life, and imagined himself in the continuum of life even after his death. "That would be the thing to do," thought he inwardly, as he slowly rose from the chair. "If anyone can make the task of his life to bring these things to others, that'd be a life worth living."

When the morning broke and Sita came in, she found the cold, lifeless, dead body that had once belonged to Rushi.

27

Everyone Caring the Same, As One

ON THE MORNING OF THE First Day of the Ourdhva Daihika Karma, in accordance with Srivaishnava sampradayam, and in a resolute hope that though people on this earth submit their will in the pursuit of that elusive relation with the Lord Almighty, only a proper aparaprayogakarmam will set the soul on its destined path, they lowered the body of Rushi, which had not yet began to thaw, on the dry-grass mattress directly in the middle of the courtyard, where the stairs from Anasuya's house descended.

Earlier that morning, though Anasuya tried to discourage Arya – she was afraid her boy's heart would break – he went to the hospital, where the deceased body was kept in the cold storage.

At the hospital, at the sight of the lifeless body of Rushi, Arya burst out into an awkward cry, not taking his eyes off its reclined head. He saw that the mortuary attendants kept on looking at him. Becoming self-conscious of his position as one who lives in America, Arya believed that his expectations, that he deserved an extraordinary sympathy from the attendants, were being fulfilled in their surprised looks. In their looks he saw a curiosity that even this foreigner-looking person was crying like them. He followed the hospital stretcher with his hand on it, afraid to touch the body, which shook a little here and there when the rusted wheels bumped at the hospital door.

When Arya swallowed his tears and looked up a bit, he again became conscious of the mortuary attendants. He imagined them thinking, "Look, how pitiful! What a misfortune has befallen him, even after all these thoughts of improving himself and his following them diligently!"

When they came into the long hallway a dull suspicion rose in him that one of the attendants did not believe him, and this discovery made Arya even more resolute in his intolerant mood. If anyone had come in the way of the stretcher he would have thought them as animals with no feelings, even towards the dead.

SOON THE VAN FROM THE hospital arrived at Anasuya's house where hundreds of men and women, old and young, who had belonged so much to the core of Rushi's life when he was alive, now stood at the periphery with reddened eyes.

Then the back door opened.

Protruding out of the confused movements and the subdued sounds of men inside the van, the two pale white under feet of the deceased became visible, frozen at an awkward angle.

At this sight an inexplicable disbelief entered the men

and women's consciousness. With a grim terrified look on their faces, they hid their mouths to squelch their wailing sadness.

Amidst the synchronous voices of the elders who recited the services, five men carried the deceased body from the van to the center of the courtyard, lowering it at the predetermined spot, around which sat the elders.

Sarangapani rose and motioned the five men to clear.

With slightly swollen eyes, but not swollen enough to contain an intense glitter that emanated from them, Anasuya sat on the chair behind the clothesline, away from everyone, her gaze fixed on the movements of Arya in the courtyard below.

Seshu came near Arya, who now stood there meekly. Then in a manner of a teacher guiding a young child, he set off Arya into a series of movements, beginning with covering the deceased body with garlands and flowers.

The recitation ceased as some men brought the sacred bier, placed it next to the body, and commenced preparing it with flowers, turmeric powder and kumkuma for the final walk to the cremation site.

"Oho, this too is happening to me then," Anasuya thought, knowing that soon she will be led to a place where everyone in the society would agree she would no longer be visible.

When Arya saw, from below, his mother leaning forward in her chair, staring intensely at him, for a brief moment he thought she raised her eyebrow mischievously teasing him, as was her habit.

The next moment it occurred to him that his mother waited for a thousand years to reveal to him a thousand desires and expectations in her eyes, as though he was the friend she had always wished. Now those very same eyes looked at him as if he was a far-away stranger to her, though still a son. Arya experienced an urgent desire to be near her.

Eagerly, determined to perform the rites with utmost sincerity, Arya placed flowers and garlands on the body. With quivering fingers, he carefully removed a petal that fell on Rushi's eye.

Sarangapani turned to the elders and motioned the completion of the movement.

The ladies near him, who took this as a signal to commence their next movement, stepped forward, calling Sita.

SITA, WHO HAD BEEN SITTING motionless all this time, staring at her father's body, at once became alert on hearing her name, and following Sarangapani's instructions came near Arya.

"Take him upstairs, give him a complete head-bath, put these new clothes on him and come down," said Sarangapani.

As Arya turned and followed Sita's lead, he felt everything blurred as he stepped on the stairs. He stared at his sister's pale face. He experienced a peculiar restraint in his forward motion, and he felt unable to move away from his father's body lying on the ground.

He stopped, and began to revert back toward his father's body, as if to correct a childish mistake.

At that instant he suddenly became embarrassed. He kept feeling that he had forgotten something, that he was not doing what he was told, and that somehow everything was going in the wrong way.

Correcting himself, he turned to resume his climb, but the stairs in front of him were not what they were before, and all angles seemed messed up and he was confused even more.

Seeing the disorientation Arya was feeling, Sita held his arm tightly, nearly bursting into tears. In that moment the brother and the sister experienced, as one, a growing feeling resembling that of a glory, and a myriad emotions flooded their souls at once.

With the help of Sita he regained his step and they both reached upstairs. Still thinking of his mother near the clothesline, Arya stepped inside the washroom. He sat on the plastic stool, and Sita raised the blue bucket and poured water over his head. Suddenly a feeling of horror rose in him, and at once an uncontrollable pity, affection and concern for his father overcame him.

"He is all alone downstairs among all those people, how lonely he must feel!" he muttered to himself in a low voice, as Sita poured bucket after bucket of biting cold water over his head, and they both laughed nervously at his shivering spasms.

Seeing the wet-haired figure of Arya coming down, the elders, who were engaged in a small talk with the dignitaries and with other men in trousers, then resumed with the next phase of the aparaprayogam.

YASHODA, WHO UNTIL NOW STOOD by herself among women, not talking to anyone, came up to Arya with a towel on her arm. She then wiped the drops of water on his neck and gave him the towel, staring at him with intense, piercing eyes, ready to burst into tears.

"Do you feel the shivers? Wipe those glasses."

Arya took the towel.

"No, no. Just a bit. Now the sun is already high so they'll go away."

Then in a lowered voice he said, "Are you crying? What can we do? He is peaceful. Nothing, no words can hurt him. That's the most important thing, is it not?"

Yashoda could not control herself anymore, and leaning into him she cried without speaking a word, making an effort to contain herself. She then stood erect, wiped her red eyes, and softening her face a bit with relief, she smiled weakly and stepped back.

"Why is Amma not here?" Arya wondered, thinking that perhaps the ritual required her to stay indoors.

Sarangapani, hiding his tears, and reminding himself that the proper execution of the aparaprayogam was all he could do for his deceased brother, beckoned Arya toward the sacred bier.

"Now, look here. While repeating this prayer inwardly, without the sound," Sarangapani uttered the short prayer-phrase, "Go around to your father, sit near his head and whisper these words in his right ear." He then leaned close to Arya's face and pronounced slowly and clearly the phrase "Aayushyaha praanagum-santanu."

"Aayushyaha praanagum-santanu," Arya repeated eagerly.

"Yes, Aayushyaha praanagum-santanu" Sarangapani confirmed.

Though Arya did not comprehend the purpose of what he was told to do, though he could decipher the meaning of the phrase only vaguely, and though a persistent feeling gnawed at him that despite all these people who surrounded the deceased body he left his father alone somewhere far away, not here, Arya obediently repeated the phrase in his father's right ear, and stared, with a suspended thought and with pity-filled eyes, at the frozen white chin and at the protruding nose of the deceased.

He then stood up and looked eagerly and meekly at Sarangapani and the elders, in a manner of asking if he did that correctly. He was filled with satisfaction that he had indeed followed their instructions minutely.

Sarangapani, who was already thinking of the next step in the sequence, did not acknowledge Arya's satisfaction and instead signaled to him to follow his next movements.

The homam that followed lasted for half an hour.

Then the moment arrived to move the deceased on to the sacred bier.

THE ELDERS RESUMED THEIR SYNCHRONOUS recitations.

Then four short strips were cut from a new white cloth. Someone then tied them into knots on the right and left thumbs of the deceased, and on the right and left toes, and the body itself was then covered with new clothes.

From the old garment that was pulled off the deceased body, Sarangapani yanked a single thread, by catching it between his forefinger and thumb, and gave it to Arya.

But either owing to the sound of recitations that drowned what was said to him, or because a strange finality suddenly descended upon him, Arya did not understand at first what they were all telling him to do with it. Tiruvengalam then looked steadily toward his eyes with such a calm reassurance that Arya forgot entirely his abrasive feelings towards him.

Two or three uncles, who had just arrived, came into the midst of the elders after a change from the city clothes. They briskly joined the recitation by first staring intently at the elders' mouths, so as to catch their cadence, then instantly matching it and synchronizing with them after a second or two. Infected by their success, the elders renewed their synchronous emphasis, suddenly elevating the solemnity that disseminated around them.

Sarangapani took the cloth containing unbroken rice grains-made-saffron, prepared just then by Seshu. He then turned toward Arya and said, "Now, look here. Hold it like this, go around, and give everyone a few, don't miss even one!"

As if a shot was heard, men and women then suddenly stood up with a collective anticipation. They solemnly received from Arya's hands, calling out his attention to whomever he missed. They then cast the saffron rice grains on the deceased body, prayed, turned away and stepped back with crying faces.

The recitation ceased.

By now they all began to feel the heat from the rays of the sun, already high in the sky.

THE ELDERS ROSE IN UNISON, and made vigorous, repeated movements with their hands, indicating sternly for the others to rise urgently. The five men who kneeled around Rushi's body at once became alert with readiness.

Arya wished to be near his father all by himself. He was afraid that so many men around Rushi created a nuisance and would wake up his sleeping father. He did not understand why there were all these men around his father, though he knew them to be Rushi's cousins, brothers and brothers-in-law.

"Who are all these strangers? Now they all act as if he belongs to them! What nonsense!" Arya thought.

But before he spoke, the five men began to place their hands under the deceased body, causing Arya irritation.

"They may do what they want, but I am here and will not let even a single fly touch him," thinking like this Arya stooped down fully, intending to embrace his father.

Just as he pushed his arm under Rushi's shoulders, he at once felt the deceased body being lifted. Stepping sideways and backward he followed the men, who placed it on the sacred bier.

As soon as they settled the body on the sacred bier, Arya adjusted the garland, pushing back a tender green stem that poked at Rushi's cheek. An extraordinary love and affection that earlier rose in him, seeing the swaying and jerking movement of his father's head, now reached its peak in his soul.

The smooth, shiny, large forehead of Rushi now rested prominently and quietly. The thin sunk in cheeks, the wrinkles that froze below the jaws and on the throat, the closed eyes, all appeared to Arya in a hazy translucence. At once he recalled a memory of that drawing room of his schoolteacher's house, where his father took him when he was a child. Arya recalled how, when he was scared of the cat that suddenly jumped on the wicker chair next to his, Rushi came to him instantly, held him in his arms and took him to his chair; and how he leaned back on his father's stomach and stared at the teacher's face.

In an instant Arya completely forgot why his father's deceased body was here, lying down like this and what he himself was doing next to him. He touched its cheek, ran his fingers gently against the frozen skin, and suddenly felt shy, as if his father had just awakened and caught him in this display of affection, and expected Rushi to beam his infectious smile any moment.

In that instant, the knowledge that his father had passed away, though Arya would not have denied it, seemed to him so remotely unconnected from the inexhaustible, overwhelming presence of Rushi he now felt, that Arya would not have been surprised if someone told him that such knowledge was indeed erroneous.

In that moment Arya became aware of something else: an inexplicable resistance, which he could not have described but he felt its strong force. An incomprehensible blankness appeared in his consciousness, by virtue of which Arya surrendered himself to the two conflicting possibilities at the same instant, without any turmoil in his soul: that his father was both dead and alive. Arya felt an inexplicable calmness at the presence of this blankness, which enveloped him completely, and all at once, in that split moment, he lost all the urge to resist it.

Just as quickly as the moment overwhelmed him, it passed, and Arya recovered himself, once again reminding himself to perform these rites with utmost dedication and attention to details.

"YES, ISN'T IT TIME?" SARANGAPANI gazed around him, going over the sequence inwardly, and looked towards the elders, seeking confirmation for his next movement. "Aadeeyamaanam?"

"Yes, yes. No need to deliberate anymore. Proceed with it," came a vigorous reply. "Then, is bhandam ready?"

Sarangapani took the new copper urn that had a long yellow twine tied around its neck. He then went over to the homam fire, and, turning his face and cheeks slightly away from the heat, he waved a stack of newspapers at the embers. The thin, transparent smoke swirled, grew into a large cloud, was caught violently in the volatile up and down and sideways movement, and rushed towards Sarangapani. Then a distinct, bright, red-and-blue color flame suddenly appeared at the underside of the burning wood, and with a sudden *"Bhlubh!"* a bright yellow fire erupted, pushing the cloud of smoke up into the air.

A pair of kitchen tongs was handed to Sarangapani. Peering into the fire, Sarangapani carefully pushed the tongs with his right hand into the fire, pulled them back with a large piece of glowing wood, and placed it quickly on the bronze plate that Seshu extended.

Moving from one angle to the other, Sarangapani repeated the motion and collected five or six pieces of burning wood, until the elders prompted him, "That's enough now. They will suffice. Now place them in the bhandam."

Having carefully placed the burning fire in the copper urn, and fanned it one more time, Sarangapani took one end of the long twine and lifted the urn gently above the ground, swaying it slightly.

Walking up to Arya he said, with a tremor in his voice, "What grace your father will receive from God, to see you like this, with such attention! Now look here," and handing him the twine, he instructed Arya, "With your right hand hold this urn by this twine, and walk slowly in front, without looking back."

"Like this? Now?" asked Arya, thinking if he should

commence as he was told at that very instant, and dissuading himself from looking back.

But Sarangapani had already turned away and, with a stern expression, he silently motioned to the men with an upward wave of his palm. He then turned, stepped towards Arya and placed a hand on his shoulder, calming Arya's urge to look back.

As long as the deceased was lying there, a peculiar relief pervaded the men and women. They stood staring at the corpse and listened to what the others were saying, comparing it with their own inner feelings.

A strange magnetic power bolted their looks on the deceased so that soon they drifted with a recollection, now of his bright smile, now of his resolute generosity, now of his cigarette smoking; and for a few moments the knowledge that he was dead evaporated from their consciousness, until suddenly remembering their present condition, their eyes became fixed once again on the lifeless body.

All their recollection was abruptly destroyed when the deceased was at once surrounded by six men blocking their view, who elevated the sacred bier so that the crowd of the people, even those at the outer circle near the gate, had a clear view of the deceased body.

"Now, walk slowly forward out through that gate," Sarangapani said to Arya and immediately wiped the tears flowing from his eyes.

The throngs of people near the gate parted and silently stepped back, as the pall-bearers approached and passed through. They paused for the sacred bier to completely leave the premises, and moving forward together again watched with pity and curiosity at the family of the deceased that followed.

After a second or two the small group that was with Anasuya paused its movements.

"I can walk down the slope myself fine, it's only the uneven stones down below that are a problem," Anasuya's voice rose above the rest. "You go, if we delay because of me then you'll lose time," she then added in a weak tone.

Sita and Yashoda, who experienced the same feelings at these words, did not look at her. A dull feeling of despondency passed through them.

When the pall-bearers reached the van that was stationed at the end of the road, Seshu held Arya by his arm, so that they stepped aside to allow the sacred bier to go inside first.

"You come around, and hold it here. Slowly! Don't slope that much!" Arya heard his uncle's urgent voice. Several voices spoke with animated movements. "Not like that! Here, hold it here!"

"You climb first and pull in. Like that, Aaaa….slowly!"

Arya stepped to his side and asked Sarangapani in a pale voice, "Can Amma come?"

"Why shouldn't she come? No need for such strict rules," Sarangapani said tenderly. "She can even sit next to you with no concern! I will sit her next to you, why do you worry?"

Amid the bustle several moments passed.

"Did he say that she could come?" Sita and Yashoda who came near him a moment later asked, and proceeded to sit in the second car.

The vehicles drove towards the cremation center, which was forty minutes drive in the city.

WITH THE SACRED BIER AT the center on the van floor, Arya sat at the edge of his seat, near his father's head, holding the fire urn between his knees, raising it a bit above the floor.

Anasuya was seated next to him, her body shaking with the jerking movement of the van, her hair disheveled and her face pale.

As the van increased its speed, driving through the city, stopping, starting, jerking forward through the heavy afternoon traffic, the occupants, sitting silently, stared constantly at Arya and Anasuya, mentally encouraging them to endure all this. In their souls they turned over and over again the present condition of Rushi that continually surprised them.

In the moments that passed, a whole world, with she in it, flashed in Anasuya's imagination. She recalled the little girl that she had been, imagining her father she never knew; she recalled being given away in a marriage to a stranger; she recalled the face of Rushi who betrayed her; she remembered the sensation, and the fear, when he beat her; she recalled her children, her very own children, always out of her reach, always on the edge; and at once she recalled the figure sitting next to her, how he turned to her, dragging her to the floor, and the sensation of his heavy legs and arms striking her body. An intense feeling of pity rose in her, before another feeling, of an utter estrangement from this world, flashed in her consciousness. She alternately winced, frowned, looked askance, and cast her glance at the roof of the van with curiosity.

Through the glass window near Arya's seat the traffic was visible, with the view of the scooters, auto-rickshaws and city buses that bustled on the street.

A scooter – driven by a young man – approached them fast from behind. Just as Arya thought he ought to apply the brake, the young man deftly swerved around the van, emerged on the side and, at the instant of speedily overtaking them, the pillion rider stared at them curiously.

Arya at once felt disdain for the young man and scowled at him inwardly, "What do you know about all this?"

"Here I am," Arya said to himself. "If there's one thing I had so desired for so long – his peace of soul – it is coming to pass like this," he repeated to himself for the fiftieth time.

"Seeing me like this, what would all of them think?" he wondered, thinking of everyone who collectively made for his life in America.

"That doesn't matter. None of that matters now. Only one thing matters," he said to himself resolutely.

Though he could not be certain of the meaning of all that was happening to him and around him, Arya questioned, probed and confirmed repeatedly in his soul that, "He is at peace now. That's all that matters," and he derived extraordinary strength and calmness at this one single inevitability.

Staring at the large buildings on both sides of the street, at the numerous scooters and motorcycles that filled the parking spaces, he thought, "These are the same streets he drove in his office Jeep."

At one large building, where the van slowed for a moment, an angry watchman suddenly lurched forward with an agitated blow of the whistle and stopped an auto-rickshaw from entering the gate.

"Same petty rules, daily drudge and same hot afternoons," Arya observed with disdain. A momentary anger, at the matter-of-fact attitude of the people on the street, rose in him, before the thought that "nothing in this universe can hurt him" came rushing back to him, and he once again grew calmer.

ARYA GLANCED AT HIS MOTHER and saw a pale expression-less face.

It appeared to him that she did not even acknowledge the sadness, but was filled with a bleak weariness, waiting quietly for the ritual to be over; and that she did not even think about *that*, that ghastly act, at this moment. His heart was filled with a desire to suspend every thought and to be with his mother, to join her in her expressionless state of mind.

Strangely, he was glad of the absence of emotion in her face.

Then another thought occurred to him. He suspected that the pallor in her face was not what comes from an extreme sadness in one's heart, but from a suspiciously ordinary feeling of boredom. He desperately wanted to know which was it.

A few moments later that agitation subsided and he was flooded by the involuntary replay in his head, of various movements of the ritual he had carried out earlier.

He turned to his mother and looked at her arms and at her forehead, having just remembered something unpleasant.

"Did you have to remove all the bangles?" he asked her.

Anasuya nodded without reply.

After a moment's pause she leaned over to his side and said in a reassuring, low tone, "After all this is over I will ask if I am allowed one or two and wear them, but now we must do this."

Tears flooded Arya's eyes.

"She knows me, understands me completely," he said to himself inwardly, feeling an uncontrollable pity and love for his mother.

Then, as though remembering something else, he looked away from her.

Then came a voice, "Open the window, let the smoke go out."

He realized only then that the smoke from the urn filled the compartment. He hurriedly slid open the glass window behind him, following others who did the same above their seats.

As soon as he sat down and looked up, he saw his uncle Tiruvengalam staring at his direction. On Tiruvengalam's face was an expression, not of pity, not of commiseration, but of a perplexed brood.

Until now Tiruvengalam viewed all his associations with Rushi only as a means that kept him closer to his sister Anasuya. Now the memory of these associations shot forward into his consciousness like a coiled spring that had snapped and taken hold of him. As a result, Tiruvengalam now would have insisted that he had *always* felt wholeheartedly closer to Rushi.

"How did I not see such a simple man before? How quickly life simply ceased to exist, without any regard for the anxiety that pestered him! And now all those urgencies, all those life pressures which seemed to us as so important, they are all gone too!"

He glanced at the large figure of Arya, at his heavy thighs, at his enormous back against the rexine cushion of the seat, and at his yellow yagnopaveetam quivering against his pale shoulder muscle and his sweaty stomach.

"Just like his father," Tiruvengalam thought, turning his eyes away from Arya, who was staring at him through his spectacles.

Just then the van stopped with a violent jolt, jerked forward, and started to move again, which made everyone hold the sacred bier tighter. Then the van's movement reversed and it came to a halt. Evidently the driver was not allowed to proceed further into the Cremation Center, so he parked a few paces from the Center entrance.

Seshu turned his head, peered through the window into the street and with an unexpected loudness, said, "It's arrived! We are here!"

SUDDENLY LURCHED INTO A HURRIED consciousness by these words, the occupants made several disjointed movements. A door opened with a loud noise, and a pair of dark hands swung open the second door, exposing them to several pairs of curious eyes of the passers-by. Bursting into the van, a breeze of the hot city air hurriedly rushed into the space that just opened for it, and carried with it the smell of the burnt road tar that glistened in the sun. To the left of their view was a large entrance. Its heavy, brown iron gates were already wide open, tied with a discolored nylon rope to the two granite pillars behind, one on each side. To their right extended the dirt pavement on which the van now stood. The pedestrians, who came into Arya's view on the right, inquisitively turned their heads towards the van, stared with an alarmed expression at the half-naked figure of Arya in a white garment, and at once softened but continued their look with curiosity.

Arya glared angrily at this violent sight.

In the smell of the petrol exhaust from the hissing and heaving buses and lorries, from the sounds of *"Kot, Kot, Kotrrr...!"* with which those relentless auto-rickshaws crowded the streets like the incessant swarms of worker bees, at the sight of the men and women across the street standing under the shade of the bus stop, at the sight of that young boy, with oily hair and glistening forehead, running out of the café into a paint store with a tray full of dull white tea cups, and at the sight of no one that he recognized and everyone who only aroused a feeling of an intense estrangement in him, Arya experienced a terrible, terrifying sensation that even in these last few moments, all these strangers, all these busy sights and sounds, and this strange brown monster that stood with its enormous mouth open, were prowling for his father, waiting with their fearsome jaws open; and the indifference of the men and women around him intensely amplified this terrible, terrifying sensation in him. A sound like a piteous whimper, like a faint squeal concealed under a heavy sigh, emanated feebly from his throat. The disjointed movement among men behind him continued. He experienced a sensation of someone who suddenly started descending into the ground beneath that has turned into quicksand. It seemed to him that a large freezing cold object had been inserted inside his stomach, which turned everything below his chest into ice and he expected any moment to collapse. He wanted to say something to someone, to stop everything that was moving so fuzzily, to plead to someone that this was so terrible and terrifying, and to make them know that if only they stopped moving Rushi this horrible sensation would stop. But no sound came from him, and no one noticed anything.

He then saw the sacred bier being lifted by some men, and was conscious that he himself was one of them. The faces of Yashoda and Sita appeared in front of him for a second or two, and then were lost in the bustle of proceeding through the gate, into the Cremation Center.

From the gate the path descended lower into the large open grounds of the Cremation Center, and from this high ground Arya could see crowds of men and women over on the far left. Beyond them were visible two or three large open sheds, with raised concrete platforms, arranged in one row. Evidently another party had just completed the rites and was leaving.

As they carried the sacred bier forward, the elders, Sita, Yashoda, Sarangapani, and other familiar faces that stood near the sheds gradually came into a clear view. The path, strewn with scattered growth of green grass, merged into where they stood.

The elders motioned silently and pointed to the area in front of them, towards which the sacred bier moved.

Just as they were placing it on the ground, a rush of urgent, excited voices erupted, "No! No, no, turn the other way!" indicating that the corpse's legs were pointing in the wrong way.

The men hurriedly positioned themselves correctly, and the sacred bier was then lowered. The men straightened their backs, wiped their perspiring foreheads and necks and stood back.

THROUGHOUT THE ENSUING MOVEMENTS, GESTURES and

utterances that he was made to perform, made to repeat, and amidst the continuous stream of Sarangapani's commands which he meticulously obeyed with complete concentration, Arya thought of nothing but did what he was told, observing carefully each gesture of Sarangapani, submitting himself wholeheartedly to what was expected of him.

Arya felt that there was no duplicity in these rituals, as if he was answering a question that sooner or later would show itself. He was convinced that a mysterious, complex force surrounded them, walked with them as one and that they, he and the others with him, collectively submitted themselves to it. He directed all his thoughts, gestures and actions towards this mysterious being, which was outside of them, and towards which they were all being gradually drawn.

Their experience was just as when, on seeing someone suddenly take a pleasurable plunge in the water, the splash infected all those who remain on the shore, momentarily making them feel as if they themselves were rollicking in the waters with unfettered joy.

He experienced a similar sensation: that the sudden plunging of his father into this mysterious, joyful state infected them all with a momentary surpassing of their selves. Like the wistful looks of the people on the shore, he too looked upon his father with a pure, child-like envy.

When he was told to remove the white knots from the toes and thumbs of his father, neither by loosening them with his fingers, nor by untying them with his hands, but by cutting them in quick short snaps with scissors, he did it with no other thought, and no question arose in him.

When they told him to climb on the platform and prepare the cremation site, he forgot everything else and swept the marked area with the tree brush, spread the thick mattress of dried straw, arranged freshly dried cakes of cow-dung, and laid the thick, heavy blocks of firewood, with their green bark that still smelled fresh.

The dried grass bedding, the evenly spread firewood, the cleaned cement surface around the bedding, all these for him were not an aid that burned and disintegrated the body of the deceased, but a fine, carefully prepared resting place, made by his own hands for his tired father.

He kneeled, reached the far corner of the bedding, and made sure no uneven spread of grass or a wobbling piece of wood would disturb his father's sleep. "There...that should do it. There..." he muttered to himself. Several pairs of hands touched where he adjusted, and spoke to him with a reassurance, "Yes, this is how it should be." Several other hands looked into his eyes enquiring, "Shall we bring some more wood?"

THE CORPSE WAS THEN REMOVED from the sacred bier and was placed on the firewood on the prepared bedding.

The throng of men and women, now moving as one, quivered silently, pressed closer, and surrounded the funeral pile.

Someone tore open a new can of melted butter, poured some into a silver vessel. Handing it to him, Sarangapani instructed Arya to pour some into the corpse's mouth, and to touch some on the ears.

Arya looked up.

Seeing the kind expression on men who gazed at him

with disbelief and reassurance, and seeing the women who covered their mouths with the hems and transfixed their large eyes towards the sight in front of them, Arya lowered his head, and resumed pouring.

Then one by one they gave the firewood to Arya, and he placed it all around the corpse.

Two or three others joined.

More and more firewood was placed, now on top, now around, now near the head.

Someone reached near the exposed feet, and soon several other hands began covering it with more firewood.

With raised arms Seshu, Sarangapani and others shook cans of melted butter over the pile. With a peculiar, *"Glugg, glugg"* sound the translucent unction fell like a glittering cascade over the pile.

More firewood, now sandalwood, was placed near the head of the pile.

Though the enormous mass of firewood now completely covered, enclosed and removed any sight of the corpse, Arya saw only his father's body – with his eyes closed – in his imagination. He only thought that nothing could do his father any harm, protected by the armor that now surrounded him. He felt a sudden, overwhelming urge to see his father's face, to make sure he did not open his eyes, with all that wood pressing his face. A low, persistent voice from somewhere inside Arya, that until now continually whispered weakly, *"Nanna!"* now rose louder in his consciousness, and flooded his heart with an overwhelming feeling of gratitude. His chest heaved heavily. He wanted nothing, thought nothing, but the gratitude he now felt for the presence of his father in him. His face contorted, tears flooded from his eyes, he could not breathe. A dull pain crept into his face.

From somewhere in the background, behind him, he heard a faint voice. He looked up but could not decipher the movement in front of his eyes.

A second passed, he cleared his eyes of tears, and following the same voice he now heard next to him, he received the fire from an outstretched hand, and touched the pile near its head with it, until a small chip of wood caught it. Thick swirls of smoke filled the gaps between the green barks.

Then a figure stepped forward, breathing heavily, carrying a large clay urn filled with water, and saying, "On your left shoulder...!" it lifted the urn up until Arya balanced it on his own left shoulder.

Arya then heard a voice, "Go around three times to your right!"

As he walked around the pile, which had not yet caught on fully to the burning wood at its head, he saw that after each turn someone stepped behind him and with a quick hammer-like motion poked a hole in the urn, releasing a stream of water that spouted behind and away from him.

He wished to turn his head and see the pile and see his father. But he was constrained by the weight on his left shoulder, and the awkward manner in which he was made to walk forced him to keep his eyes in front of him, away from what he wished to see.

Just as he completed the third go around, the water now streamed vigorously from the three holes, and he said to himself impatiently, "What is this, and why doesn't someone..."

"Aaah... Now drop the urn! Let go of it...quick!" cried

several voices.

Arya hurriedly released his hands, at which the clay pot – already nearly empty – fell with a crash behind him. A pair of strong hands then took hold of him forcefully, and before he turned his face, led him away from the funeral pile, which suddenly began to blaze intensely.

When they were a few paces away, Seshu's trembling voice spoke, "You should not see, nor turn towards it. That was why you had to be taken away…"

Soon the blaze intensified.

Just when the moment came, for which the elders were waiting with pricked ears, a dull popping sound was heard from inside the burning pile. The elders nodded their heads in agreement, and in satisfaction.

Cremation was completed, and the men and women left without taking leave of one another.

The family returned home.

2 8

Tomorrow

GRADUALLY, OVER THE NEXT THREE days, the relations departed. During the days that followed, the house was quiet.

On the day after the ashes were dispersed in the river Krishna, the family was sitting in the bedroom near the window where the old tree was visible.

Yashoda and Sita were lying on the bed.

Arya stood near the window, staring at the tree.

A moment or two later they heard the chirping of the birds, coming from the old tree, which swayed in the wind. A new state of being, in which everything appeared in a new light, descended all by itself into these three siblings.

Until now they had experienced an intense longing for home, but only that home with their mother and father fully in it. But now they were filled with a new sense of belonging, and they felt that any strange place, even America too for Arya, had become home for them. Tears swelled in their eyes. It occurred to them that this was what their mother and father always wished for them. They saw Rushi in that yellow grass under the old tree, in that breeze that swayed its thick branches, in that bird that flew from one branch to another, riding the wind, and they each thought, "How simple it is! This is all he wanted of me. What a precious gift this is! Is this what he wanted me to feel? But I have always known this, haven't I?"

Just then the sound of an airplane, far above in the sky, entered their awareness. In that awareness, Rushi was saying, as though he too overheard the sound of the airplane, "This too is part of everything that you should feel. I am here, closer to your feelings, in your emotions, than ever before."

His children's eyes, their cheeks and their faces became numb with the intensity of the emotion. They experienced this up-swelling with a strange clarity. They wanted nothing else, desired nothing else, but experienced gratitude for this state, for this realization, and for being shown this. Arya became conscious of his lower lip's quiver, and felt a dim pain in his lips, in his cheeks, and on his nose, at the tingling rush of blood and emotion.

"What is it...? Oh, I am crying," he mumbled, and felt the blood recede from his face, leaving the imprint of the truth that seemed to elevate him.

"Yes, it is that simple," he said to himself once again, slowly slipping into absentmindedness, in which his thoughts drifted here and there, and he felt light-hearted.

After some time like this he rose and went near Anasuya. In his consciousness there was only one thought, "I know what I must do."

A<small>NASUYA WAS SITTING OUTSIDE IN</small> the chair with a newspaper.

"There's still that tomorrow for me, I still have to carry on," she sighed. She felt as though a part of her still insisted in her allegiance to her husband, but another part of her was a spy, watching and smiling with disdain at her allegiance.

Just then she heard, from the corner, near the stairs, familiar voices.

Kadir had just come upstairs and seeing Suri on the steps, began talking to him.

"Just as you see me, like this," replied Suri's voice to Kadir, who was asking him how he was.

"Then one must go one like this, what choice do we have," thought Anasuya.

"See how it happened, just like that, Suri, see how life has moved on, like that? Went away, just like that, and now what else is left?" said Kadir's pale, choking voice.

"Whatever *can* one do? Can one stop a passing soul? The man's time arrived, how could he not abide? Wouldn't He be angry then?" said Suri's voice.

"When did he ever have time to be properly old?" Kadir's voice continued. "He was a good man, poor soul, lived fully as long as he stayed on this earth. And where did we all go to when we needed anything, but to him, ah, did he serve us any less?"

"Why did he serve us less? Aren't these from him?" Suri pulled his shirt a bit. "Why talk nonsense..." his voice suddenly angry, carried away by a wish to silence his master's detractors.

ﷺ

Explanation of Non-English Terms

All explanations are highly simplified.

veena: A stringed musical instrument

harathi: A small oil-light, used to wave off evil spirits prior to the beginnings of a significant event, in Hindu religion.

kaman: An arch, usually straddling the street. Old City of Hyderabad is famous for its kamans near Charminar.

namaaz: Prayer, in Muslim religion.

payasam: Sweet pudding, in south India.

rangavalli: Attractive colored patterns, drawn with chalk powder on the floors during festive occasions in south India.

kumkuma: A cosmetic red mark in the middle of the forehead.

charka: A wooden flywheel-like drum, on which the kite string is wound.

zebia: A type of a kite, favored by skilled kite-flying youngsters.

nanna: Father, or dad.

Ourdhva Daihika Karma: Last rites.

Srivaishnava sampradayam: In the tradition of Srivaishnava.

aparaprayogakarmam: Act of last rites.

aayushyaha praanagum-santanu: One of the twelve phrases uttered in the right ear of the deceased during the last rites.

aadeeyamaanam: Literally, to be taken away. A phase during the last rites when the deceased body, having been prepared appropriately, is ready to be taken away.

bhandam: An urn, usually of bronze, used during the last rites.

Acknowledgments

Over the course of more than ten years, friends and strangers helped shape this book from the first draft to its present form. I thank them. Here they are, in no particular order: Kavita Bhanot, Fran Bigman, Namit Arora, Usha Alexander.

About the Author

RAJ KARAMCHEDU has spent the last twenty-three years in technology business in Silicon Valley, California, USA. He is the publisher of Saaranga Books, a small literary publishing company. This is his first novel.

www.ingramcontent.com/pod-product-compliance
Lightning Source LLC
Chambersburg PA
CBHW051332250626
47155CB00007B/2572